Evergreen Academy

BY

HEATHER SCHNEIDER

Summary: A teenager discovers an academy for magical botanists in the woods of her hometown.

Editor: Red Adept Editing Services

Cover Design: Krafigs Design

ISBN: 979-8-9850507-6-9

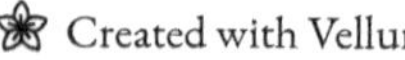 Created with Vellum

Evergreen Academy

BY

HEATHER SCHNEIDER

Property of
Evergreen Academy Library

For those who have ever wished they would stumble upon a
secret garden.

Prologue

THE SUMMER SOLSTICE

The darkness of the forest engulfed me like a cloak as my friends and I crept through the underbrush just before midnight. It was the height of summer, and it had taken forever for the sun to set. But now that it had, darkness had settled completely. We made our way through the thick forest from where the road had ended to the grounds that housed the elusive Evergreen Academy, a fount of speculative rumors within our small town.

"There's the gate," Mitchell said, a note of roguish exhilaration in his voice, and I squinted ahead to where a large metal gate with some kind of symbol loomed. My stomach kicked up a notch. We were really doing this.

"Let's make this quick, okay?" Maci asked for the second time that night. "Get in, get the pictures, get out."

"Maci's right. No theatrics, you two," I whispered to Mitchell and Jace, who feigned looks of innocence.

"You're the boss, B," Jace said smoothly. "We just need a picture of ourselves in front of the gate to prove to Javi that we did it."

Javi—Jace's cousin—was the reason the four of us were all

here. He'd made a bet with Jace that if he snuck up to the gate, he would give him twenty bucks. Somehow, that had morphed into Jace roping us all into the scheme. Still, I hadn't been too reluctant. These were my high school friends, and now that we'd graduated, this felt like a final mildly reckless bonding experience before our lives headed in separate directions.

"Is this close enough?" I asked, examining the tall metal gate, a clear indicator to keep out if I'd ever seen one. Maci snapped my picture as I struck a pose. I stood slightly off-center, the swirling vine symbol and the letters *EA* clearly visible with the flash of her camera.

Task completed, I glanced through the gate with a surge of curiosity, but I glimpsed nothing but dark forest. While the other three took turns getting their pictures—Jace and Mitchell turning theirs into a photo shoot opportunity—my eyes roved over the dense, dark forest that surrounded us.

Attached to either side of the iron gate was a massive brick wall that surrounded the grounds. It was covered in trailing ivy and moss and went on as far as the limited distance my eyes could see in the dark. I tripped on a rock and took a step back, looking down at where I'd just stepped.

A ring of round stones formed a circle the size of my aunt's small dining room table.

"Never step in a fairy ring, Briar!" Maci called with a laugh.

I startled, not realizing that the three had finished their photo shoot.

"That confirms it, then," Jace said. "This place is some kind of mystical cult."

"Seriously, though. What do you think this academy is about?" I asked.

"My money's on the California equivalent of Area 51. People already claim to visit Mount Shasta because it's a touch point for aliens. Maybe this is where the government experiments on them," Mitchell said with a completely straight face.

I rolled my eyes.

"I still say it's a cult." Jace shrugged, squinting through the gate as I had a few moments earlier. "Think there's anyone in there that needs rescuing?"

"My mom said it's a private school for rich kids," Maci said practically, letting some of the air out of our wild speculating. "Are we ready to go?"

I nodded, and Jace and Maci linked hands and began to walk down the road to the car, Mitchell right behind them. But I didn't immediately follow. Instead, I turned back to the circle of rocks.

A fairy ring. I shook my head but smiled. So-called fairy rings were made of mushrooms, not rocks. And there was no magic to it, just a scientific phenomenon caused by some kind of fungus in the soil.

If anything, this circle of stones was more interesting. It was man-made. The question was, who had created it, and why? And why place it just outside the gate of this creepy abandoned academy?

I reached out a hand, inexplicably compelled to feel the soil inside the circle.

"I wouldn't do that if I were you," a deep voice said from somewhere behind me.

I jumped so quickly that I stumbled, feeling my ankle give a slight twist. I steadied myself and whipped around, searching for the source of the words.

A young man about my age, somewhere between eighteen and twenty, was leaning against a tree. He had olive skin and chestnut-brown hair and was dressed in all black, or maybe his jeans were dark enough to look black at night. I tensed immediately and cast a look over my shoulders. My friends were already out of sight.

I turned back to the newcomer and straightened my shoulders. "And why shouldn't I? It's just a circle of rocks."

"Are you sure about that? What did your friend call it? A fairy ring?" There was a hint of amusement in his voice.

So he'd overhead that. "It's obviously not a fairy ring."

"How do you know?"

I rolled my eyes, feeling less tense at the presence of a stranger than piqued by curiosity at the weird line of questioning. "Because fairies don't exist, so this can't be a magical ring."

A slight smile pulled at the corner of his lips, as if I'd said something funny. "That's partially true."

This conversation had taken a strange turn. I took a step back, ready to join my friends. But something kept me from turning away completely. A bit of moonlight caught his arms, illuminating black tattoos. The bits I could see looked like leaves or vines.

The stranger noticed my gaze, and he crossed his arms. "What are you doing out here?"

"I came with some friends."

"It's the middle of the night."

"It was a dare," I said, straightening my shoulders slightly. In his presence, all of that felt a bit juvenile.

"Did you get what you came for?" There was a hint of amusement in his tone again, and I suddenly had the feeling he'd known why we were here all along. A small voice reminded me of what Maci had said. *My mom said it's a private school for rich kids.*

I studied the stranger's dark collared shirt, pants, and shoes. I didn't know much about designer clothing, but they looked expensive. And tattoos weren't cheap. I'd never seen anyone our age with that much ink. Could he be a student at Evergreen Academy?

The idea was intriguing. I'd lived in the small town of Weed, California, for eighteen years, and I'd never met anyone associated with the academy. I'd thought the place was probably abandoned, a relic of an earlier time.

"I'm not sure," I said, struggling to remember what he had just asked. *Get it together, Briar.*

"I think your friends are waiting for you. Be careful walking back. Wouldn't want you to trip." By the way he said it, I knew he'd seen me lose my balance against the rock and almost fall into the ring. I narrowed my eyes.

"I know my way around. I grew up here." I wasn't sure why I'd said that, but I felt the need to defend myself for being in this forest. If he truly was here to attend this Evergreen Academy, then he was the newcomer, not me.

His eyebrows drew up incrementally. "Well then, happy midsummer, local." He smirked, and I frowned. *Happy midsummer?* I wanted to study him more closely, but it was difficult to get a read on him in the dark.

We stood there like that for a moment—locked in some strange staring contest, his expression infuriatingly relaxed—until I heard Maci call, "Briar! Where'd you go?"

I glanced behind me and saw her emerging from the trees with Jace right behind. The headlights from Mitchell's car shone in the distance. "Who are you talking to?"

When I looked back toward the fairy ring, the dark-haired man was gone. I shook my head, scanning the forest. There wasn't a soul or a sound besides us. "No one."

By the time we were driving down the long dirt road and into town, I'd begun to wonder if I'd seen him at all.

Chapter One

"Tomorrow's the big day. I can't believe my niece is going to be a college student. It's making me feel old." My aunt wiped her hands on her apron and tucked a dark curl behind her ear. Her flower-embroidered apron hung from her neck and was tied securely around her waist, her ever-present uniform when she worked in the café.

"You? Old? Never," I said with a grin, and my aunt—barely forty and the receiver of plenty of attention from our male customers—nodded approvingly.

"Have I told you lately you're my favorite niece? I wish we could rewind the clock on summer, though. It always goes by too quickly."

My brain conjured a memory from the summer, the one that had replayed in my mind in the weeks since, and before I could think twice, I asked my aunt about it. "Have you ever heard of anyone around here celebrating Midsummer?"

"Midsummer? It's a lovely tradition in many countries. But no, I don't think many people celebrate it in the US."

I'd done a little research on it immediately after the day in the woods outside Evergreen Academy and learned that it was

another term for the summer solstice, the longest day of the year. But the way the stranger had said "Happy Midsummer," as if it had been as common as saying "Merry Christmas" in December, had thrown me. It was a strange salutation.

"When I was in culinary school, one of my classmates was Swedish," Aunt Vera continued. "She told me that Midsummer is a holiday there, and people make flower crowns and wear them around. It sounded delightful. Why do you ask?"

I shifted my weight and poured my attention back into stirring the batter in the large commercial mixing bowl between my hands. I didn't want to tell Aunt Vera that I'd been sneaking around on Evergreen Academy grounds at midnight, having conversations with strangers. Aunt Vera was lax compared to most of my friends' parents, but that one wasn't likely to go over too well.

"It's just something I heard about this summer, and it's not a common holiday here."

"That gives me an idea. We should start selling midsummer-themed cookies. We could do the same when the seasons change to fall, winter, and spring as well." I could see my aunt's brain—creative, like my own—running through ideas for decorating the cookies, cakes, and cupcakes that she was famous for. New themes always excited her.

"I like that. Want me to mark it in the calendar for fall?" I was headed to the wall calendar when I heard the soft ting of the bell from the front room.

"I've got it," I said. I went out to mix up a lavender latte for a customer, grateful for the distraction from my memories of the stranger in the forest. I noticed a middle school student, Emma, seated in the corner. She often sat there and sketched while her mom worked on a laptop at the window.

I walked over to her. "May I see?"

Emma nodded and moved so that I could look at her sketch. It was of a field of wildflowers.

"Wow. That's beautiful, Emma. I like what you did with the contrast there."

Emma beamed. "Thanks. I got a new pastel charcoal set for my birthday."

"When was your birthday?"

"On Monday."

"Just a second." I walked to the pastry counter, took out a cupcake, then used one of our piping tools to draw a purple flower and a cursive *Emma*. I riffled through the drawer and found a candle then nestled it into the frosting.

Emma's mom paused her work when I came over with the cupcake and a lighter.

"Briar! That's so thoughtful!" she said, squeezing her daughter's shoulder. "How did she know purple is your favorite color?"

"We can't let our town's best thirteen-year-old artist's birthday go by without celebrating." I lit the candle and set it in front of Emma. She grinned at me, closed her eyes, and blew it out.

My aunt was watching from the counter when I returned. "Where'd you get such a heart of gold, Briar Rose? Certainly not from me." She winked.

I laughed but knew it wasn't true. My aunt had some sass, but she was a big marshmallow at heart. It came through in a million different ways, the most significant being when she'd invited me to live with her after my mom—her twin—had died unexpectedly and I'd begged not to have to leave my friends to move in with the dad I wasn't close to in Seattle. She was the reason I'd been able to finish middle and high school in Weed, the small town my mom had wanted me to grow up in.

"Maybe it came with my auburn hair," I joked, fluffing the wavy tendrils that fell to my waist. The dark red-brown hue was apparently a signature of my dad's side of the family, while most relatives on my mom's side had raven hair.

As we cleaned and closed the bakery that evening, I tried to shake off a slight sense of melancholy. Emma had just turned thirteen, the birthday age my mom had never lived to see for me. I hoped that Emma and her mom would cherish every moment they had together. The impending start of college was another moment my mom wouldn't be there for.

I paused to take in the feeling of the café, which helped ground me and lift my spirits. Vera's Café always smelled of sugar. Walking into the place was like entering a cozy cottage, with plants trailing along the walls and soft music playing in the background. Real candles were a fire hazard, but battery-powered ones littered shelves around the room, stuffed between books and other curiosities. And on one wall, nestled inside a gilded frame, was a striking painting of a local pasture.

My mom had painted it not long before the accident, and customers commented on it regularly. Every time that happened, my heart expanded a little, grateful that people were still admiring her work.

The café had been my favorite place to do homework in high school, and I didn't expect that to change once I started at the local community college. My seat of choice was a counter stool that faced the street, where I could watch the traffic that came off the highway, with people stopping for a food and refueling break.

I only had two more years in this little town, and then I'd be off to a university. It felt like an eternity and nothing at all at the same time.

"Grab one of the sourdough loaves, will you? I'm making soup tonight," Aunt Vera said, dissolving my thoughts of the future. The musings had become more frequent recently as I wondered if my plans were going to work out the way I'd always dreamed they would. The way I'd been striving for for six years.

I wrapped a loaf of sourdough in paper, removed my daisy-printed mini backpack from the hook in the back room, and joined my aunt as we locked up.

"That afternoon rush was intense," I said as we turned and walked up the stairs to our apartment above my aunt's business.

Summer was always the busiest time at Vera's Café, since people passed through for road trips to the Oregon coast or even farther up to Washington or Canada. Other travelers made their way south, destined for San Francisco or the Southern California beaches and amusement parks. This week, it seemed that everyone was heading home, just in time for the start of the school year.

I'd been working full time in the summers for the past few years, but I always dropped down to weekends only once school started. I'd been tucking away my small hourly wage into my tuition and book fund, and with the semester starting tomorrow, I would need to begin spending it.

I rolled my shoulders as we entered the apartment and went to check my list of classes for the millionth time. *This* was what I needed to be focusing on—my future and continuing my mom's legacy.

I did not need to be dwelling on the strange sensation I'd experienced during a random summer encounter in the woods. But the curious part of my brain that I struggled to turn off refused to forget it.

Chapter Two

On the first day of college, I was as ready as I could be, and I embraced the controlled chaos of finding my new classes and getting a feel for my instructors. Maci and I had Biology together, but other than that, my classmates were mostly people I didn't know.

At Siskiyous Community College, students were a combination of high school graduates from around the county, students returning to get a degree or take career-oriented classes, student athletes from all over, and sometimes, retirees and other community members who took elective classes for their own enrichment.

When I walked into my art class, that diversity was represented more than it had been in history or math, with students ranging in age from sixteen to sixty.

I scanned the art studio and saw an empty workspace next to a striking girl with a long dark ponytail and deep brown eyes.

"Is anyone sitting here?" I pointed to the seat next to her.

"Nope. All yours." The girl smiled warmly and gave me a little wave. "I'm Yasmin."

"Briar. Nice to meet you. Are you a freshman here?"

Yasmin nodded. "I am. I have to say, art is a bit outside of my comfort zone, but it seemed like an easy elective."

"I'm the opposite. Art's the one thing that comes easily to me. Science and math, on the other hand..." I made a face, and Yasmin laughed, her ruby earrings swaying softly. "I love your earrings."

Yasmin's hands went to her ears, and she made a facial expression that caught me off guard. She almost looked nervous. Finally, she gathered herself and said sweetly, "Thanks. They're my birthstone."

"Where did you get—" I began to ask but stopped speaking as our instructor came in and started to pass out the course syllabus. Yasmin and I both turned our heads to the pieces of paper in front of us, and I scanned mine with excitement. Most of the topics listed were ones I was already familiar with. I'd taken AP Art in high school, and my goal was to transfer to an art school, like my mom had.

The period flew by, and I said goodbye to Yasmin on the way out. "See you Wednesday."

"Definitely. I'm going to need a buddy to help me survive this class. That syllabus looked intense."

"I'm going for a walk on the Wildflower Trail with a friend right now. Are you free? Do you want to join us?"

Yasmin smiled apologetically. "Can't. I have to be somewhere in thirty minutes. Rain check?"

"Of course." We parted ways, and I continued to Wildflower Trail to meet Maci, who was waiting at the trail's entrance when I arrived.

My friend talked nonstop as we walked the trail, which looped our campus. Like so much of our town of Weed, forest surrounded Siskiyous Community College, and trees dotted the campus, as much a part of the environment as the buildings that housed our classrooms.

We paused at one of the letter boxes along the trail. The

boxes were attached to a few special trees along the path, and visitors were encouraged to write the tree a note and leave it in the box.

As Maci scrawled on a small piece of paper, I pulled out my notebook. I studied the large pine tree and sketched it as Maci finished her quick note and tromped around, worrying herself sick about calculus.

"Hopefully, my pleas to the tree will bring me a little luck with this class. I never had a problem with math in high school, you know? But we had an assessment today that we self-scored to see where we're at, and I didn't do great. I can already see my 4.0 GPA goals going down the drain." She huffed out a breath. "I think I might actually have to sign up for tutoring."

Laughing, I looked up from sketching a pinecone. "Oh, the horror."

Maci laughed, and I could see her relax a little.

"If it makes you feel any better, most people don't take calculus as a freshman. I'm taking college algebra, and I'm probably going to struggle." I focused harder on my sketching, trying not to think about all the math homework I'd be doing that semester.

"I know. I sailed through math in high school, and the entrance exam tested me into calculus, so I really didn't think it would be this hard."

"I already know you're going to crush it." I added a shade of dark green to the edges of the pine leaves, signed the corner with my signature *BR*—for Briar Rose—then tore the page out of the notebook and tucked it into the tree's letter box.

"What did you write to the tree?" I asked.

"To send me good tree-ish vibes for calculus."

I laughed. "Good tree-ish vibes? Is that a thing?" I stopped to ponder the box in front of us. "I wonder what whoever collects all the tree letters thinks about them. Do they read them or just use them for fire starters or something?"

"I don't know, but I'm glad it's anonymous. It's kind of cathartic, in a way. Writing to the trees that can never reply. Or drawing, in your case."

"I guess that's the point. It is nice to slow down and really study the trees for a moment." I wondered, not for the first time, who ran the Letters to the Trees program. It had been around ever since I could remember.

There were fifteen trees of different species and sizes along Wildflower Trail that had names and letter boxes attached. We'd just visited the tree named Frank, a large oak that was unofficially labeled the oldest tree in town. I'd left drawings for each tree over the past few years, and for Maci it had become a bit of a ritual to send a letter whenever she needed something. Apparently, a scary first day of Calculus justified a visit.

I made to follow Maci along the path, but my attention snagged on a large leaf that sat on the bench near the tree. It was bright green, as if it had fallen well before its time. But the color wasn't what had drawn my eye.

The veins of the leaf weren't in the typical arrangement, with one central vein that had others coming out of it on either side. Instead, the veins rose in shaky lines from the bottom, almost like roots, and then swirled upward. I could swear that they made the shapes of tiny leaves.

"B? Are you ready to head back?"

Startled, I looked up at Maci then back at the leaf. But the wind kicked up and carried it away before I had a chance to examine it further. I rubbed my eyes. All the nature sketching I was doing lately must have been playing tricks on me.

"Yeah," I murmured and tried to focus on clearing my head as we walked back to campus. There was nothing I needed less on my first week of college than odd tricks of light messing with my brain.

Chapter Three

"Okay, everyone, now that we've had a few sessions getting comfortable with the microscopes, we're going to look at some live plants today." Professor East indicated the screen where his microscope view was being projected on the whiteboard.

We were in our second week of Biology, and our instructor had grown on me already. He was kind, with a pinch of humor that occasionally went over our heads.

"Your goal is to get your view to look something like this. All the materials are in the back of the room. Work through your lab instructions, and ask your neighbor if you get stuck. I'll be circulating to check on your progress."

There were sounds of chairs screeching across the laminated floor as the students in my biology class began to rise to gather their supplies, and I joined them. When I returned to the lab bench, Maci was already looking through her microscope's eyepiece and adjusting the focus.

I studied my plant for a moment before slicing off a piece to put on the wet mount slide. The elodea was a tiny green water plant that looked like a miniature version of sea kelp and was wet to the touch. I made a quick macro-level sketch on my lab sheet then prepped the plant for the slide.

After switching on the microscope's light, I focused the lens, taking the view from something blurry and abstract to a clear shot of the elodea's cells. The long, rectangular cells came into focus, and I frowned, glancing up at Professor East's projection on the whiteboard.

I reset the lens and zoomed in again, my eyebrows pulling together. Professor East's screen showed a bunch of green circles piled up inside clear shapes like peas in a pod. The green circles were the chloroplasts—that much was clear. But they were moving along tiny strings. I closed my eyes, feeling the fatigue from focusing through the microscope already, and then looked through the viewfinder again. The movement of the green dots along the strings was still there.

I raised my hand. Professor East noticed and made his way around the room toward me. I studied the cells through my eyepiece one more time. "Yes, Ms. Whelan?" He glanced at my lab paper.

"I see some strings in my cells. What are they?"

Professor East nodded, moving toward the microscope as I leaned out of the way. "These elodea were collected fresh from the water, so it's common for other things, both biotic and abiotic, to show up under the microscope. Let's take a look."

He leaned over and looked through the eyepiece. "Hmm. I'm not seeing anything unusual here. Maybe it moved out of the view."

"The chloroplasts seem to be moving along the strings." I thought I saw Professor East still at my words. But then he pulled back and motioned for me to look into the microscope again.

"Describe what you're seeing," he said.

"They are extremely thin, like little hairs." I looked more closely. "And they seem to be flowing with some kind of pattern.

It's like the chloroplasts are clinging to them and being moved along."

I leaned away from the microscope to let Professor East look again, but he was studying me, expression intent. I motioned to the microscope again, wanting him to confirm what I was seeing. I wasn't sure why, but the movement intrigued me.

But Professor East didn't look through my eyepiece again. Finally, he spoke. "Ah, yes, those. They are just a bit of debris. No need to include it in your lab report. Just sketch the chloroplasts and cell walls."

Professor East turned then and went to help another student who was raising their hand. I frowned, but I did as Professor East had suggested.

I fished out my colored pencils and got to work sketching the cells. Afterward, I continued to follow the instructions on the lab sheet and was surprised when I noticed my classmates cleaning up around me.

By the time I'd finished, I was the only one remaining in the classroom. Maci was outside the door, waiting for me. I slipped my lab sheet onto the stack on Professor East's desk, and he turned to me from his laptop. "Do you have another class right now?"

I nodded.

Professor East flicked through my lab report, eyes scanning the pages. "Nice drawings," he said, and I felt my chest warm slightly, as it always did when someone complimented my art. "Can you come see me in my office before you leave campus today? Do you know where it is?"

I blinked. I knew where his office was—on the second level of the science building—but I had no idea why he wanted to see me. "Um, yeah, sure. Professor," I added quickly, worried my language had been too informal.

A trace of a smile quirked at the corner of his mouth. "Nothing to worry about, Ms. Whelan. I just want to discuss this lab a little further with you. I may have a research opportunity you can help with."

I raised my eyebrows. A research opportunity? Wasn't that the kind of thing students did in upper-division classes? This was my freshman year, and I was at a community college. But I was intrigued and wanted to know more, so I nodded and smiled politely. "Sure. I'm done at noon."

"See you then." Professor East turned back toward his laptop, and I took that as my cue to leave.

"What was that about?" The question was out of Maci's mouth as soon as we stepped out of the science building, preparing to go our separate ways. Her shiny, near-black locks spilled across her face as she turned toward me, eyebrows raised.

"Not sure yet. He said something about a research project." A sense of interest stirred again, and I felt my heart rate increase ever so slightly as I tried to imagine what the meeting held in store.

"Weird. I didn't even know they did those here."

I shrugged, a lingering feeling that his invitation was related to my lab report gnawing at me. "Me either."

"Well, I'm glad you're going to hear him out. Stuff like that is great for your transfer application."

I smiled. Maci was a great friend for many reasons, and her determination and knowledge about all things "going places in life" was one of them. Who needed an academic advisor when your best friend knew all the transfer requirements from memory?

"Yeah, that's true. Have a good weekend."

"Text me how the meeting goes."

"I will. See you later. Have fun with Jace." I smiled coyly at her, and she waved me off.

I hurried to Psychology. We were working through the first unit on sensation and perception, which I normally found quite interesting, but I was unable to focus on Professor Tara's words today. The impending meeting with Professor East had my mind wandering.

I wasn't used to meeting with instructors one-on-one, so that was slightly intimidating, but I also couldn't shake the feeling that his request had something to do with what had occurred during the lab that day. Why else would he single me out for a project?

When the class finally ended, I tuned in just in time to look up at the screen and jot down my homework assignment. Most of my classmates took a picture of the screen, but I preferred to use an old-fashioned notebook. Maybe because it was another place for me to doodle. I scribbled quickly as Professor Tara erased the board.

Sure enough, I finished writing the homework assignment and realized I'd been scribbling plant tendrils around the edges of the week. There were a series of leaves sprouting out of the *m* in *September*. I quickly cleaned up, preparing myself to return to the science building.

The nerves that had changed target while I hurriedly noted the Psychology homework shifted gears again as I entered the science building and made my way to the second floor, where Professor East's office was nestled in the corner.

I took a deep breath and knocked on the door of Office 213. Professor East called, "Come in," and I entered. He waved me into the seat across from his desk, and I slipped my backpack off my shoulders and sat.

"How was Psychology?" he asked. I opened my mouth to answer before looking at him in confusion. Had I mentioned that I was going to Psychology after his class?

I shook it off and replied, "It was good. I enjoy that class."

Professor East nodded. "And how about Biology? What do you think of the class so far?"

Was this a trap? Of course, I wasn't going to say anything less than flattering about his class. Though, in this case, I didn't have to lie. "It's fun. So far, I think it's my favorite science class I've ever taken."

"Are you planning to take any other science courses?"

Yikes. I was walking a dangerous line. I was planning to take the bare minimum of science required to meet the general education requirements. Same for math. Those were subjects I had always struggled with during high school. I intended to pack my schedule with as many art and humanities courses as I could over the next two years and, ideally, keep my grades high enough to be accepted to art school.

I swallowed, not wanting to offend my instructor, who was looking at me kindly. "Just the two that are required for transferring. I plan to major in art, so more than that won't be needed."

"Ah, yes. I looked over your lab report and was impressed with your drawings. It's a valuable skill in a science class."

I sat up a little straighter and smiled. "Thanks. It's always been a hobby of mine, and I love when I can apply it to my classes."

"I think your... skills could be useful in another program I work with. I'm guessing you're eager to know more about why I asked you here. As I said, there is a research opportunity I think you might be a good fit for."

Professor East turned toward the microscope that was stationed on his desk. Based on the placement, I had a feeling that it didn't normally reside there and wondered if he had pulled it out for this meeting.

He quickly confirmed my suspicions when he slid the microscope my way. "Can I have you look at that slide and let me know what you see?"

I bit back my question about what the microscope had to do with the program and bent my head to the eyepiece. The slide was already in focus. "I see plant cells."

Professor East nodded in my limited peripheral vision, and I took that as a cue to keep going. "There's movement in the cells.

It almost looks like there are cells between some of the cells. They're more oval-shaped. And it looks like little bubbles are going in and out of them."

"Could you sketch it for me?" Professor East asked, sliding a piece of paper toward me.

"Can I use my colored pencils?"

"Of course."

I reached into my backpack and pulled out my favorite pencils then tilted my eyes back to the microscope. I spent the next few minutes sketching what I saw and providing color to highlight distinct features. Once finished, I slid the paper back to my instructor.

He picked it up slowly and scanned the page, his expression guarded. I wasn't sure what to think. Was this research project he was alluding to in need of someone to draw diagrams?

It wasn't totally unappealing to be a sketch artist for some more scientifically adept students as an extracurricular assignment, but I still wasn't sure why that position would be so important or why it hadn't been filled by an art student already. Shouldn't there be a formal application process for that sort of thing?

Professor East put the paper back on the desk and leaned back slightly in his chair, steepling his fingers.

"Thanks for taking the time to do that. I think you could be a good fit for the program. It's very selective. Many of the students in it are enrolled concurrently here at the college, and they do very well in their studies. It is extra work, to be certain, but it will open a lot of doors for you. Ones that would never exist otherwise."

My mind was racing. A selective program? Like the AP and dual-enrollment courses I'd taken in high school?

Professor East must have seen the confusion on my face because he cleared his throat and continued. "You may know the program as the Evergreen Academy."

Chapter Four

I forced my expression to stay neutral as surprise ratcheted through my body. Had Professor East just said the Evergreen Academy? The mysterious school out in the woods? The one with the fairy ring by the gate?

"I take it you've heard of it?" Professor East asked calmly, putting an end to my spiraling thoughts. My intense curiosity about the place and the stranger I'd met there in the woods had diminished over the past few months, but it was back as if it had never left.

I leaned forward, crossing my legs at the ankles to try to tone down some of my excitement.

"Of course. I mean, I don't know much about it. But I grew up here, so I've heard it mentioned."

"Well, I know there are a plethora of rumors about it in the local community. But it's an incredible program. People come from all over the country to study there."

"What do they study, exactly?"

A trace of a smile crossed Professor East's lips. "It's hard to explain. A visit to the academy will paint a more accurate

picture. From there, should you choose to attend, you can complete... orientation and officially enroll."

I frowned. That he had paused before saying the word "orientation" hadn't escaped my notice. My mind swirled. I had been wondering about Evergreen Academy since the summer solstice, and now here was my Biology professor, offering to take me there for a visit. I felt like the world had slipped sideways a few degrees.

Curiosity overflowing, I let my eyes meet Professor East's. "Okay. I'm interested."

He nodded and pushed back from the desk, preparing to stand.

I mirrored him.

"Great. What is your Monday class schedule like?"

"I only have morning classes. I'm done at noon."

"Meet me here after your last class. We'll drive out to the academy together."

I nodded and picked up my backpack, slipping it onto my shoulders again. "Do I need to bring anything special, or..."

"No, come just as you are. Though that is a good reminder that cell phones are not allowed on the campus. It's due to the nature of the research there being... sensitive."

The idea of going anywhere without my cell phone felt stranger than the idea of actually seeing the mysterious academy grounds. But I nodded in agreement and stepped out of the door that Professor East had opened.

"Have a pleasant weekend," Professor East said, already turning back to his laptop.

"You, too, Professor." And I left the room with far more questions than when I entered.

<h1 style="text-align:center">Chapter Five</h1>

"The Evergreen Academy?" Maci squeaked over the phone. "You're joking, right?"

"I'm not. This is so surreal."

"I've never heard of anyone local being invited there. This is... incredible." I could practically hear the wheels turning in Maci's brain over the phone.

"I know. I'm a little nervous but mostly excited. I've been pretty interested in the place since we went there for that picture."

"Have you told your aunt yet? Is she okay with you going?"

I sighed and shook my head, even though Maci couldn't see me. "Not yet."

"Your aunt is cool, so she'll probably say yes."

"True. I'll probably wait to tell her until after I go check it out. Then I can dazzle her with either how interesting or how boring the place is."

"You better take some pictures. I'm dying to see what that place looks like inside."

"Actually... Professor East said there are no cell phones allowed." I cringed and braced myself for her response.

Maci gasped loudly. "*What*?"

"He said the research there is sensitive or something like that."

"Okay, now I'm even more intrigued."

"I don't know how I'm going to concentrate on anything else this weekend."

"You can come do your homework at my house, if you want. You can try to tackle some calculus with me. That will take your mind off the Evergreen Academy."

"Yes to your house. No to calculus."

"I gotta go, B. My mom's calling me for dinner. Text me." I pictured Maci's tiny mother prepping their dinner around the family table. While the Phouthavongs had been in America for a few generations, Maci's family still observed the Laotian tradition of sitting on the floor and eating from a low table, and I'd joined them many times.

"Bye. Say hi to your mom."

After hanging up with Maci, I prepped a few things for work the next morning, trying not to obsess about the Evergreen Academy and what it might be like. I was worried that I had built it up too much in my head and had to repeatedly remind myself that I had been invited by Professor East, a prestigious instructor at Siskiyous Community College. If he was involved, it couldn't be anything too mysterious.

Could it?

My curiosity failing to ebb, I flopped onto my bed, opened my laptop, and began to search.

The online results for Evergreen Academy were mostly things that I had seen or heard about before. There was a short Wiki page describing Evergreen Academy as a private college, with very little information given. There were no pictures provided beyond those of the symbol on the gate attached to the brick wall of the grounds, and I'd already seen that in person.

I zoomed in and studied the logo more closely. It consisted

of the curving letters *EA* with curling leaves and vines surrounding it. Pretty nondescript but somehow charming. Did the leaves and vines have any significance, or were they merely objects that looked nice to the eye of the designer?

I switched to an online discussion forum, where a post that was eight years old had received a few replies. The original poster had asked if anyone knew about Evergreen Academy, located in the expanse of forest between Weed and Mount Shasta, California.

There were a few replies but none that I could put any credence in. The theories echoed what my friends had said when we were at the gate.

It was a mystical church.

It was an elite private college for the very rich.

It was a wellness retreat full of hot springs and yoga.

It was a secretive government research site.

It was a second home for the mythical lemurians, when they weren't living under Mount Shasta.

I sighed as I closed my laptop. Whatever Evergreen Academy was or had been, its online presence was tiny and unremarkable. Whatever research was going on at the campus today, its leadership certainly didn't want the public to know about it.

Next, I searched for Professor East and found his bio on the Siskiyous Community College webpage. After a slew of accolades and degrees from well-known universities and publications in academic journals, there was a single-line entry noting that he was a distinguished researcher with the Evergreen Academy.

If Professor East was a biology instructor, with a Ph.D. in Ecology, that had to mean that Evergreen Academy was science connected, didn't it? Or was it a full-service college like SCC and bigger than I'd been imagining?

I changed tactics once more and did some digging into the property that encompassed Evergreen Academy. After a deep dive into public records on land ownership, I came across something curious. The area registered under the academy's name was about forty acres, but there was an attached parcel registered to Perennial Farms for another one hundred acres. I recognized the farm name from our local farmers' market.

Was there a connection, or did the two pieces of land happen to be neighbors? If there was a connection, the academy grounds were sitting at nearly one hundred fifty acres, much larger than I'd anticipated.

I dug around for another hour, finding a very basic website for Perennial Farms, but didn't manage to uncover anything revealing. Like that of the academy, its digital footprint was incredibly thin. I didn't know what to make of that for either place, especially now that I knew the academy was active. It seemed impossible for an individual, let alone an entire academy, to keep such a low profile online these days.

The dark-haired guy from the forest entered my mind again. The whole interaction had been so strange. He'd been there in the middle of the night, all alone. If I hadn't been about to touch the stone ring, would he have made his presence known at all? I had a thousand questions about the academy, and I knew myself well enough to know that I was going to struggle to relax my curiosity between now and Monday.

I took a break to water the flowers on the tiny balcony of our building, paying special attention to the climbing rose plant— lovingly nicknamed Rosie—that had been in my family for generations. The petals were a vibrant watermelon pink, and my mom had always told me I'd been named Briar Rose after the plant.

Aunt Vera and I had been carefully keeping it alive since my mom passed away, not wanting to let down either my mom or any previous generations of Belroses. As I looked at Rosie climbing a trellis against the siding of the house, I pictured the entrance to Evergreen Academy and the swirling leaves and vines on the logo.

"Stop worrying about it," I finally said aloud before letting out a deep breath. I put in my headphones, settled into the red Adirondack chair with my sketchbook, and stretched my legs out under the hanging string lights.

My heart rate slowed as I allowed the work with my hands to calm the endless questions. Come Monday morning, one way or another, I'd have answers about Evergreen Academy.

Chapter Six

When I showed up for my Friday morning shift at the bakery, Aunt Vera was already in the back room, rolling out dough for the homemade cookies that flew off the shelves.

"Good morning, B."

"Hi, Aunt Vera. Sugar cookies today?"

She nodded. I pulled on one of the floral aprons and washed my hands in the sink, the smell of the lemon soap invigorating me. The morning shift at the bakery required rising before the sun. Fortunately, I was an early bird. It was the one superpower I felt I could truly claim.

As I washed and towel-dried my hands, I debated telling my aunt that I would be visiting the Evergreen Academy on Monday. I'd told Maci I would wait until after, but now I felt strange not mentioning it.

My aunt had been my guardian since I was twelve, and we talked about almost everything. Still, she'd always encouraged me to have my independence, and part of that was respecting my personal space. She'd made an even bigger effort to convey that now that I'd turned eighteen.

Aunt Vera spoke before I could. "How was school this week?"

"It was good. Actually…" I steeled myself, deciding I wanted her opinion more than I wanted my privacy. "Something interesting happened in biology class. The professor thinks I might be a good fit for a research project."

"Really? That's wonderful. What kind of project?"

"I don't know the details yet, but"—I turned away from her, hiding my face by sifting through the mixing bowls—"it's through the Evergreen Academy."

"The Evergreen Academy?"

"You know, the one off of Highway—"

"Yes, yes, I know it. I'm just surprised. I didn't know they invited local college students there."

"I didn't either. To be honest, I'm not sure *why* I was invited. Professor East said he would explain more once we were out at the campus."

"And when are you going?"

"Monday. After my classes."

My aunt finished rolling and began to section the dough with various floral-shaped cookie cutters. "Well, that sounds exciting. You'll tell me all about it afterward?"

I felt my shoulders relax, relieved that she didn't seem to have any concerns about my going. "Of course."

Using a spatula, she transferred all the cookies to a few massive sheets and stuck them in the oven then turned to look at me. She put a hand under my chin and tilted my face upward. "Have I told you how beautiful you are lately?"

I grinned and pulled away. "Okay, Aunt Vera. That's enough with the ego boosting. You want me on the register when we open?"

"Yes, please."

I walked to the front of the bakery, which was filled with the familiar, enticing smells of freshly baked goods and perfectly brewed coffee, and got to work.

familiar, enticing smells of freshly baked goods and perfectly brewed coffee, and got to work.

Chapter Seven

On Monday, just after noon, I approached Professor East's office and forced myself to take a deep breath before entering.

My art class before lunch had allowed me to relax a little, helped along by a few self-deprecating jokes from Yasmin about how figure drawing was going. Now, I felt prepared to go in with a completely open mind and no expectations.

The door to the science instructor's office was propped open when I arrived, so I cautiously took a step inside.

"Ah, you made it. Welcome, Ms. Whelan."

I was about to return the greeting when Professor East stepped to the side, revealing another person behind him.

I instantly straightened my shoulders and swallowed. I hadn't expected anyone else to be here, so the sight of the young man standing in front of me immediately sent my nerves rocking again. And then my stomach dropped as I realized I recognized him.

It was *him*.

The mystery guy I'd seen that night in the forest outside the Evergreen Academy gate was here—in Professor East's office.

The one I'd thought about many times since and who I'd occasionally wondered if I'd conjured up in some kind of delusion.

The fact that he was real and standing in front of me sent my thought process out the window. So much for being cool, calm, and collected.

"Allow me to introduce you to Callan. He's a student at Evergreen Academy. He'll be accompanying us to the campus today."

Callan nodded in acknowledgement of the introduction, but his hands didn't leave his pockets, and his eyes didn't leave my face. His dark hair was a little unkempt, and he had thick, near-black lashes that I hadn't been able to see at night. He was a handful of inches taller than I was, and he had the lean muscle tone and defined jaw of someone who was very active. There was an easy posture in the way that he stood, but his eyes were a little too discerning as he gazed at me. What did he think he saw?

I swallowed. He had, after all, seen me sneaking around near his campus over the summer. Had he reported that to Professor East? Did I dare hope he didn't recognize me from that night? It *had* been dark.

I tried to keep my expression smooth. I'd see how he let this play out before acknowledging that I recognized him.

"Nice to meet you. I'm Briar," I said, trying to keep a frog out of my throat as I levelly met his gaze. Callan gave me a nod of acknowledgment before turning to look at Professor East. I followed his lead.

"Let me just…" Professor East closed his laptop and slid it into a dark brown bag then slung the satchel across his body. "Okay, let's go."

We walked in silence to the parking lot, the trees that dotted the entire campus providing welcome shade on the warm September day. Professor East stopped in front of a white van and pressed a button on the keys. He opened the sliding side door for me, and I climbed inside. Callan slid the door closed behind me, and he and Professor East got into the front seats.

Once I'd buckled my seat belt, I noticed some unusual things about the van. The front dashboard was covered in little mosslike plants, and a seemingly live string of pearls plant hung in a crocheted holder from the rearview mirror. The van smelled strongly of pine and lemongrass.

Oh no. This *was* a hippie cult.

"Professor East tells me you're... unfamiliar with the academy," Callan said from the front passenger seat as Professor East eased us out of the parking lot. Callan hadn't mentioned our interaction. So either I'd gotten lucky and he didn't recognize me or remember it, or he wasn't going to out me to Professor East just yet.

"I'd heard of it, since I grew up here. But I don't know much about it, no."

"Of course. You're a local." I thought I heard a tone of amusement in his voice, and I racked my brain through our interaction that night in the forest. Hadn't he called me "local" then too? Was this his way of telling me he *did* recognize me? I was glad he was facing forward and couldn't see whatever emotions were playing out on my face.

"Born and raised," I said, shifting slightly in my seat.

"We don't have many locals at the academy," Professor East added. "Our students come from all over the country, as I think I mentioned before."

I wanted to ask them more questions but decided it was best to wait and see what was in store for me at the academy.

Professor East received a phone call, and he answered on a headphone, seeming to have a normal conversation with a fellow faculty or staff member at SCC. Callan and I both sat in silence, our gazes mostly set out the window.

We were headed deep into the forest down a side road I'd never been on before. It wasn't the same one I'd taken with

Maci, Jace, and Mitchell the night we'd gone to Evergreen Academy together, but I assumed it led to the same place.

After about twenty minutes on the road, we pulled up to the large gate that connected the tall brick wall on either side. Professor East had done a bit of off-roading to get us there, but the van seemed unscathed.

I took in the logo on the gate immediately, which was much easier to see in the daytime. There was the symbol of the academy, a cursive *EA* surrounded by curling leaves. It was identical to the logo I'd seen online during my mostly unfruitful research.

We stopped before the gate, and Professor East nodded to Callan. "Go ahead."

Callan opened the front door of the van, and my eyes tracked him as I wondered what was going on. Then he pulled open the sliding door on my side. "What's your birthstone?"

"What?" I sputtered, the question catching me completely off guard.

"What month were you born?"

"Emerald," I said quickly, realizing he thought I didn't know my birthstone. "But why—"

"A May birthday, then." He paused for half a second, and there was a slight look of annoyance on his face that I wanted to question, but I was soon distracted by the small bag of gemstones he had pulled from his pocket and begun to sift through. Who carried a bag of gemstones in their pocket? Those couldn't be real, could they?

When he found an emerald—imitation, it had to be— Callan walked a few paces away and stepped into the circle of rounded stones on the ground.

I suppressed a gasp. It was the same circle I'd seen with my friends. The one Maci had referred to as a "fairy ring." The one Callan had warned me to stay out of.

I continued to watch as Callan knelt, held the emerald against the earth, said a few words I couldn't hear, then stood up again and made his way back to the van, stride even and assured, like what he'd done wasn't anything unusual.

What on earth had just happened? I glanced at Professor East, but he was staring casually at his phone. It appeared that the rule about no cell phones on campus didn't apply to the instructors.

"Do you prefer a necklace or a ring? I only have one emerald, so we can't do earrings."

"I'm sorry. I don't understand," I said, struggling to comprehend whatever was going on here as my attention snapped back to Callan. Was Callan making me *jewelry*?

Professor East turned from the front seat. "Everyone needs a charged gemstone to fully experience the academy."

A *charged* gemstone? I was now full of more questions than ever before, but Callan was looking at me expectantly.

"Ring, I guess," I said meekly. I watched as Callan easily set the brilliant green gem into a basic gold ring with some small tools, as if he were an expert jeweler, then he handed it to me.

My eyes went to his forearms and were immediately drawn to the tattoos again. I realized I'd been wrong about the ink in the dark. They weren't all black but a mixture of shades of onyx, gray, dark green, and deep blue. It was a work of art.

I pulled my eyes from the stunning design and to the ring he was holding out. I slipped it on my index finger, and it fit perfectly. "This isn't real, right?"

I looked up at Callan to see his eyebrows drawn together, but he quickly relaxed them and smirked a little. He closed the sliding door without saying anything and climbed back into the front seat.

"Of course it is real. Fake gemstone can't hold an earth charge." Professor East's voice was perfectly serious, as if we were still back in class, discussing photosynthesis. What the heck was an earth charge? I'd heard of crystals being charged but...

gemstones? Maci was going to lose her mind when I told her about all of this.

As the van rolled up to the gate, Professor East tugged a braided necklace from underneath his suit and held it up to something that must have been a scanner. I couldn't see anything against the brick wall, though. Wherever the scanner was, it was covered in thick tendrils of trailing ivy.

I felt a vibrating pulse around my finger and looked down in alarm, but the feeling was gone. A second later, the gates swung open inward, and he inched the van forward.

We drove a few dozen more yards through the forest, and then my breath caught in my throat at the sight that appeared before me.

"There's no way..." I whispered to myself.

A beautiful building the size of a small castle lay ahead of us down the trail, with glass-paneled floor-to-ceiling windows lining each of its multiple stories. Green vines snaked up the corners and between each panel of glass. A sprawling field of flowers—composed of more colors than I'd ever seen in one place, so vibrant it could have been a painting—lined the entire front garden leading to the building.

In the distance, I spotted a few white gazebos, each overflowing with flowering vines. And the trickle of water drew my attention to a fountain that looked like it belonged in Italy.

I sucked in a breath. This was no abandoned facility. This was the enchanted garden of childhood stories with a diversity of plant life that I knew couldn't possibly grow in this Northern California climate.

We climbed out of the van, and I stood there, staring at the greenhouse-like castle before me, so encased with plants that I thought it might be living itself. I caught Callan watching me, what looked like a genuine smile on his face, but his expression switched back to neutral the moment I met his eyes.

Professor East waved his hand in front of the building. "Briar Whelan, welcome to Evergreen Academy."

Chapter Eight

A butterfly flitted across my vision as I continued to take in the building in front of me, still enchantingly perplexed that the overgrown greenhouse castle was an academy of some sort.

The spell was broken when Callan said a quick goodbye and headed for the stunning building, and I briefly pulled my mind away from the awe of the moment to wonder why he had even been with us. Had he simply been catching a ride to campus? It was obvious that he wasn't sticking around to be my tour guide.

"This is... incredible." I let out a deep breath, and Professor East smiled.

"It is, isn't it? Let's go up to my office, and I can tell you more."

I followed his lead through the mass of flowers, some wild and others planted tightly in formation. The smell was like walking through a perfume store, though one that didn't instantly cause me a headache. Instead, I wanted to pull out the notebook that was tucked into my backpack and spend the entire afternoon drawing the blooms.

As we walked, two young women came from a covered area,

carrying buckets of potting soil. They greeted Professor East and eyed me curiously as we passed by. I glanced back to see them squat down by one of the flower beds.

We passed under a trellis-covered entryway, where vines of grapes were mixed amongst the vibrant flowers dangling overhead. Professor East reached up and grabbed one, popping it into his mouth.

And then we entered the academy, and I was completely unprepared for what I saw. The entryway was an atrium—the kind you might see in a fancy hotel that was attempting to bring the outdoors in.

Plant life sprouted from every direction, and I got the odd sense that the plants felt as welcome inside as they did outside. A few more students brushed past us, chatting loudly, arms full of books or scientific equipment.

We passed through the atrium and into the body of the building, where white stone made up the walls, columns, and massive curving staircases that stood on either end of the oval room.

"This is the central vein of the academy. From here, you can access any of the rooms on the first floor or take the stairs up to the second and third floors. My office is on the second floor."

I followed him, all the while letting my eyes soak in everything around me. Even here, plant life seemed to seep through the white stone, twining up the marble columns. Glass windows in every direction let in natural light. And more students, all appearing to be around my age, bustled about, heading into various rooms or outside.

Professor East ushered me into his office on the second floor. It was a corner room walled entirely in glass on two sides. Plants lined nearly every free inch of the space, plus a compilation of microscopes and other tools I recognized from biology class. A large bookcase was filled with botanical books and curiosities. A massive mortar and pestle sat on his desk.

"So, Ms. Whelan, it's time to tell you why I invited you here. Everyone who attends this academy has special... gifts."

I swallowed, wondering if he was going to mention the overly detailed sketches in my lab reports. Had they really been that memorable?

"The things you were able to see and sketch in class last week... Those aren't things you could normally see under a microscope. You would need a much more powerful electron microscope, if even that, to see those structures. During the lab class, you noticed the chloroplasts moving. But beyond that, you were able to see what was actually moving them—actin and myosin filaments. And then, in my office, you saw guard cells and gas exchange. These are things that are impossible to see at that magnification."

I stared at him, my eyebrows pulling together in confusion. "But it can't be impossible if I was able to see it, right?"

To my surprise, Professor East let out a laugh that was more like a guffaw. "Well reasoned. You are correct. It is not impossible for everyone. Not for those with certain... abilities."

I stopped short, eyeing him with skepticism. Was he saying I had extreme eyesight? "Abilities?"

"This might be a lot to hear, but there are some people on this Earth, a very rare few, who have, let's say, an extra affinity for plants."

I squeezed my lips together. I was brimming with questions, but I sensed that he planned to continue, so I held them in.

"Those with this extra affinity can see things in plants that those without it cannot. And, with training, those with this power can tap into and amplify the characteristics of some plants. They can work together in a sort of... symbiotic relationship."

I tilted my head slightly, trying to make sense of what he was saying. I understood that Professor East's scientific knowledge was much more advanced than mine, but this didn't even seem in the realm of modern science.

Professor East seemed to read my thoughts. He lifted a hand, and with a soft rustle, tendrils of a trailing plant snaked along the floor between us and crawled up his pant leg. It winded its way around his arm, a tiny green sprout landing softly in his hands.

I let out a soft gasp and jumped out of my seat. "What... What is this?"

Professor East released his hand, and the tendril fell gently to the floor. "I have a strong affinity for this type of plant, among others. Here at Evergreen Academy, we teach people how to tap into these affinities."

I suspended my disbelief for a moment and dove in with my first question. "So you think... you think that I have some of these... affinities?"

"Based on what you were able to see through the microscope, yes."

"I'm sorry, but that's really hard to believe. No plant has ever come and snaked up my arm like that."

Professor East's lips quirked. "Again, training is needed to truly capitalize on these gifts. It's not unusual that you wouldn't have noticed any dramatic signs of your powers yet."

"You said you have an affinity for certain kinds of plants. If I did have this ability, how would we know what types of plants I have affinities for?"

"Now that is an astute question. The academy will conduct a series of tests that will determine your affinities. Do sit down, won't you?"

I took the seat across from his desk once more.

"But... why? Why do some people have affinities? And what are you supposed to do with them?" My mind was whirling as my entire view of the world tilted like I was inside a fun house.

A half smile formed on Professor East's face. "That is the ultimate question, isn't it? As to why, who can say? As for what we're supposed to do with them… Magical botanists go into a variety of career fields. But that will come later. What's important to know now is that, as a magical botanist, it's imperative to attend school here to learn how to master your ability so that you can use it safely and ethically."

I choked. "I'm sorry. You said I'm a magical—"

"Botanist. Yes, everyone here is. It's a rare gift indeed and needed now more than ever. Plants and humans are at odds with one another, and that's not how it's meant to be."

My head was spinning. There were such things as magical botanists, and Professor East was claiming that I, Briar Whelan, was one of them? Before I could realize what was happening, Professor East was pressing a thin wafer into my hands.

"Eat this. You'll feel better."

I caught flashes of green and white and realized the room was spinning around me. I couldn't think coherently enough to argue, so I popped the wafer into my mouth. Nearly instantly, my vision began to clear.

"It's just a bit of ginger, maca, peppermint, and a few other herbs. It's proprietary and was invented here at the academy. You looked like you were about to faint, and these help you stay more alert."

The strong aftertaste of peppermint and other herbs I couldn't place lingered on my tongue, distracting me from the spiraling thoughts I'd been having a few seconds ago. I sat up a little straighter, my dizziness gone. But the confusion and shock remained.

Evergreen Academy was a school for magical botanists. And, apparently, I was one of them.

Chapter Nine

"Many students dual enroll here and at SCC. It helps to keep up our façade in the community. I looked at your schedule and saw that you're done by noon each day. We offer morning and afternoon classes here, so we can work out an afternoon-only schedule for you. And you're not currently taking any classes on Fridays at SCC, which is perfect, since that's our affinity studies day."

Professor East chattered on as we left his office and made our way down one of the two grand staircases. The windows all around let in rainbows of light that must have sustained the plant life that seemed to cover every free inch of the school's interior. A few students hurried past us, arms loaded with books and plant materials.

I tried to force my focus back to his words. My class schedule. I had purposely crafted it to end by lunchtime each day so that I could do my homework in the afternoons. That left my three-day weekend available for working at my aunt's bakery.

"I work at a bakery Friday through Sunday. It's how I pay my tuition. I could cut back to only working on the weekends, but that wouldn't leave me much time for homework."

45

Professor East nodded. "I guess I forgot to mention that being a research fellow with Evergreen Academy comes with a stipend."

My eyes widened, and I gulped as everything finally started to sink in. Was I really going to become a student at the Evergreen Academy, a school for... magical botanists? I suddenly felt lightheaded again, and I took a sip from my water bottle, wishing I had another of Professor East's wafers.

"And I get this stipend just for attending? Is it dependent on my grades?"

"We don't have traditional grades at Evergreen. So no, this isn't like a scholarship that's dependent on your maintaining a certain grade point average. Success here is measured in many ways. A lot of it has to do with your affinity powers and the areas of research you eventually take on. The grade is not the goal. The outcome is."

I swallowed another big gulp of water, wondering if I was dreaming all of this. I was going to attend a magical school where I would be paid for attending, and where I didn't have to worry about my grades. I was truly in an upside-down world.

"Hello, Ms. Ortega. Right on time." Professor East's voice interrupted my thoughts, and I turned, mouth falling open in surprise.

"Yasmin!" I gasped, shock coursing through my already adrenaline-fueled body.

Yasmin smiled broadly. "Briar! What are you doing here?" She glanced at Professor East. "That's a dumb question. Obviously, you're going to start attending the academy."

Professor East gave a slight smile. "I see you two know each other already. Yasmin here has a very strong affinity for mosses and ferns."

My eyes widened.

"I know, I know." Yasmin put her hands up. "It doesn't

sound that cool, but trust me, it is. Mosses and ferns are some of the unspoken heroes of the forest."

I smiled, my stomach relaxing for the first time since I'd arrived at Evergreen Academy.

"Mr. Rhodes didn't have time to give you the full tour, so I've asked Ms. Ortega to take over," Professor East said.

I blinked, realizing that Rhodes must be Callan's last name. The knot in my stomach that had been nagging me loosened at the thought of touring the school with Yasmin. Since I knew her from my art class at SCC, her presence made things feel more normal. As normal as was possible under the circumstances, anyway. I eyed her ruby earrings with a new appreciation and glanced down at my emerald ring.

Professor East said goodbye and slipped into a glass elevator behind the stairs, presumably returning to his office.

Yasmin looped an arm through mine. "So, you've already seen the entrance atrium when you came in and Professor East's office upstairs. We call this area down here the central vein because it connects everything else in the building. Like a leaf."

She turned us toward an open archway made of the same white stone that comprised the rest of the building. "This is research lab one. The first floor has most of the research labs, plus the teahouse. Most of the classrooms are on the second floor or outside. The dorms and the library are on the third floor. Don't worry about remembering all this. You'll get the hang of it when you start classes."

Start classes. The idea was dizzying. My brain snagged on another thing she'd said. "Teahouse?"

"Our affectionate little term for the cafeteria."

Yasmin tugged me from room to room on the first floor, and we poked our heads in to see a handful of students in each lab room. The rooms were an odd mix of modern scientific equipment and materials that looked like they were from an earlier century. Mortar and pestles were common, as were glass bottles, test tubes, and vials. And everywhere I looked, bits of plant material were scattered on the tables.

"What kind of research do people do here?"

"Oh, all kinds of things. It can really be up to you, depending on what your interests and affinities are. Most of the research happens during the second-year or third-year internships. The first year, we just do our foundational classes and our affinity studies."

We popped our heads into the last research room on the first floor, and I spotted Callan peering through a microscope while simultaneously scribbling something in a notebook. He lifted his gaze when we looked in, nodded at us, then got back to work.

"So, Callan is a second-year, then?" I asked Yasmin once we'd left the room.

"Oh no. He's a first-year. But he's very advanced. Are you ready to see the classes upstairs? Most people are still at lunch, so they should be fairly empty."

We went up the curved stone staircase again, and Yasmin showed me each of the classrooms on the second level. Some were similar to the lecture halls and lab rooms on the SCC campus, except each room was connected to the exterior of the building, so one wall was always made entirely of glass. The clear windows were scattered with the plants that climbed inside and out.

"And now for the third floor," Yasmin said. "I'll show you my dorm room in a minute. But first, the library."

My breath caught as we walked into the massive room. The walls that weren't glass were lined from floor to ceiling with books, and the entire roof overhead was glass, as if we were inside a human-sized terrarium. Cozy alcoves of cushioned chairs and even some hammocks were scattered around the corners of the room. Tables with books, pens, and what I dared to hope were art supplies were stationed at the tables. Plants poured out of every nook and cranny, vines and flowers snaking across the fronts of the books and along their shelves.

But the showstopper was the towering tree in the center of the room, its gnarled trunk somehow both living and hollowed out, opening to a miniature reading room inside it. The soft glow of tea lights flickered invitingly. The remainder of the tree ran upward through the library, the top somehow flowing seamlessly out of the glass so that no gaps existed.

"Spectacular, right?"

"I never want to leave," I admitted. I let my eyes roam over the oil paintings that covered the few open areas of the walls. There were paintings of leaves, flowers, roots, and portraits of a few people who looked like they were from a much earlier century.

"You can spend as much time as you'd like here when you're not in classes," Yasmin said. "Ready to see the dorms?"

"Does everyone live on campus?"

"Almost everyone. I do know of at least one student who lives off campus. Does this mean you'll be moving in?"

I blinked, mind racing. Professor East hadn't mentioned anything about moving on to campus. "I don't think so. I live locally with my aunt a few streets from the SCC campus," I offered.

"That's cool. So you'll be one of the rare ones who lives off campus. I think most people like to live here so they can work on their research at any time, and we have social events that span evenings and weekends. But sometimes I wonder if there isn't a benefit to living off campus and interacting with the real world instead of just magical botanists all the time." She winked, and I smiled.

"There are two wings: men's and women's. Men are to the left of the staircase from the library, and women to the right. My room is right"—she turned the knob to a door we'd just approached and pushed it open—"here."

My eyes widened, and a grin spread across my face. It was like I had stepped into a storybook home. "No way."

"Yep, I feel like I live in a tree house sometimes."

The window in this room was curved and rounded, popping her room slightly out into the forest. Outside, a massive tree was sprawled in front of us, its branches and bright green leaves extending toward the window.

A large round bed was nestled under the window, with shelves of books surrounding it. Potted plants in vibrant planters ran along the low windowsill above the bed, while hanging ones snaked down from the top of the window. I forced my eyes away from the glass to examine the rest of the room.

As would be expected in a college dorm, there was a wooden desk with floating wall shelves above it, and they were all covered with papers, plants, and a few teacups. There was a small closet, the doors wide open and revealing clothes in browns, whites, blues, and greens. Oversized fern plants adorned every corner of the room, both on the floor and hanging from the ceiling.

Yasmin waved her hand, and the ferns shimmied, as if waving hello to me, a dramatic reminder that Yasmin had a fern affinity. Aside from the one demonstration with the vine in Professor East's office, I'd yet to see anyone using their affinity powers.

"Okay, I am officially jealous of this room."

Yasmin laughed. "Well, you always have the option to move in if you want to. If not this year, then the next."

I looked around the room and tried to imagine it. It was too strange to even contemplate. And she'd mentioned next year. I couldn't begin to fathom what an entire year would be like at this school, let alone the idea of a second year. But a warmth bloomed in my chest at the thought that I could belong here.

Standing in this room with Yasmin, in the heart of the forest, calmed me in a way I couldn't explain. It was art come to life. And I wanted to explore every inch of it.

"This is a two-year school, then? Like SCC?"

"Technically, yes. Though most students go on to do an internship with a magical botanical field office during their third year, which is run through Evergreen Academy."

I wanted to ask her about the magical botanical field offices, but the existence of the academy was already a lot to process, and Yasmin was continuing her explanations.

"So, now you just have to do all your affinity tests this week, and then you'll officially be ready to start classes."

Reality snapped back into place. Right. It wasn't all fun and games and leisurely time in the library. We still had to figure out where I fit in the field of magical affinities, which I didn't at all understand.

The reminder that I'd never felt any kind of unexplainable pull toward plants snuck into my consciousness. Was there a chance that Professor East had been wrong in his assessment? If so, it would mean I didn't belong here after all.

I didn't look back as we left Yasmin's room, and she softly closed the door behind us.

Shortly after our tour, I caught a ride back to the SCC campus with Professor East, my mind swirling the entire way. Despite the wildest theories people had proposed about Evergreen Academy, not one of them was as wild as the truth.

It was a school for magical botanists.

Magical *freaking* botanists.

My thoughts were broken when Professor East spoke as we pulled into the parking lot at SCC. "Well, I'm sure that was a lot of new information today. I can drive you back to campus after classes again tomorrow to start your affinity testing, or you can drive yourself. Do you have a car?"

I nodded. "I can drive myself."

"Great." He pointed toward the ring on my finger. I'd nearly forgotten it was there, and I ran my opposite pointer finger across the smooth emerald.

"Just make sure you have that on you. Hold it up near the

gate, and it will open for you. And Ms. Whelan"—his voice lowered an octave—"in case this hasn't explicitly been said, Evergreen Academy operates in strictest secrecy. Only other magical botanists know of it. I know this may be difficult, but you can't tell your family or friends about it."

I met his eyes, heart racing. Perhaps deep down I'd known that I was being let in on a secret that others in my life couldn't be, but could I really keep it a secret... forever? What about Aunt Vera? Maci?

"Can we count on your confidence?" His eyes were steady on mine, then they flitted briefly to my ring again, and I wondered what would happen if I said no.

But I swallowed and replied, "Yes, Professor East."

The intensity in his eyes relaxed, and he smiled. "I thought so. See you tomorrow, Ms. Whelan."

Chapter Ten

"Tell me everything," Maci said, pulling me aside into an empty classroom before Biology.

I'd rehearsed what I was going to say to Maci the previous night, and the words flowed out of me now.

"There's not too much to say because students are required to sign NDAs, but I can tell you that they do scientific research there. Mostly involving plants."

I let out a deep breath, upset about the lie in the first part of my answer, but I felt that it would help me prevent future lies. If I was under a nondisclosure agreement, Maci wouldn't constantly ask about my time there. And with the way Professor East had looked at me and the emerald ring on my finger, I couldn't help but feel I *was* operating on some sort of magical NDA anyway.

I could see the disappointment in Maci's face. "An NDA? Bummer. But I guess that makes sense, seeing how they maintained their secrecy all this time. Isn't there anything you can tell me? Did they say why they selected you?"

My stomach churned. *Yeah, they selected me because they think I have magical plant affinities.* I cleared my throat. "Not

exactly. I still think it might have something to do with my drawing skills."

"So do they have classes, or is it more like research labs where you pop in, or what?"

I bit my lip, trying to determine how to avoid giving away more than I should. This was going to be as hard as I'd imagined. "They have classes, but I can't say much more about them." The honest truth was, at this point, I didn't *know* much more about them.

"Well, if you're ever able to tell me more, *please do*. The suspense is killing me."

I laughed and agreed then tried to change the subject in the last few minutes before class started. "How were the movies with Jace this weekend?" Maci and Jace had been on and off for the past year, and I was never sure if a new weekend was going to bring news of a breakup.

Maci made a little lovestruck sighing sound. "So much fun. You should join us next time! We could invite Mitchell too."

I cringed. "Maci, I've already told you, I'm not interested in Mitchell."

"All right, fine. But I'm going to find someone to fix you up with by the end of the semester. There's got to be someone worthy of your attention here at SCC."

"Something tells me I'm not going to have time for guys this year."

"Never say never. You know I'm a firm believer in 'work hard, play hard.'"

I was saved from responding as students began to spill into the biology class next door, and Maci and I followed them in.

"To be continued," she whispered, eyeing me meaningfully.

Biology passed in a blur. Maci was chatting with me constantly during the lab—during which time we were dissecting lily flowers—and I tried my best to give appropriate responses, but my mind was on my upcoming afternoon at Evergreen Academy.

Psychology would have been the same, except once I took my seat, someone settled into the usually empty one to my left.

"This seat taken? I don't like sitting so far in the back." The voice was smooth and friendly. I turned my head to see a guy with sandy-blond hair and a casual smile.

"All yours," I said, suddenly feeling flustered. Had this guy been sitting behind me for the past two weeks? He was undeniably cute.

I forced myself to focus on the conversation. My mind must have been all twisted up due to Maci's prodding about my nonexistent love life. I glanced at the front of the room. Professor Tara was still in the process of setting up her laptop.

"I'm Alex," he said.

"Briar. But everyone calls me B."

"Nice to meet you." Alex's voice and slight smile were smooth, and I tried to match his ease. "Do you live on campus?"

"No, I'm local, so I live at home. You?"

"With some friends off campus."

"Where are you from?"

"Southern California."

I raised my eyebrows, intrigued. Maybe he knew people at the art school I wanted to attend down there. "And you came all the way up here for school?"

"Yep. Wanted something a little slower paced. Besides, who doesn't want to go to college in a town called Weed?"

"It's named after a person." I laughed. I'd grown up with our quirky town name, so I often forgot how unusual it was to nonlocals.

Professor Tara began to speak then, so our conversation ended, but I couldn't help feeling aware of Alex's presence a foot away for the entire class. Now, instead of academies for magical botanists, I was distracted for a whole other reason.

Alex picked up the conversation at the end of class.

"So, do anything fun last weekend?" he asked.

"I mostly worked and did homework."

"Where do you work?"

"Vera's Café."

His eyes widened. "Home of the world-famous lavender scone?"

I laughed. "You've heard of it?"

"Oh yeah. Part of unofficial orientation at SCC is sharing the best places to eat. Vera's is number one for baked goods. I've heard her scones sell out in minutes."

"Good to know. I'll pass that along to Aunt Vera."

He angled himself toward me then. "You're related to Vera? This is perfect. You can text me when she's making a fresh batch of scones, and I'll come get them before they sell out. I'll be a hero with my friends." We were walking out of the building now.

"I'll text you, huh?" I asked, arching an eyebrow.

He reached out a hand. "Can I have your phone?"

With a nervous simmer in my belly, I fished my phone out of my bag and handed it to him.

He typed a few clicks. "There. I just texted myself. Now we have each other's numbers."

"For the scones," I said, voice conspiratorial.

"For the scones," he said with a grin, walking backward easily as he moved away from me.

I turned around and let out a breath as I walked back to the science building. This week was full of surprises.

Chapter Eleven

I drove to Evergreen Academy after my psychology class with my heart in my throat. While the spark of friendly flirting that had flared up in Alex's presence had pushed my concerns about the affinity tests out of my head temporarily, they were back in full. I was acutely aware that I had no idea what to expect, and that set me off balance.

As I approached the gate, I searched the area where Professor East had scanned his necklace the previous day and noticed a little carved leaf in the brick wall. I held my ringed hand out the window and felt that tiny pulse of energy again, and then the gates to the school grounds creaked open.

The sight of the massive glass-encased, vine-covered building was just as enchanting the second time. I parked in a small clearing where a few other cars were nestled in the shade then made my way to the building.

Yasmin met me in the entrance atrium and handed me a deep-green notebook engraved with a few leaves. I took it from her, noting the soft feel of the cover against my palm. On the front of the notebook read the words *Anno Uno*.

"Latin for year one," Yasmin said, correctly realizing that I

didn't know the translation. "This is the basic level that everyone works to complete during their first year of training. Next year, you'll get the *anno duo* notebook."

Carefully, I opened the first page and saw a place to inscribe my name. That page was followed by a table of contents listing the classes I would take as a first-year.

I swallowed as I reviewed the list.

FALL:
Latin for Botanists
Basic Plant Biology
Biostatistics for Botanists
Affinity Studies

WINTER:
Latin for Botanists
Chemistry of Plants
Biological Applications of Physics
Kitchen Botany rotation
Affinity Studies

SPRING:
Latin for Botanists
Flowering Plant ID
Ecology in Action
Affinity Studies

DESPITE A FEW EXCEPTIONS, WHICH STILL LOOKED challenging, it was chock-full of science and math courses. My stomach flipped. I navigated to the section for affinities and saw that the last quarter of the journal was reserved for Affinity Studies.

"Take this everywhere you go. As you complete your classes, there will be key pages to fill in. Once your affinity is determined, you'll start doing small group and independent research and practice that will be documented in that section throughout the year."

I relaxed a little as I skimmed the pages. My eyes were drawn to places on the soft pages to press flowers and sketch plant anatomy. Maybe there were a few areas in the classes where I could excel.

"I have to get to class now, so you'll meet Professor Tenella for your first affinity test. Affinity tests are conducted from most to least common affinities, so florals are up first. Her office is out in the flower gardens. Do you remember where that is?"

I nodded, picturing the luscious blooms we'd walked through on the way in. "Thanks, Yasmin. Do I need to bring anything?" I could feel my palms start to sweat at the thought of doing my first affinity test, nerves and excitement mixing in equal measure.

Yasmin inclined her head toward my hand. "Just your journal. Good luck."

After Yasmin disappeared down the wide hall of the indoor oasis that was the school's central vein, I turned toward the entrance atrium and made my way out to the gardens.

At first, I wasn't sure where I would find Professor Tenella's office. I hadn't seen one on the previous occasions I'd had to walk through the garden. But this time, I turned and took the first narrow row through the overflowing bins of canna lilies, petunias, creeping phlox, verbena, and dozens of other flowers I didn't know the names of.

As I followed the slender path, it spiraled through the garden and to a corner covered on three sides with trellises where flowering vines crept from the earth, stretched skyward, and dangled above my head. Underneath the spacious makeshift room were three wooden workbenches that blended into the trellises, each strewn with piles of gardening tools and dirt-encrusted notebooks.

A tiny woman with tanned skin and dark curly hair piled into a loose, springy bun by a floral bandana got up from a stool she'd been sitting on. "You must be our newest botanist," she said with a smile.

"Hello, Professor Tenella. I'm Briar Whelan."

"You're right on time. And the test is mostly completed. The floral affinity tests are considered to be some of the easiest, and it's the broadest group, so that's why we usually have new students experience it first."

I blinked. What did she mean that the test was mostly completed? I'd just arrived in her office cantina.

Professor Tenella gave me a coy smile. "Caught the meaning of my words, did you? Yes, this test started as soon as you walked into the gardens. I was observing how the flowers responded when you walked through. Typically, when someone passes through these gardens who has an affinity for florals, the blooms perk up and lean out of their planter boxes, as if drawn to the affinity in the botanist."

I glanced around me in slight alarm to see if I noticed any unusual leaning of the flowers around me, but they all appeared as they always had. "You said the test was 'mostly' completed? Is there more you'd like me to do here?"

The professor, who I deemed to be in her mid-fifties, nodded. She reached onto the workbench behind her and picked up a round plant container that was made of natural material rather than the plastic ones I was used to. She beckoned me over.

"I'm going to have you plant a flower. Do you know what to do?"

"I've planted flowers before. So just proceed as I normally would?"

When Professor Tenella nodded, I grabbed a trowel and scooped out a big pile of soil from the bag on the bench then placed it into the container. I continued to add soil until there was just enough space left for the nursery flower that Professor Tenella held out. I took it from her, carefully nestled it into the soil, added a bit more to top it off, and patted the whole thing down.

As I worked, I remembered my mom's advice about planting depth and felt confident that I'd done fairly well.

"Now, give it a little water." Professor Tenella held out a clay pitcher, and I took it and poured a small amount into the pot. I stood and looked at the professor, wondering what she was watching for. Her eyes studied the flower for a full minute before she finally spoke.

"Well, Briar, you don't have an affinity for florals. They're a huge group, so we usually need to do some more detailed testing to get specific affinities, but these first two tests determine if there's any affinity at all. If you had an affinity, we would have seen the flower you planted grow and bloom in seconds."

Professor Tenella went through the motions I just had with another plant, and I watched in amazement as a small green sprout stretched and opened into a vibrant pink snapdragon within moments. It tilted slightly toward Professor Tenella.

My shoulders fell, and she smiled kindly. "Don't worry about it, dear. This is the first test of many." She reached out a hand toward my journal, and I released it to her.

I watched as she flipped to the affinity pages. The first page had a list of each of the affinities. She went to the one for the category of florals, posed her pen below it, and scrawled *non par* in a looping script.

Was that Latin again? I was beginning to understand why Latin was listed on all three trimesters of my first year. I needed to start learning it—and quickly.

"So *non par* means..."

"No affinity match. But as I said, don't worry about it. You'll be with Professor Variegata next for a few other tests. I saw her a few minutes ago. She should be around the other side of the building somewhere." Professor Tenella pointed at a path that led through the flowers along the building, and I nodded.

"Thanks, Professor Tenella. Nice to meet you."

"Nice to meet you, too, Briar." There was a slight twinkle in Professor Tenella's eyes, and I found myself smiling as I left the cantina.

I glanced down at the flowers with renewed interest as I walked to the other side of the building. It was hard to imagine the mass of blooms bending toward botanists who had a floral affinity, as if the person were a ray of sunlight.

But a moment later, two students emerged from the glass building, and the nearby flowers strained toward them.

A little spark of excitement ran through my veins at this dramatic display of magic, and I headed to my next affinity test with a renewed sense of anticipation.

Chapter Twelve

After following Professor Tenella's directions toward the other side of the academy's exterior, I spotted another woman in an area of the garden where the plants went from ordered rows to more unwieldly patches, overflowing from barrels and running across the ground in every direction.

"Professor Variegata?"

The woman nodded. "Here for your affinity tests? How did it go with Professor Tenella?"

"I didn't have any affinity for the florals."

"*Non par?* Well, let's see how you do with these. I'll test you for what we call harvesters, which are foods like fruits, vegetables, lentils, grains, etcetera. I'll also be testing you for an affinity for grasses. Let's start with the fruits."

I watched Professor Variegata as she spoke. Her voice was smooth, but her hands were constantly moving. She held a long vine of some sort in her hands, and her fingers traced and twisted it. My eyes widened as she released the vine, and it snaked around her wrist like a bracelet.

She lifted a tray of fruit from atop a barrel and set it in front of me. There were dozens of fruits, including familiar ones, such

as apples and oranges, plus others I had never seen or tasted before. "Sort these."

I shifted my weight from one foot to the other, waiting for her to offer further instruction. "What criteria should I use to sort them?"

She clasped her hands together. "Whatever feels right to you."

Ohhhkay then. I went for my first instinct and sorted the fruits by color then by size in their color groups. Once finished, I looked at Professor Variegata.

"It looks like no affinity for fruits, but let's test a few other harvesters. If you had the affinity, you would have sorted these fruits into groups like stone fruits, citrus, melons, etcetera instinctively."

She led us out of the overflowing rows of flowers and into a cacti garden. I looked around, admiring the variety that spanned from smaller than my hand to nearly as tall as the school building.

We approached one that looked particularly protected by thick spines, and I recognized the prickly pear cactus that my grandmother had made jelly from.

"Reach out and touch it," Professor Variegata said, the vine moving in her hands once more.

My eyes widened, but I followed her instruction, carefully touching the cactus and pulling back quickly once I felt the sharp spines.

"Most harvesters are unaffected by the spines," she explained.

I wanted to say that touching the prickly pear hadn't been necessary, since I'd poked myself on many cacti over the years, but I bit my tongue. I still wasn't entirely sure how affinity magic worked and if it was something I would have manifested before coming to the academy and receiving my birthstone jewelry or not.

Professor Variegata took my notebook, flipped to the page for affinities, and scribbled *non par* under the cacti section.

"Now, the legumes. Are you familiar with them?"

"Um," I began, not wanting to let on how ignorant I was of plant classification. "Beans are legumes, right?"

"Right. And lentils, peas, some nuts. We grow almost all of them in our gardens here, and they're staples in our pantries." She approached a leafy green plant that looked like some sort of pea, and I realized it was the same one that encircled her wrist.

"Snow peas," she said with a soft smile.

She looked at me expectantly, and I quickly said, "It's beautiful." She nodded, seemingly satisfied by my answer. We kept walking and paused again at a small wooden table where brown cloth bags of recently harvested beans sat open.

"Grab a handful." She pointed at a bag of beans that looked like kidney beans, but they weren't all the uniform cherry color that I was used to seeing at the store. Instead, some had bits of a whiteish yellow.

As instructed, I reached into the bag and collected a fistful into my palm then held it out flat. I waited, and Professor Variegata watched my hand expectantly. A minute passed, and when nothing happened, she gestured back toward the bag.

"You can put them down. Do you know why you must soak or boil beans before eating them?"

Again, I felt ignorant, as if she were asking questions a fifth-grader should know. My knowledge of preparing beans was limited to opening them with a can opener and popping them into the microwave.

"Many legumes, including beans, have levels of lectin that can be harmful—even toxic—to humans. Boiling or soaking inactivates the lectins. It's an interesting area of research that some of our second years are engaged in. Those with an affinity for harvesters—and legumes in particular—will be able to inactivate the lectins just by holding the beans in their hands."

My eyes widened. "And you'd be able to see the inactivation?"

"The beans would soften a little and the color would fade slightly, yes." She was still holding my notebook, and she wrote what I assumed was another *non par* on its pages. "Grasses are next."

We continued to walk around the back of the school, where a large field of various grasses stretched to a massive pond. I spotted a few students in a rowboat, leaning over the edge with jars to collect some of the pond water. Beyond the pond, there were fields of wheat, oats, corn, and other varieties of grain that I couldn't identify.

"Walk through the grasses," she prompted, once again playing with the snow pea vine in her hands.

Stepping forward, I began to walk through the large field. About halfway across, I heard her call me back, and I turned around.

She wrote in my notebook again. "When someone has an affinity for grasses, the grasses will bend out of the way for them as they walk. The opposite of what happens with the flowers, which arch toward you."

I tried to mask my disappointment at having failed so many tests in a row already.

"The last test for harvesters will take place inside. This one is a rarer affinity, and not every harvester has it. I'll explain more in the Mendel Atrium."

The damp humidity of the Mendel Atrium hit me as soon as we stepped inside. The room was stuffed to the brim with palms and other tropical trees with air plants and orchids clinging to their branches. I recognized the distinctive heads of bird-of-paradise plants lining the walkway, and butterflies flitted overhead. A massive jackfruit protruded nearby.

My entire body relaxed, as if I were experiencing a tropical vacation.

"Now, this test is a little dangerous."

I turned sharply to Professor Variegata, all feelings of relaxation melting away. She'd asked me to poke myself on a prickly pear cactus and hadn't felt the need to warn me about *that*.

"Some harvesters take on the characteristics of plants that can survive the high winds of hurricanes. Like coconut palms, which only lose a few fronds."

She walked toward a box on the wall I hadn't noticed, hidden by plant life. "We are able to simulate all kinds of weather in here. Botanists with an affinity for palms are unaffected by storms. The wind and water bend around them. I've experienced it myself many times."

My chest tightened, realizing what she was going to do. "I don't think it's necessary to run this test, Professor Variegata. I've been in many storms, and I can assure you they do *not* bend around me."

"Maybe so, but you didn't think to look for this power then. It's possible the powers were weak, and you didn't notice that you weren't feeling the effects of the storm as acutely as others."

Acknowledging that she could be right, but still skeptical, I braced myself. Professor Variegata flicked a few switches in the box then came to stand by my side. Within a few moments, the room darkened, and the plants began to rustle as wind formed.

"Don't worry. It doesn't get to hurricane levels. There are plenty of plants in here that are more easily disturbed than palms."

Small comfort, I thought, wondering how strong a storm could get before being classified as a hurricane. My hair began to swirl around my face, propelled by the wind that was now gusting through the atrium. I peeked at Professor Variegata out of the corner of my eye and saw that her hair lay perfectly still, and she didn't seem to be squinting against the wind like I was.

She nodded, as if she'd seen enough, and returned to the control box. Within moments, the wind died down, and the full daylight returned. She signed my notebook once more then extended it back to me. "Well, Briar. It looks like you do not have any harvester affinity."

I tried not to let the disappointment show on my face, but I felt my shoulders crumple slightly, and my gait was shallow as I followed her out of Mendel's Atrium.

When we emerged in the central vein, the instructor and I went separate ways. Yasmin had said I would only be doing tests with Professor Tenella and Variegata today, so I wasn't sure where I should be headed next. Should I go home? But then I remembered the library, and I strode purposefully to the stairs.

The library was even more breathtaking than I remembered. A few students lounged in hammocks or papasan chairs, some with books, others with plants. I tried to stroll in casually as I entered the room, hoping none of them found me out of the ordinary.

I turned my attention to the nearest bookcase, scanning the titles. The entire shelf seemed to be dedicated to plants local to the area. There were nature guides like you might see in any bookstore, but there were other tomes as well, which looked much older. I took one off the shelf, carried it to a nearby table, and opened it.

After a few minutes of paging through the book, I wasn't sure what to make of it. Each page contained botanical images and illustrations, but most of the writing was in Latin. There were lists of phrases next to scientific processes, such as *Accelerated root growth*.

I was getting ready to turn the page when I heard my name and looked up to see Yasmin.

"Hey! How did it go?"

I shook my head. "No affinities yet."

"Well, that's nothing to be worried about. A part of me always wished I had an affinity for florals just because they're so pretty, but I've learned they're really not the coolest plants. Mosses and ferns have way more going for them."

I perked up a little at that. The idea of sharing an affinity with Yasmin was promising.

"So, tomorrow you'll do your aquatic plant affinity test with Dr. Lemna first. She can be a little... brisk, so just be prepared. It's nothing personal."

I swallowed. "Thanks for the heads-up."

"I'm heading down to dinner. Want to join?"

We both pushed back our chairs from the table and stood.

"Thanks, but I'd better get home." I wasn't entirely sure why I turned down her offer. It wasn't like I had a fancy dinner waiting at home. But the idea of eating the evening meal here, like I belonged, didn't feel right. I wondered if it ever would.

"No problem. I'll see you tomorrow."

"Oh, Yasmin, I have a question. Can you tell me what the Latin phrases in this book are for?"

Yasmin smiled. "Those are the phrases we use when we need to get our plants to do something. We call them *Floracantus*. But you might think of them as spells." ·

Chapter Thirteen

Yasmin and I traveled to Evergreen Academy together after art the next day. As it turned out, she didn't have a car and usually caught rides with other dual-enrolled students or with Professor East in his van.

Once we were at the academy, she directed me to the greenhouse by the pond for my aquatic plant affinity test with Professor Lemna. I breathed in the heady fragrance of the flowers as I passed through them toward the back of the academy.

A group of students were walking ahead of me, and I saw the flowers arch their stems toward them. Would I ever get used to seeing little signs of the affinity magic that the botanists here supposedly had?

The pond emerged into view, overflowing with flowering plants. A few ducks of various shapes and sizes floated across the glimmering surface of the water. As I drew closer, I recognized some of the plants from the summers we'd spent at my grandmother's cabin. The otherwise clear water was covered with water lilies, hyacinths, and hawthorns. Dragonflies flitted from plant to plant, their narrow bodies seeming to skim the water.

I itched to sketch the scene in my journal, but I wasn't sure if Professor Lemna knew I was on my way, and I wanted to make a good impression on each of the instructors here. So I reluctantly turned away from the pond and walked toward the greenhouse at its edge. Like all the other buildings at Evergreen Academy, the glass shelter had plants creeping all over it.

The temperature felt a full five degrees warmer as I stepped inside and saw a small group of students tending to fruits, vegetables, and other plants. One of them—a tall student with dirt all over the front of his shirt—looked up at me. "Can we help you find something?"

"I'm here to see Professor Lemna."

He nodded toward a far door. "She's just through there."

I thanked him and passed through the greenhouse to open the door he had indicated. My eyes widened at the sight before me. The room—an extension of the greenhouse—had a floor made entirely of glass. The clear material stretched out over a portion of the lake, so I had an unobscured view of the clear water and the fish and plants that were moving below the surface.

Hesitant to step on the glass, I lingered in the doorway.

Professor Lemna spotted me. "Yes?" she asked.

This professor couldn't have been more different from the two professors I'd met yesterday, despite my guessing that they were around the same age. She was taller and thinner than Professor Tenella, with short shoulder-length blond-and-gray hair that was fashionably cut. Her eyes were coated with a sparkly blue eye shadow and mascara of deep ocher. When she looked at me, her irises were a piercing bright blue.

I cleared my throat. "I'm here for affinity testing, Professor Lemna. My name is Briar Whelan."

She frowned. "No one told me I had an affinity test today. And I prefer Dr. Lemna."

"Sorry, Dr. Lemna," I said quickly. "Today is my second day

of testing. I did the floral, harvester, and grasses tests yesterday and was told this was next."

"And?" She arched an eyebrow at me, though the rest of her body language seemed uninterested.

"Excuse me?" I asked, unsure of what she was asking and starting to get nervous about the whole interaction.

"And what were the results of those tests?"

"Oh. No affinity. *Non par.*"

"Well, I guess I'll have to make time for you." Dr. Lemna let out a sigh as she cut across the glass floor in my direction. "Luckily, I have a few chemicals prepared already."

I didn't know what she was talking about, but I decided to stay silent. Unlike Professors Tenella and Variegata, who'd given me warm feelings, this instructor had my shoulders tensing.

Dr. Lemna stepped back into the main greenhouse room and indicated that I should follow her lead. We made our way to her office, which was enclosed with the same glass that made up the walls of the greenhouse. She reached into a wooden box and began to pull out small glass vials of various shapes, each containing some type of liquid.

Once she'd placed about a dozen vials into the portable container, she opened a door from her office that led outside. "This way," she said primly.

I hurried to follow her.

At the edge of the pond, Dr. Lemna knelt and opened the container she had just packed. She handed me a mason jar.

"Collect a sample of the pond water."

I took the jar, knelt, and pushed some water hyacinth out of the way to dip the container into the water. The water was cool as it pooled over my fingers.

"You're going to be running a series of chemical tests on the water."

I looked up at Dr. Lemna in confusion. Wasn't this test supposed to determine if I had an affinity toward water plants, not water chemistry? I steeled myself for whatever was coming, remembering how challenging Chemistry had been in high school. My mind went to my course list for the year, which indicated that I'd be taking Chemistry of Plants in the winter, and realized that Dr. Lemna was likely to be my instructor. A knot of dread formed in my stomach.

"Flip to the Chemistry of Plants section in your journal. There are some reference sheets there, and the first one is for a series of water quality tests. You'll be learning how to conduct these with much greater accuracy in the class, but for today, the basics will do. Follow the steps for dissolved oxygen, nitrate, and phosphate levels."

I took a deep breath and began to read the instructions in the notebook. I'd long ago learned to read through all the steps before attempting step one of a new process, especially when it involved chemicals. Dr. Lemna stood a few feet away, watching.

Twenty minutes later, I'd fumbled through all three tests, and I turned to Dr. Lemna for my next instruction. Instead of saying anything, she took the mason jar from my hand and studied the water. A few moments later, she looked at the values I'd recorded in my journal. She pursed her small lips together.

"There were a couple steps that weren't executed well in the testing, but as I said, you'll get practice with that in Chemistry. The main area of interest for the affinity evaluation is how the water reacts when you're studying it. When someone has this affinity, the water bubbles during the dissolved oxygen test, turns slightly green during the nitrate tests, and whips into a small whirlpool during the phosphate test."

My eyes went to the mason jar. The water had remained calm as I'd performed the various tests. "So I'm assuming I don't have the affinity?"

"Not a strong one, anyway. But some have weak affinities. *Infirmi par*. Let's go back into the greenhouse."

I followed her into the glass building, and we returned to the place where I'd first found her, in the room covered with a glass floor. "Walk out on the glass," Dr. Lemna prodded.

Tentatively, I stepped a foot onto the see-through floor. When nothing strange happened, I stepped out with my other foot and walked a few paces across the glass.

"Walk slowly back this way."

I took a few slow steps back to Dr. Lemna, who shook her head. "None of the plants floated over in response to you." She reached out a hand for my journal, and as she flipped to the page for my affinities, I knew what was coming. She wrote *Non par* in straight, even lettering.

My stomach clenched, and I couldn't help feeling disappointed. One of my favorite activities growing up, besides drawing, had been swimming in the lakes and ponds at my grandmother's cabin. I hadn't realized that I had been secretly hoping to have an aquatic affinity until that moment.

"I'll have you wash out your glassware before you go. You can use the sink in my office."

"Okay," I said, unsure of what washing the glassware would entail and hoping she didn't have a strict procedure I would unknowingly violate. "And then I should head to..."

She turned her head and looked at me sharply. Then her features softened a bit, and she sighed. "It's always so disorganized when we have out-of-cycle enrollees. Let me see your journal again."

I handed it to her, and she studied the index. "I believe Dr. Bowellia is free this period. You can find him by the tree houses."

Grateful that she'd offered some guidance, I thanked her and made quick but careful work of cleaning the glassware then left the greenhouse—and its clammy warmth—behind.

Chapter Fourteen

I had to wander around in the forest for a few minutes before I found the tree houses. In the end, it was a familiar voice that helped me find my way.

"Try not to crush the leaves as you load them," Callan's clear voice said from straight ahead, and I followed it to see him and several other students collecting leaves. Air seemed to swoosh the leaves into piles and then into the bags with a subtle movement of the students' hands.

I emerged in the clearing where they were working, and Callan's eyes flicked to me immediately. He raised his eyebrows then walked over to me. "What are you doing here?"

"I'm looking for the tree houses. I have my affinity test with Dr. Bowellia. What are you doing here?" After I asked, I realized the answer was obvious and that he was there for a class or affinity studies.

"Everyone here has a strong tree affinity. The time around each equinox and solstice is important for collecting plant specimens as the seasons change. There's a lot we don't know about these transitional periods. The opportunities are greatest at the equinoxes, and the fall one just passed."

I was surprised by the thoroughness of his answer. Callan crossed his arms, and I again noticed the tree-inspired tattoos that painted his forearms. I quickly glanced away and saw Callan's classmates continuing to collect and sort leaves without touching them.

"Interesting," I said, and I meant it. People often had the misconception that nature was fixed and that our knowledge of things like plant properties had long ago been determined and catalogued in textbooks. But I'd always known that what we knew was only a fragment of what was possible.

"P.B.'s office is in the first tree house."

"P.B.?"

"Professor Bowellia." Callan looked up, and my eyes widened as they made out the shape of wooden huts and pathways nestled in the canopy above, nearly perfectly camouflaged.

"Woah. Good thing I stumbled across you all. I don't think I would have found those on my own."

Callan grinned. "They were originally crafted by some botanists with tree affinities about fifty years ago, and we've been upgrading them ever since. Wait until you see the inside."

A little thrill of excitement coursed through me before his words dawned on me. "Um... how do I get up there?"

Callan nodded toward a nearby tree that had wooden rungs clinging to its trunk, leading up into the canopy. I gulped but didn't protest.

"Those of us with tree affinities can climb the trees without issue, but we added the rungs for the other students and faculty. Since we don't know if you have this affinity yet, it's safest to use the rungs. What other affinities have you tested so far?"

"Florals, harvesters, grasses, and aquatics. All *non par*."

Callan gave me a strange look but quickly smoothed his face. "Well, good luck with the tree tests." There was something in his voice that set my nerves working again.

"Thanks." I flicked the word at him and approached the tree

with the rungs, hoping Callan wasn't going to watch me climb the whole time. I took the first few rungs easily but slowed as I neared the top. I paused for a moment to catch my breath then suddenly felt a rush of wind push up from underneath me and plop me onto a platform the size of a doormat.

I leaned back against the tree, breathing hard as the shock of what had just happened hit me. I heard a soft laugh from below and looked to the ground.

Callan was standing there, arms crossed, a smile tugging at his lips. "Looked like you could use a little help."

Still trying to catch my breath, I tipped my head back against the tree and said, "A little warning would have been nice."

I heard Callan laugh again, but when I looked down, he was gone. I followed the wooden path that led from the platform I was standing on to one a few trees away, stepping carefully as the rope that held the slats of the path together swung lightly. I ended on a small platform again, but this time, it stood before a doorless entryway to one of the tree houses I'd seen from below.

I had to work hard to keep my mouth closed as I carefully stepped inside. The tree house seemed to be carved *into* the tree, which had to be at least the size of one of the world's largest redwoods. Like so many of the plants I'd seen on campus, I knew redwoods didn't normally grow here, but I didn't have time to dwell on that as I took in my surroundings.

In many ways, the inside was a miniature version of the classrooms in the main building, with a few tables, stools, microscopes, and solar-powered lanterns that hung throughout the space. They weren't on now, but I imagined it would be a magical place to work in the evening.

The scent of pine and other fresh woodsy aromas I couldn't place was strong, and I inhaled deeply as I approached the desk where Professor Bowellia sat. His skin tone was similar to the deep, rich color of the trees, and he wore a local SCC baseball team cap. I deemed him to be in his thirties, and his style was more that of a college student than a professor. No wonder Callan had referred to him as P.B.

"How was the climb up?" He asked, lifting his gaze to meet mine. There were slight crinkles at the corners of his eyes.

"Fine, though Callan helped get me over the last little bit," I admitted.

Professor Bowellia chuckled. "No surprise there. So, you're here for your affinity test."

It wasn't a question, but I nodded. Professor Bowellia stood and looked out the window to where I assumed Callan's group was still collecting leaves below.

"Are you afraid of heights?"

I braced myself, wondering what this task was going to ask of me. "A little."

"Let's start with the tree ring, then." He returned to his desk and handed me a tree ring the size of a hubcap. "Tell me how old this tree is."

I took the ring and set it on a nearby table, starting to count the tree rings as I'd learned in elementary school.

"Not like that," Professor Bowellia said, voice kind. "Hold on to it for a moment. For most of those with tree affinities, you will be able to tell how old it is without counting the rings."

Startled, I gripped the ring in both hands and studied it, but I didn't feel anything.

"Nothing?"

"It... just feels like a piece of wood," I said, feeling slightly embarrassed.

"That's all right. Some people have an affinity to the forest, even if not to individual trees. Trees are social creatures, after all. On to test number two."

I relaxed at his words and followed him out the other side of the tree house with a little more confidence. He seemed so easy-going after the near hour I'd spent with Dr. Lemna.

"We're going to see how you do with tree walking."

My feeling of calm quickly evaporated. "Tree *what*ing?" I repeated, trying not to panic at the chance I might have heard him correctly.

"All with tree affinities can walk effortlessly through the canopy, just like they can climb them with ease. The branches in this portion of the canopy are thick and close together. They'll move even closer to make a path for you, if you have the affinity. It'll be no more difficult than walking along the plank bridge like you did when you first came up here."

I tried not to let my shock show. "But, Professor Bowellia, what happens if I don't have the affinity?"

"Don't worry. You won't fall. Remember how Callan helped you up those last few rungs?"

I looked over the railing and saw Callan leaning casually against a tree below us. *Great.* Of all the people who could be watching as I fell to my death, I would prefer it not to be him.

Professor Bowellia nodded toward the next tree over, and I took a deep breath. If I was going to fall out of a tree today, at least no one could say I hadn't tried.

I eyed a nearby limb that looked sturdy and, after one last nod of encouragement from P.B., stepped away from the roped path. I let out a sharp gasp of fear as my full body weight transferred to the branch and it sagged slightly.

"Good. Now step to another branch."

I felt, more than looked, for a close branch and removed one trembling foot from the first branch to step on it. I tried to imagine my fearless childhood years of scrambling up trees, but my legs shook. As I went to transfer my second foot, I let out a scream as I felt myself fall.

Half a breath later, I was still screaming as a gust of air tucked underneath me—as it had when I'd climbed the rungs— and I was floated like a feather to the ground, where I landed with a soft rustle. I could feel my arms and legs shaking, and Callan calmly made his way to my side.

"Are you all right? I've never done that without a tree affinity, but I've heard it's no joke. You're safe on the ground now."

Professor Bowellia called from the path above. "There's no surer test than that one. Callan, float me her journal."

Callan reached for the journal I'd left at the base of the tree with the rungs and floated it on a gust of air and leaves into Professor Bowellia's hands. A few moments later, he sent it back, and I knew the affinities page now had an additional *non par* signature.

Chapter Fifteen

"Let's get dinner. You look like you could use some food." Callan reached out a hand to help me up from the ground, and I took a deep breath, trying to tell myself I hadn't just had a near-death experience. I also wondered if I should be offended by his statement.

I glanced down at my clothes and immediately wished I hadn't. My jeans and T-shirt were crumpled and crisscrossed with dirt.

I decided to change the subject and flip it back to him as I wiped some of the dirt off my jeans. He'd probably breezed through every test even if he didn't have the affinity. I realized then that I didn't know which affinities Callan did or didn't have, aside from the trees.

"Which affinities did you have when you tested? I'm guessing trees, but do you have others?"

Callan looked away, and I wondered if I'd been overstepping to ask. Were these the types of things that magical botanists considered to be personal?

I hurried to cover my faux pas—if I'd committed one. "You

don't have to tell me. I think I'm just looking to make myself feel better, since I haven't passed any yet."

"There are still a few tests left." Callan hoisted open a door to the side of the academy building, and I noticed that he hadn't answered my question. Still, I was glad that he was acting less frosty than he had when he'd escorted me onto the academy grounds the first day.

Callan led me to another massive glassed-in room where students were piling thin wooden plates with loaded salads, steaming pasta and vegetable dishes, and plump fruits that looked like they were from a Greek painting. Several students were bustling back and forth from the serving table to the kitchen, slicing the food and replenishing the supply.

Callan saw me eyeing them. "Harvester affinities. Or those on Kitchen Botany rotation. You'll get a taste of that in the winter."

I briefly wondered how he knew my schedule. Yasmin popped up at my side then, her long, dark ponytail swishing around her shoulders. "If you're ever here for breakfast, they make the most incredible smoothies, super-fruit bowls, and loaded oatmeal."

"That sounds amazing."

"Hey, Ortega," Callan said. "I'll leave you two to it." He gave me a quick nod then went to join some of the students I recognized from the leaf-collecting activities.

"Tree affinities," Yasmin said with a sigh. "They always take their food and run." She let her eyes drift out the massive glass windows, where the sun was beginning to set. "They eat up in the tree houses most of the time. That was so weird to hear my last name from him. I didn't even realize that Rhodes knew who I was. By the way"—she looked at a delicate watch on her wrist that had a tiny fern engraved into the plate—"do you need to get home at a certain time? I know you left before dinner yesterday."

I blinked at her words. She was correct. Yesterday, it hadn't felt right to be eating dinner with the other magical botanists, but this evening, as I'd walked back from the tree houses with Callan, the idea of eating here had felt completely natural. Could my comfort here really have changed that quickly, even without having identified any affinity powers yet?

We loaded our plates with food that was more perfect than any I had seen before. The leaves of my salad greens were more vibrant than usual, with a variety of berry and nut toppings that added crunch and color. There was homemade bread to eat with cheeses or eggs that were bursting with flavor and a fruit salad containing some fruits I had never tried.

"Where does all this food come from?" I asked Yasmin as we took a seat in the courtyard. I studied our surroundings as Yasmin took a bite of her salad. The white stone tables were in the style of something you might see in an ancient European courtyard, and trellises with grapes and other vines provided shade overhead.

"The majority of it is grown here. There are some nearby farms that we pick up weekly orders from for the dairy and meats. We don't keep livestock on campus, so only plant-based foods come from here. Which is honestly most of our diet. There's the fruits and vegetables, of course, but we have wild grains, corn, oats, rice. With the affinity powers of the students who tend them, we don't need to take up the normal amounts of space to grow a large quantity of those. Plus, everything has magically enhanced nutrients, so we don't need to eat as much of those types of items."

"That's incredible," I said after tasting the first few bites of my salad while Yasmin spoke. I wasn't sure if my praise was more for the flavor of the food or the wonder of the abilities of the other students here. My brain clicked on something then, and I paused eating. "I saw that Perennial Farms is connected to campus. Is that part of Evergreen Academy?"

She gave me a strange look. "Yes, though that's not widely known. How'd you find out about it?"

"Online research. I saw their parcels are right next to each other."

"Got it. Yeah, Perennial Farms has a booth at the local farmers' market. We have to sell our blandest, non-enhanced stuff there, since they might be suspicious of why our food is so much more flavorful, but it's still more nutrient dense than most of what they're getting. We have some devoted fans who order seasonal boxes from us every week."

"Does that help cover the cost of running this place and the stipends we get for attending?"

Yasmin nodded. "Plus, we have magical botanists in high places. Most of the academy's operations are donor funded."

I thought about the high-tech lab equipment I'd spotted in some of the rooms, more fitting for a PhD-granting university than a small college. But nothing about Evergreen Academy was normal, and having access to industry-leading technologies should not have come as a surprise.

Yasmin pulled a piece of paper out of her bag. "Professor East told me your schedule, so I made a little table for when you officially start classes next week. It can get complicated when you're dual enrolled. It's a good thing all your SCC classes are in the morning. Hopefully, you can get a similar setup next semester."

I looked over the schedule she handed me. She had neatly categorized my SCC and Evergreen Academy classes into Monday/Wednesday and Tuesday/Thursday columns. Friday simply listed Affinity Studies.

"Wow, this is great. Thanks." I studied the names of my Evergreen Academy classes again, and nerves seized my stomach. With all the affinity testing, I'd nearly forgotten that I would be attending classes soon. "I'm already a month behind, though."

"It might be a little challenging at first, but you'll be fine.

These aren't like traditional college classes, with tests and all that. Yes, we need to learn everything, but I think you'll find that it's kind of fun because it's so applied."

Her words echoed what Professor East had told me about achievement at Evergreen and that there were no grades. I tried to relax, but that blend of excitement and nerves that had been my constant companion since finding out about Evergreen Academy still kicked in my stomach.

I tucked the schedule into my bag and couldn't help thinking that Yasmin reminded me a lot of Maci. They were both so organized, not only for themselves but for me.

"Thank you again for this, Yasmin. I don't know what I would do here without you."

"It's my pleasure. I've always wanted to mentor someone, and you're super great to work with, so honestly, you're doing me a favor."

Just then, two other girls came and sat beside us. "B, this is Coral and Aurielle. They're both first years with fern affinities, so they'll be in your classes as well as your Friday Affinity Studies, if you end up having a lead fern affinity."

Coral, her dark-brown skin smooth as silk, waved. "Hey, B." I caught a trace of a Southern accent.

"Yes, we need more people in ferns!" Aurielle said, smiling at me in greeting before diving into her dinner. Her soft blond waves framed a round face that was sporting a slight sunburn.

"Nice to meet you both. I'd be happy to have a fern affinity like you all."

The ferns in the corners of the courtyard began to rustle.

"I know Yasmin has affinities for mosses too. How do people determine what affinity group to study in on Fridays if they have multiple affinities?"

Coral was the first to answer. "You typically study whichever your strongest affinity is. We call that your lead affinity. You can train your trailing affinities as well, but most students only have one trailing affinity, if any. I'm a one-trick pony with ferns."

I couldn't help but smile at the slight twang in her accent, and she quirked an eyebrow at me.

"You're wondering where I'm from, aren't you?"

I smiled. "I wasn't going to ask, but…"

She rolled her shoulders back and grinned. "It's not a problem. Proud Louisianan here. Though I have to say, I like studying around the lakes here rather than the swamps back home. There are far fewer bugs too."

"I'm from Connecticut," Aurielle offered.

"And I'm from Arizona," Yasmin said.

Aurielle and Coral looked at me expectantly. "I'm from here."

"California?" Coral asked.

"Yep, but also *here*. Weed."

Their eyebrows rose in surprise.

"Woah. A local. Your family must have moved here at some point because of the academy?" Coral asked.

I shook my head, questions swirling through my mind. Why did they assume there had to be a connection between my family and the academy if I lived here? Despite the friendly tones of the group, discomfort twisted in my stomach. There was still so much about this world—and myself—that I didn't know.

I smiled at the three girls and stood. "I better get going. I live off campus, and my aunt is expecting me home before it gets too late. It's great meeting both of you."

Yasmin joined me on the walk to the entrance atrium. "I hope you didn't feel like too much of a specimen back there. It's just rare to have a local attending school here, so they were being a little nosy. Botanical magic runs in families, but most move away after finishing their studies."

My head whipped toward her. "Botanical magic runs in families?"

She raised her eyebrows. "Of course. It's a genetic trait. Professor East didn't tell me much out of privacy for you, but he did mention that you were... new to all of this. So, you don't know which of your parents it came from?"

My mind reeled. There was no way my father was a magical botanist. We'd only met a handful of times, but deep down, I knew it wasn't possible. And my mother... My brain went wild at the thought. Though she'd loved plants and nature deeply, she'd never mentioned—and I'd never noticed—anything out of the ordinary.

Had my mom been a magical botanist? If so, what had been her affinities? My thoughts shifted to Aunt Vera, my mom's twin sister. Did *she* have plant magic? I blew out a breath, suddenly feeling unsteady.

"I'm sorry," Yasmin said, seeming to sense my discomfort. "I didn't realize you didn't know your magical heritage. Typically, affinities run in families too. All of the recent generations of the Ortega family have also had affinities for mosses and ferns, so they've been able to pass down some tips."

"Maybe that's why we haven't discovered any affinities for me yet. There's no way it came from either of my parents. Wouldn't there have been signs if they were magical botanists?"

Yasmin's forehead pinched. "You should talk to Professor East about it. He's a genetics expert, among other things."

A million thoughts formed again as I drove home that night, and when I slept, I dreamt of vines of green plants swirling around strands of DNA.

Chapter Sixteen

Thursday morning, I had Biology with Maci. On the way to class, she grilled me about Evergreen Academy again.

"Are you *sure* you can't tell me anything else? Do you swear there are no weird rituals? No cult? No private school for the children of billionaires? It's just a scientific research program?"

"Pretty much," I said.

"Huh. Well, that's a little disappointing. But, seriously, what an amazing opportunity for your resume. I imagine if you decide to major in science, this program will help you get into several prestigious four-year schools."

I coughed. Majoring in science? That wasn't in the forecast for me. Maci had hinted previously that I should consider other majors besides art, but that was not an option.

It wasn't that I'd always been terrible at math and science. I actually liked both until my mom passed. After that, I had the energy to focus fully on only a few things at school. I chose art, which was the passion we had in common and the subject that allowed me to get the most lost in work. I'd gone from being a grade ahead in math and a constant questioner in science to being in the middle of the pack with my classmates.

I'd known for the past six years that I would follow in my mom's footsteps and do all the things she'd never had a chance to do. It was the only way I knew to honor her memory.

"It is a good opportunity. I'm not going to be majoring in science, though, Mace. My focus is set on the art school my mom attended, with a few backup schools in case I don't get in."

"Fair. But think about what's going to pay the bills. Maybe this is sending you in a direction you never considered before. Maybe it's a good thing?"

I tried not to frown at her words. Why were people always saying that art couldn't pay the bills? Obviously, I couldn't sit around drawing all day, but many people had successful careers in graphic design, animation, teaching, game design. Even my aunt had managed to carve out an artistic career for herself as a cake and cookie decorator.

"Maybe," I said softly.

We passed through the door to our biology class, and Professor East greeted us as we walked in. He didn't show any signs of knowing me beyond as a student at SCC, and I made sure to do the same. Once the clock hit the top of the hour, he said, "Good morning. Today, we continue our lesson on photosynthesis."

"Better pay close attention," Maci whispered. "This may be your new major."

PROFESSOR EAST INVITED ME TO HIS OFFICE WHEN I arrived on the Evergreen Academy campus that afternoon. It was strange to now know him in two different contexts—as my regular biology professor at SCC, and as a sort of advisor of all things magical botany at Evergreen. I still wasn't quite sure what his role was at Evergreen Academy, aside from being a professor. It was clear that he was in charge, but he'd never introduced himself as a president or headmaster or whatever term would be used at a school like this.

"How were your first few affinity tests?" he asked once we were settled around his desk.

"So far, I've done the tests for florals, harvesters, grasses, aquatics, and trees. I didn't have any affinity for any of them."

"Okay, we'll see what shakes out in the remaining tests. You'll test for mosses and herbs today. Then you'll start your classes next week, with Affinity Studies every Friday."

I nodded and looked back at the schedule Yasmin had given me, my stomach tightening. How would I manage to keep up with my five classes at SCC and now four classes plus Affinity Studies at Evergreen?

As if sensing what I was thinking, Professor East nodded toward my schedule. "It's a full load, but many of the students at Evergreen are enrolled concurrently at SCC. It helps us to maintain our cover as an enrichment research opportunity for students there."

I didn't tell him that the cover wasn't working as well as he thought, given the amount of conspiracy and rumors that swirled about Evergreen Academy. Or maybe it was working a little *too* well.

My mind jumped to Callan for some strange reason. I remembered the bit of humor on his face when he'd whisked me onto the tree house platform and then the calm concern when he'd caught me as I'd failed my affinity test for the trees.

Was he enrolled at SCC? I'd never seen him there, but if he was enrolled, it was likely that he was in more advanced classes than I was. I imagined him taking Calculus with Maci.

"Do you have any questions for me?"

His prompt pulled me back, and I thought about the

conversation with Yasmin, Coral, and Aurielle the previous day. Had Yasmin told him that I was questioning the genetic component of magical botany?

"Since you ask, yes. Yasmin told me that botanical magic is… inherited. But neither of my parents have it." I didn't feel like telling him that my mom was no longer alive to ask about it.

Professor East steepled his hands. "We don't know everything there is to know about the genetics of it, but yes, it runs directly in families. Many of the students here grow up learning basic botanical magic from a very young age. It's so rare that members of our community tend to remain… close. Most magical botanical families are fairly well documented. I must admit that finding you was a surprise but not unprecedented. If no one in your family was ever trained, they may not have known about their powers."

I latched on to that explanation. Had I really come from a line of magical botanists who didn't know what they were?

"We can discuss this more, Ms. Whelan, but I've got to get to class. Professor Sato is waiting for you at the edge of the woods. She will conduct your moss affinity testing. Good luck."

Chapter Seventeen

As I walked to the woods, I tried not to worry about what the day's affinity tests were going to throw at me.

The test for aquatics, though challenging, hadn't been too terrible, and the one for florals and harvesters had been downright easy except for the hurricane machine, but trying to walk along tree branches had knocked the wind out of me. I wondered if the tests were going to keep increasing in difficulty.

You're being dramatic, I told myself. Callan had been there to catch me with his unexplained leaf-wind powers. There had never truly been any danger, except embarrassment. I took small comfort in the likelihood that Callan wouldn't be present at any more of my tests. I'd gotten the feeling that he was one of those people who were good at everything, and I didn't need him seeing how epically I was failing all the time.

When I reached the edge of the woods, I saw a woman with a broad straw sunhat, holding a small basket. I judged Professor Sato to be the oldest of the professors I'd met so far—probably in her late sixties—though her skin was so smooth that it was difficult to know for sure. She was wearing earrings that appeared to have tiny sprigs of moss encased in them.

"Greetings, Briar. Yasmin has told me that you're a local and that you share classes at SCC. She's a wonderful pupil." There was warmth in Professor Sato's voice, and I tried to return the friendliness while simultaneously wondering what this test had in store for me.

She placed a piece of moss in my hand, which I held out flatly, unsure of what to do.

"We must wait a few minutes. You can relax."

About three minutes went by, and Professor Sato examined my hand. "One of the tests for affinity toward mosses is that the moss, which has rhizoids instead of roots, will attach to the person and begin to grow across their skin."

I must have looked alarmed because Professor Sato chuckled and said, "It's not permanent." She placed the moss in her hand, and I watched with amazement as the fuzzy substance quickly spread across her palm and up her arm. Then she gave a subtle shake, and the moss fell to the ground.

"The mosses also have antiseptic properties, so our healers use them in addition to herbs. It's a wonderful thing to find a botanist who has an affinity for both mosses and herbs. Have you been tested for herbs yet?"

When I shook my head, she continued, "Okay, another test. Mosses are very unassuming, so it can take a few different trials to draw them out. We may have to test you against some of the other bryophytes as well."

I had no idea what a bryophyte was, but I nodded. It was clear that I needed a crash course in basic plant taxonomy. Professor Sato walked to a clear area, away from the trees. I saw a small stone circular wall on the ground. She pulled a lighter from her pocket, and I watched with interest as she lit a few strands of grass on fire, allowing the small area to burn until there was nothing left but soil.

"There. The soil should be cool now. Go ahead and place your palm on the ground." I followed her instruction, squatting to touch the soil and charred grass remains. "Hold it there for a minute."

Much like with the first test, we sat there in a relaxed silence while the time passed. Finally, Professor Sato said, "You can stand up now."

"I take it something would have happened if I had the affinity?"

"Mosses are one of the first living things to recolonize an area after a forest fire. It's a major area of my research focus, with the prevalence of wildfires in the state." She reached down and set her hand against the soil, where mosses instantly burst through the ground and covered the entire area inside the rock circle. "Those with moss affinities can amplify that power."

I crouched to the ground again and reached out to touch the moss, which felt like a soft, moist carpet underneath my fingers. "That's... amazing."

Professor Sato nodded as I stood. "I think so too."

She ran me through a series of other tests with mosses and some plants called liverworts and hornworts, but I tested negative for affinities to each of them.

"We're not exclusive like some of the other groups," Professor Sato said as we walked to the academy together. "You're welcome to pop in on our affinity studies classes on Fridays if you'd like to learn more about the bryophytes."

"Thank you. I'd like that." I had to admit that I was awed by the capabilities of the tiny plants that Professor Sato had demonstrated throughout our lesson, with the post-fire spreading powers one of the most interesting. It felt relevant to our local area, which had been hit hard by fires in the past. I experienced a small twang of sadness that I wouldn't share this affinity with Yasmin.

As I walked back to the academy, I tried not to dwell on the fact that I was another affinity test down and still wasn't showing signs of aptitude for anything. But I had to have some affinity. Otherwise, Professor East never would have invited me here.

I repeated that mantra until the massive glass academy stood before me once more.

Chapter Eighteen

The herb affinity test took place in the kitchen, where baskets and canisters of fresh herbs lined an entire wall and those still living overflowed out of planters along the counters under the wall of windows.

Professor Mendoza greeted me when I entered the kitchen. His wheelchair was covered with delicate vines, and a butterfly rested on his shoulder.

"Call me Sage. They're way too formal around here. We're all magical botanists. I'm not sure how much our non-magical PhDs should mean here."

"Okay," I said, still not wanting to refer to an instructor by their first name.

"Well, let's get right to it. Most herb affinities can be identified through cooking or through healing. We will test both today."

Sage clapped once then swiveled to the counter, where cooking utensils were neatly organized in labeled bins both on and underneath the countertop. "You can cook any recipe you want from this cookbook." He hefted a large book onto the counter and opened it.

"Feel free to freelance and fudge the quantities. Cooking is an art, not a science."

I'd heard that phrase before, and though I was an artist, that ability had never transferred into food preparation. I'd mastered the most popular recipes at Vera's Café and was good at baking and decorating our desserts, but my cooking skills were limited. I peered at the giant cookbook and began to flip through the pages, seeking something simple.

When I landed on a description of lentil soup that claimed to be a one-pot recipe, I got to work dicing onions and chopping carrots. As I prepped, I noticed that Professor Mendoza—Sage —had placed a tiny bowl on the countertop near my cutting board, and I was surprised to realize that my eyes weren't watering while I diced the onions.

"What is that?" I asked, nodding toward the petite ceramic bowl.

"It's a ground-up mixture of parsley, celery, coffee beans, cardamom, and cloves. It counteracts the sulfuric acid, along with our practice of keeping our onions chilled. I'm not sure if the mixture works for the layperson, but I amplify the herbs' ability to combat the acid with my affinity powers. Pretty neat, right?"

"Very. The school should bottle that and sell it."

Sage was about to respond when the lights in the kitchen flickered once, and I felt a subtle tug on the finger that housed my emerald ring. Sage rolled out of the room, and I hesitated, wondering if I should continue making the recipe.

Ultimately, I finished preparing the soup and left it on the stove to simmer. The spices quickly turned fragrant, much stronger than the herbs in the little spice jars in our kitchen at home.

I heard soft voices in the hallway outside the kitchen and moved near the door, bending my ear toward the sound.

"I thought the shield was charged at midsummer?" a voice I couldn't place asked.

"It was. It seems to be... weakening."

I stilled, recognizing Professor East's voice. What was this shield they were talking about? I glanced at my ring, realizing it must be related to how they kept people off the campus.

"We've known it's been losing strength, but to flicker like that? Should we be concerned?" That voice sounded like Sage.

"We're exploring our options. Let's just be glad it came back on immediately," Professor East said.

"And what about—"

The voices faded out as the speakers seemed to move farther away. I hurried back toward the stove and gave the soup a little stir. A few moments later, Sage rolled back into the room. He seemed surprised to see me, as if he'd forgotten what I was doing there.

"Is everything okay?" I asked.

"I think so," Sage said. "How's that soup coming along? Let's let it sit while you do the healing portion of the test."

I followed Sage into a neighboring room. Like the kitchen, it was littered with herbs, but many of these were unfamiliar. The counters were stocked with heavy mortar and pestles, tiny vials, and copper glassware. It reminded me of an apothecary out of old movies but with some more advanced equipment scattered throughout. I spotted a centrifuge in the corner.

"This is the apothecary," Sage said, confirming my thoughts. But he didn't launch into further explanation, seemingly distracted by the conversation that had occurred outside the kitchen.

He whisked me through whipping up a batch of elderberry syrup. Once I'd produced a large jar of the dark, thick syrup, Sage picked it up, scooped out a bit of the syrup, and spooned a small quantity into his mouth.

I waited with bated breath, unsure what he was testing for.

"I don't feel the spike of an immune reaction, which tells me this is an ordinary recipe."

When I looked confused, he added, "If you have the affinity for medicinal herbs, this recipe will cause an immune spike that would heal someone from a common ailment instantly. If you don't, it will still help speed the healing but not as dramatically. Our elderberries are stronger than most. As you can imagine, botanists don't stay sick for long around here." He grinned, and I smiled tentatively, though I was pretty sure I'd just failed another test.

"Your soup should be done now," he said, and we returned to the kitchen.

Sage opened the pot and scooped us each a small ladleful into bowls. "This is the fun part. If you have the affinity for cooking herbs, this is going to be one of the most flavorful bowls of soup you've ever eaten."

We both took a spoonful, and I thought it tasted rather delicious. The herbs had lived up to their potent smell, adding a spike of flavor that hit my tongue just right. But Sage took another bite and shook his head. "Just normal flavor. I'll have the students pack it up for you to take home. You live off campus, right?"

I nodded.

"I'm sorry to say you won't be joining our group of herbal affinity students. It was nice meeting you, Briar. I look forward to having you for your Kitchen Botany rotation. We'll make a chef out of you yet."

I smiled and thanked him then left the kitchen, my shoulders turning inward as I realized I'd failed yet another affinity test.

And I only had one more day of testing to go. A few botanists had multiple affinities, but I'd already struck out on most. Originally, I'd been hoping to have a cool combination of affinities, but now, I'd be grateful to test positive for just one.

I watched the butterfly float away from Sage's shoulder and out the window, then I left Evergreen Academy for the night.

Chapter Nineteen

The next morning, I approached Evergreen Academy with a sense of determination. Today was the day I was finally going to figure out what my affinity power was.

It was Friday, a day I had no classes at SCC and the first time I'd been on the Evergreen Academy grounds before noon. As I parked and walked to the campus, the air was calm and quiet, as if the academy was still waking up. But a strange feeling lingered in me as questions about what had happened with the so-called shield during my herbs affinity test the previous day arose.

Yasmin met me in the central vein that connected all the rooms on the main floor. "Hey, B. Want to grab some breakfast before your tests?"

The teahouse felt different in the morning as well. Students were scattered around the indoor-outdoor eating areas, speaking quietly and drinking from mismatched mugs. A massive tea bar seemed to be popular at this time of day, with a variety of loose-leaf teas and honeys ranging from pale gold to deep amber scattered across the shelves.

"Now I see why they call it a teahouse."

We served ourselves, and I tried a bowl of oatmeal enriched

with chia and flax seeds and topped with a mound of fresh fruit. Yasmin was eating toast with eggs, avocado, and a pile of seasonings that I was sure were bursting with flavor. A crisp morning breeze was flowing in through the fifteen-foot-tall glass doors that were propped open between the white arches that supported them.

I jumped in with my first question. "Did you feel what happened yesterday? With the shield? How does that work anyway?"

"Yeah, that was an eerie experience. The verdant shield is what really keeps the campus hidden from prying eyes. It is also tied into the powering of a few things here, which is why the lights flickered."

"Is that a common occurrence?" I asked.

Yasmin shook her head. "It's never happened that I'm aware of. Not since I've been here and not when my sisters were here either. There have been rumors that the verdant shield has been weakening over time, but that was the first time I've seen any real evidence of it."

"But why would it be weakening?"

"There's speculation that has to do with how magical botanists' powers have decreased over time."

"I heard something about it getting recharged on midsummer. Who recharges it?"

"The founders' descendants. Or, if none of them are studying at the school in a given year, recent alumni or upcoming students will come to charge it."

"Founders' descendants?" I raised a brow at the unfamiliar term.

"Descendants of the original botanists who created the school. Founders' descendants' affinities are super powerful, and most of them have multiple. Plus, when the founders created the school, they infused their magic into the soil here, effectively ensuring that their descendants would be the only ones who could charge the school's verdant shield. It keeps power in the family, I guess." She made a face suggesting what she thought of that arrangement.

Coral and Aurielle joined our breakfast then.

"So, you've got your last two tests today," Yasmin said, changing the subject. "Ferns"—she grinned at the mention of one of her affinities, and the ferns in the room shimmied—"and defensive plants."

"Do you know which test I'll have first?"

"You already met Professor Sato when you tested for mosses. She'll test you for the ferns too. Since it's affinity studies day, I'll be working with her for most of it. You can start with that then meet up with Professor East for the defensive plants test. He never arrives until after lunch since he teaches at SCC."

Yasmin finished her toast as I polished off my oatmeal, not wanting to leave one drop of the delicious meal in the bowl. "Friday mornings are a little slow around here. Everyone gets started on their affinity studies at their own pace. Well, except for Dr. Lemna's students. Do you want to do a walk around the pond before your fern test?"

When I agreed, we said goodbye to Coral and Aurielle then each prepared a mug of tea to go before making our way outside. The late September mornings were starting to feel chilly, and I zipped up my sweatshirt.

"So, what do you think of the academy so far?"

We approached the pond, and I smiled as dragonflies whizzed across it, hovering centimeters above the lily pads and water hyacinth. A few students sat in the nearest gazebo, chatting with mugs in hand. One of them was strumming a guitar.

"It's... incredible," I said, not able to fully express my thoughts. The tests had been flying at me so quickly all week that I'd hardly had time to process what I'd seen and experienced.

"I've been excited to come here for as long as I can remember," Yasmin said. "My sisters are quite a bit older than me, so I watched them come here when I was in elementary and then middle school. They had nothing but great things to say about it. It's the only time in our lives when we'll be fully immersed in a community of magical botanists our own age like this."

I wondered what it would have been like to grow up knowing that magical botany existed and to look forward to one day attending school here. Perhaps I wouldn't feel so out of place.

We looped the pond once—witnessing Dr. Lemna's aquatics students already at work at the pond's edge—then we met Professor Sato, Coral, Aurielle, and the others with fern affinities in an area of the forest that was covered with ground ferns.

"Welcome back, Briar," Professor Sato greeted me, and the few students that I didn't know yet turned toward me. "Everyone, you are welcome to get started on your affinity studies. Briar will be completing her affinity test for ferns today."

Yasmin gave me a subtle thumbs-up then walked away to join the other fern affinity students. It was time. I had a fifty percent chance of passing this test, which was higher than any I'd taken so far.

"Do you know anything about the life cycle of a fern?" Professor Sato asked.

I shook my head.

"They're unique in that they don't reproduce with seeds or flowers but with spores. And they have two separate plants through the process of growing—a gametophyte and a sporophyte. What you see here"—she ran her finger over a tall green stalk that was tightly coiled at the end and reminded me of a seahorse's tail—"is an adult sporophyte. It's getting ready to unfurl and become the ferns that you see all around us."

As soon as she removed her finger, the coil unwound, and a beautiful fan of fern emerged. "When someone has a fern affinity, the simple act of touching the sporophyte will cause it to rapidly mature and open."

She nodded toward another of the coiled plants, and I touched it delicately with my finger. I pulled my hand away, as she had done, and waited expectantly. But nothing happened.

"What affinities have you tested positive for so far, Briar?"

I felt my palms begin to sweat. This did not bode well. "None."

Her eyebrows knitted together, barely distinguishable under her broad sun hat. "And you're doing the tests in order? Which are remaining?"

"Yes. After this one, just the defensive plants test."

"Hmm. Perhaps we should try another test. That one isn't always conclusive. We'd better be sure." I followed her lead deeper into the forest, where the ferns were slightly more spread out on the forest floor.

"Ferns have a surprisingly large genome. Some of the largest, in fact, of any species, humans included. A lot of this extra DNA comes from repetitive DNA and something called transposable elements. These are often referred to as *jumping genes.*"

"Jumping genes?" I knew what a gene was from high school biology. I envisioned a picture of a chromosome, with the genes lined up to compose the shape. But I'd never heard of a jumping gene.

"So named because they move around in the chromosomes."

My eyes widened. "Is that... normal? Or is it caused by magic?"

"Normal, amazingly. But non-magical scientists don't have a good handle on these genes yet. We do." She pulled out her lighter and held it near the edge of a fern frond but didn't touch it.

"Do you... feel anything?"

I stepped closer, desperate to be able to say yes, but the only sensations I experienced were a slight breeze, the chirping of birds, and the voices of the fern affinity students beginning their research in the distance. "I don't think so."

She sighed and turned off the lighter. "I can feel the transposable genes jumping around in that fern like popcorn kernels in response to the increased heat."

Disappointment was creeping through my veins.

"May I have your notebook?"

I pulled it from my bag and cast my eyes toward Yasmin. How disappointed would she be that I hadn't passed the fern affinity test? And now, the only thing left was the defensive plants test.

After Professor Sato was finished writing *non par* under the ferns in my notebook, she passed it back to me. "Don't be a stranger. There's a lot to learn from the ferns."

I nodded and forced a smile, trying not to let my discouragement show. Yasmin jogged over to me while Professor Sato went to join her students.

"So, how did it go?"

I shook my head, swallowing hard.

"Really? I was sure you'd have fern affinity. Oh, well, don't stress. This means you must have affinity for defensive plants. That's a really cool and more rare affinity. Professor East will be here after lunch and will conduct the test. Until then, why don't you hang out with us?"

Yasmin's kindness made my heart swell, and I agreed, though I worried I would feel like an outsider the whole time.

To my surprise, though, the hours until lunch passed quickly. While I was still slightly dejected about the ferns, I had to admit that it was fun to watch the others interact with the plants during their affinity studies. The ferns were constantly shimmying around us, as if glad their affinity partners were nearby.

I watched Yasmin and the others unfurl the adult sporophytes, as Professor Sato had done during the first test, and collect fern samples for a project they were doing on fern-based sunscreen capabilities.

They used Floracantus, the Latin phrases I'd seen in the library book, to beckon their plants to do all kinds of things. I listened in awe as the Latin phrases rolled off their tongues like it was their native language.

By the time lunch came around, I was feeling much better. Watching how this group did their research, in a completely synergistic and self-directed way, made it look *fun*. It reminded me of why I had enjoyed the subject so much as a child.

Suddenly, I was excited for my last test. I was guaranteed to pass it and finally get started on classes and my own affinity studies.

I dined with Yasmin, Coral, and Aurielle again in the teahouse, making myself a salad with all different toppings this time. The options were endless, and I didn't know if I'd ever make the same dish twice.

We chatted about ferns—each of the women practically glowing as they described their affinity studies projects—and then I went to find Professor East.

"Good luck. Don't have too much fun without us," Yasmin said. The ferns shimmied in response.

Chapter Twenty

The defensive plants test took place in a clearing in the forest. Professor East and I were the only ones around, and I braced myself to finally experience a little bit of the botanical magic I'd been seeing all around the academy.

"Defensives are almost never the lead affinity for botanists. It's a trailing one for me. We still have students conduct research in the area, but since it's not primary, it can fall by the wayside. Defensive plants are... challenging to work with."

I swallowed. *Challenging?*

"Most plants tend to have some defensive mechanisms, but those we refer to as defensive plants are those with a bit of bite to them. They have defensive strategies that are beyond the ordinary measures such as thorns or unappealing leaf textures. Can you think of any examples?"

Only one came to mind. "The Venus flytrap?"

Professor East chuckled. "Yes, that one does tend to capture the imagination. It's one of the carnivorous plants, along with pitcher plants, cobra lilies, and others. Then there are those we know as poisons: nightshade, poison ivy, hemlock. The area we're standing in"—he signaled to the clearing around us—"is lined with many of these plants. We call this Perilous Grove, and students here know to give it a wide berth unless actively studying with an instructor."

Perilous Grove? Was this really going to be where I would spend every Friday? And would I be doing so alone? I was already missing the hum of activity and camaraderie I'd experienced with the ferns that morning. Aside from Professor East and me, Perilous Grove was empty.

He turned to a plant that stood about thigh-high, its leaves green and serrated. "This is a stinging nettle." He took a leaf and rubbed it between his fingers. "For those of us with defensive affinity, the nettle won't impact us at all. We're immune to the neurotransmitters and acids in the trichomes. Give it a go."

I touched the leaf and immediately felt a burning sensation against my fingers. "It burns!" I gasped, feeling like I'd just received an extreme rug burn. I looked down at my fingers and saw that they were turning red.

Professor East frowned. "Strange but not impossible. Defensive plants vary widely in their mechanisms." He pulled a glass vial out of his pocket and poured it onto my hand. Immediately, the burning ceased.

"What was that?" I asked, grateful for the relief.

"A magically enhanced concoction of jewelweed. It counteracts the effects of the nettle. All right. We're going to have to do another test. The poisons..." He looked around the clearing, and I shifted my weight on my feet.

Poisons?

"Ahh."

I eyed him warily as he walked toward a large plant with a massive pink flower that drooped toward the earth. "Yes, this should work. This is angel's trumpet, and it can cause hallucinations. I'll prepare a very mild tea for you to try. You should be immune to the hallucinations, but we need to confirm your defensive plant affinity before you start training."

We walked back to the academy's kitchen, and Professor East prepared tea from the flowers of the angel's trumpet. I eyed it nervously as he passed it to me.

I knew that—in theory—I had to have this affinity. I'd failed all the others, and this was the only one left. But on the off chance I didn't... The idea of hallucinations was nerve-racking, especially given what I'd just experienced with the stinging nettle. I glanced down at my fingers and was glad to see that the redness was completely gone.

"Just a few sips," he encouraged, and I swallowed the tea cautiously. He'd added a scoop of honey, but it still left a bitter taste on my tongue.

At first, nothing happened, and I was sure I'd passed. And then... I got the strong urge to go outside.

I left the kitchen, found a nice pool of water, and jumped in and began to swim. Why hadn't I ever decided to swim in the pond before? The temperature was perfect, and I was swimming faster than I ever had.

The water, warm and easy to glide through, rushed over my skin. I lifted one arm after the other, slicing through the water with a perfect freestyle stroke. The faster I swam, the more my arms seemed to move, propelling me forward through the pond.

But then a strong pair of arms wrapped around my waist and pulled me upward, out of the warm water. Something was shoved into my mouth, and a few moments later, my breathing slowed.

There were clumps of soil all around my feet. I looked at my hands and cried out. They were covered in dirt, and it was caked underneath my fingernails.

"What... what happened?"

Professor East's face was as smooth as stone. "You tried to swim in the flower beds."

"No, that's not right. I was swimming in the—" I glanced toward the pond, realizing it was at least half a mile away. And I wasn't at all wet.

"Unfortunately, this means you're affected by poisons, like most people. I even took a few sips myself, just to be sure, but nothing happened to me. This is most peculiar."

My brain was still foggy from the effects of the poison and the rapid removal of it from my system by whatever he had slipped into my mouth, but understanding was beginning to dawn. "So I don't have an affinity for defensive plants?"

Professor East shook his head.

But if that were true, and I'd failed all the other tests... was I not a magical botanist after all?

THIRTY MINUTES LATER, I SAT IN PROFESSOR EAST'S office. He'd sent me ahead and now walked in with two plates of a greenish-colored cake-like substance.

"Eat this. It will help draw out the rest of the poison and settle your stomach."

"I thought the poison didn't affect you?" I looked toward the cake on his plate.

"I just like the taste." He smiled softly.

I ate a few bites then voiced the question I had been wondering about since I'd come out of the hallucination. "If I don't have any affinities, then was this all a mistake?"

"It is... unusual. But there was no mistake. What you saw under the microscope cannot be seen by a non-magical eye. And the fact that your charged gemstone allows you to see the true nature of the academy can't be ignored. But that kind of power is baseline to all magical botanists and not specific to any affinity."

I contemplated his words for a moment. Did that mean that I was a magical botanist *without* any affinity powers? If so, what did that mean in practice? "So... is there still a reason for me to attend school here?"

My words came out as barely more than a whisper. I wasn't sure whether I would prefer him to say yes or no. It was clear that I was out of place, especially if I had no affinity power.

If I didn't belong here, I could go back to my normal life, in which all I was worried about was getting into art school and handling the midmorning rush at Vera's Café. But there was a part of me that had been getting used to the idea of belonging here one day. I felt like I was barely scratching the surface of this world. All of that had been hinging on me having an affinity power.

My mind roved over everything I'd seen at the academy, like a montage playing through my head. Every white stone wall covered with creeping plants, the floor-to-ceiling windows through which sunlight lit the living things both inside and out, each gazebo, greenhouse, and pond... They had seemingly sprung to life out of a fairy tale, and my desire to draw had never been as strong as it was here.

Every night before bed, I sketched the rare and exotic plants I'd encountered here. I didn't know I'd become so attached to this place in so short a time, but now that the prospect of it being taken away was on the table, the idea was devastating.

"Of course there is still a reason for you to attend. All magical botanists are welcome here, no matter how many"—he looked at me pointedly—"or how few affinities they have. Now keep in mind, classes may be more challenging for you without any affinities. You may have to work harder than the other students. But I know you're capable of that."

My chest relaxed in relief, despite the warning of more hard work to come. I didn't know if I would be successful at Evergreen Academy in the long term, but for now, at least, I was allowed to stay. And I was going to work my hardest to ensure that didn't change.

"I'll do my best, Professor East."

"Good. Now, enjoy your weekend. On Monday, the real fun begins."

Chapter Twenty-One

The following Monday, my history and algebra classes at SCC passed uneventfully, though my mind kept wandering to Evergreen Academy and what was in store for me with my first classes.

Yasmin greeted me with a smile in Art, and I was finally able to relax as we worked on drawing faces.

I completely tuned out all thoughts of plant powers, affinity tests, and Evergreen Academy itself as I sketched, pouring all my energy into capturing the tiniest of details—the curve of the jaw, the fullness of the lashes. I jumped when the instructor said that it was time to clean up.

I glanced over at Yasmin's paper. She put her pencil down with a sigh.

"I really messed up the proportions. The eyes are way too high."

"The trick is to always start the eyes much lower than you think you should. About halfway down the face. Don't worry, we're working on human faces for another few weeks."

"Holy smokes. You are *amazing*," Yasmin said, eyeing my

work. Our instructor passed behind our shoulders then and echoed Yasmin's words.

"Very impressive, Briar. You really shine in the details."

I beamed, and Yasmin gave me a high five once our instructor walked away. "Let's keep up that energy for your first Evergreen classes today," she whispered, and I experienced a jolt of adrenaline. I was really doing this.

Based on the schedule Yasmin had made for me, I would take Basic Plant Biology followed by Biostatistics for Botanists on Mondays and Wednesdays. On Tuesdays and Thursdays, I'd take Latin then another session of Basic Plant Biology. Apparently, the instructors in plant biology rotated out, and there was enough content to cover that we took it every day.

We traveled together to the academy and to my first-ever magical botany class. Basic Plant Biology was held in a large classroom on the second floor of the academy building. Wooden lab tables were arranged in neat rows throughout the room.

I was grateful for Yasmin as we entered because she immediately made a space for me at her table with Coral and Aurielle. I spotted the only other student I knew at the academy—Callan— at a lab table across the room with two other students.

Callan's eyes flicked to mine then straight to where Professor Bowellia was standing at the front of the room.

My thumb instinctively went to my emerald ring, which I'd been wearing ever since Callan had charged and assembled it for me. Why had Callan been the one to charge the ring—whatever that meant—instead of Professor East? Had it just been a convenience factor because he was in the passenger seat? Did all magical botanists have the ability to charge gemstones?

My thoughts were broken when Professor Bowellia began to speak. "We're continuing with the molecular structure of plants today. Pick your plant of choice, and claim your microscope."

Yasmin began riffling through a drawer attached to our desk

and pulled out a large fern frond. "We usually keep a stash in here," she whispered to me.

Coral and Aurielle began setting up a complex-looking microscope. It was certainly more advanced than the ones we used at SCC.

All around the room, students began to pull plants from drawers, backpacks, or the large aquarium that was nestled into a corner of the room. A few students left the class, presumably to get fresh samples from outside.

There was a soft riffling noise as papers began to drift to each lab table from Professor Bowellia's desk, and I remembered the moment when Callan had caught me with a mixture of wind and leaves outside. As the affinity instructor for tree powers, I realized that Professor Bowellia had that same ability. Though this time, no leaves were swept along with the breeze.

I looked over the handout and swallowed. Complex molecular equations dotted the page. Yasmin seemed to sense my lack of confidence because she said, "We can work as a pair. Just follow my lead. You're only a month behind, and you can start working in your botanist's notebook with the textbook for each class in the evenings to catch up."

I appreciated her words, but I knew I was much more than a month behind. If what I'd been hearing was true, most of these students had grown up in families of magical botanists and had been studying plant science since childhood. I tried not to let that discourage me and dove into what my friends were doing, closely monitoring every step.

Yasmin, Coral, and Aurielle led the way through the lab, sprinkling in small talk with the discussions of the molecules that we could somehow see moving around inside the fern plant.

"There's a garden party this weekend," Aurielle said after we'd completed the first section of the lab. "Are you going to come out for it?"

The question was directed at me, and I looked up from the paper I'd been doodling on. "A garden party?"

"They happen once a month or so. They're the main unsupervised social event around here. We have the solstice and equinox parties, of course, but the instructors come to those."

I thought of all the catching up I was already going to need to do, not to mention my homework for SCC. "Maybe. We'll see how far I get with all my catch-up reading."

"Oh, you *have* to come. Just for an hour or two. You'll have plenty of time for your academic work," Coral said, giving me a pleading pout.

"I'll try. When is it?" In reality, I wanted to go so I could get to know more about the school, including its social events. But I'd made a promise to Professor East to try my hardest. I couldn't blow off that promise so soon with the allure of a fun evening.

"Friday night. You can stick around after Affinity Studies." Yasmin's face fell in alarm, and I knew she'd just remembered that I didn't have any affinities to study. "I mean, you can study all day Friday then get ready here with us afterward. It will be perfect."

I nodded in tentative agreement, and we finished up the lab. All the while, I was wondering what a garden party for magical botanists might entail.

We went to Biostatistics for Botanists next, which was even more challenging than Basic Plant Biology had been. Professor Variegata was the teacher, and while her presence was calming, with her smooth voice and the constant movement of the vine snaking around her hands, it didn't make up for the fact that I was desperately behind. Math was a challenge for me on a good day. Throw in the aspect of botany that I was majorly ignorant of, and the stage was set for failure.

I walked out of class with my shoulders tense, feeling extremely discouraged but trying not to show it.

"Let's grab some dinner, and then we can hit up the library,"

Yasmin suggested. I followed her lead to the teahouse. We all ate together, with me mostly listening to the conversation of the other three rather than participating in it.

Today had solidified how behind I was, and my anxiety about doing well was creeping in faster than the vines that had shot up Professor East's arms on my first day here.

"You're quiet over there," Coral said when we were all almost finished eating.

"Just thinking about the mountain of studying I'm going to have to do to even begin to catch up."

"Good thing you made friends with a bunch of nerds, then. We spend most of our evenings in the library, anyway," Aurielle offered, and I smiled. At least I'd had the good fortune to meet these three.

We took a tray with a pot of steaming hot tea and four mugs up to the third-floor library and settled in to work. I'd received textbooks for my class that day, and I decided the best approach was to start at the beginning.

My friends sank onto some cushions in the corner, chatting quietly as they sipped their fragrant teas, but I peered inside the tiny room nestled in the tree hollow and found it empty. I stepped inside and took a seat at the small round table that was lit by the tea lights that were nestled inside the tree's bark. After a moment of marveling at the magic of the space, I opened my backpack and focused on the task at hand.

The textbooks at Evergreen Academy were similar to those for my classes at SCC, but there were a few distinct differences. Latin was scattered throughout, and many of the illustrations were two-dimensional. Instead of just a picture of a plant or a molecule on the page, there was texture and sometimes even smell. I leaned in to sniff a pine needle and was delighted by the sensation of being transported out into the forest.

I read the first chapter of each and found myself enjoying it immensely. While the chemical formulas and mathematical equations jumbled together, I allowed myself to relax about that for now and simply concentrate on the wonder of the story the words were telling. Magical botanists had a connection with plants, and that connection was somehow both supernatural and scientific.

The fact that this power existed and I had never known about it was stunning. Each page was like discovering a hidden secret, a forgotten language.

And somehow, even though I didn't feel it physically, this magic ran through me.

Chapter Twenty-Two

Alex was waiting in the seat next to mine when I got to Psychology the next day. "Hey, hey," he said casually. "What are you doing at lunch? Want to grab food in the food court?"

My stomach flipped in a not-unpleasant way.

"I like to crank out my psychology homework right after class, since it's usually pretty quick. We could work together," he added.

"Sure. That sounds good."

Our instructor began to speak then, and I turned my attention to her. Could Alex hear how fast my heart was beating? But then my stomach sank when I realized that I would only have about fifteen minutes available before I needed to head to Evergreen Academy.

When class ended, I quickly gathered my things. "I do have to be somewhere off campus by one, but I can grab food for, like, fifteen minutes?"

Alex smiled. "I can eat fast."

"What about our homework?"

"That was just an excuse to ask you to lunch."

Ohhhkay then. I bit my lower lip, smothering a smile. "Well, in that case," I said, trying to make my voice sound light, "I'm in."

The cafeteria was busy, but we managed to get through the line within a few minutes. I'd never eaten here before, since my classes let out at noon and I would head home and eat there or at Vera's Café. Alex swiped a meal card while I paid with cash.

"So, how do you like it here?" I asked as we took a seat.

"At SCC? Or in Weed?"

"Both."

"I like it. The forest feels like it's holding a secret, you know?"

I glanced at him in surprise but clamped my lips shut. There was no way he knew about Evergreen Academy. "Is that so?"

"Yeah, like the lemurians under the mountain."

I laughed. "You've heard about that already? I didn't realize the local lore was getting around."

"I had to do a *little* research before coming here. Just making sure I wasn't walking into anything crazy."

I raised my eyebrows. "And you heard about the lemurians and still chose to come?"

He laughed. "The stranger, the better."

"Good to know."

"So, is there anything about Weed you think I should know? Favorite dives? Local secrets?"

"Well, you already know about Vera's." I racked my brain. "There's an amazing place to get a burger and ice cream, but it's a bit of a drive and way out in the middle of nowhere."

"I'm not opposed to a drive. Or things that are in the middle of nowhere."

"What else?... We have an awesome little ski park."

"Nice. Do you ski?"

"I snowboard."

"Really? I've never tried either. I might have to check it out this year."

My brain started to swirl then, wondering if I'd have time for snowboarding this year. During my conversation with Alex, I'd almost forgotten I was attending a *magical* academy.

My world felt like it was split into two distinct halves—the time when I was at Evergreen Academy and the time when I was in my regular life.

I glanced at my phone and realized with a sinking feeling that time had run out already. I needed to get to Evergreen Academy for my second set of new classes. "Sorry, I've got to get going. See you Thursday?"

Alex's smile was bright. "I'll save you a seat."

Chapter Twenty-Three

Latin was a challenge from the very first moment. Not only was I a full month behind on the formal lessons, but most of my classmates had been using Latin at home since they were kids. I made a note in my journal to download a language-learning app once I got back to my phone.

In Latin, I was introduced to a book called the *Compendium Floracantus*, which contained all the botanical spells Yasmin had mentioned.

Despite my inability to read the language, I flipped through the book excitedly. Next to each Latin phrase was a description of what the Floracantus did, often accompanied by a picture or feature of a plant. There was a massive index, and I could search by task or by plant family. At the end of class, I tucked the new book into my backpack excitedly.

The second class was Basic Plant Biology again, though today it was taught by Dr. Lemna. Together, all the first-years who attended afternoon classes walked to the greenhouse by the pond. I remembered the affinity test I'd conducted with the chemicals by the water and swallowed.

But the class went better than I expected. Dr. Lemna asked

us to form into groups and then work through a portion of our botanical journals. We were to collect and study one aquatic plant and test it in a series of conditions of our choice. I could tell right away that it was a practice in the scientific method, which was something I was at least familiar with.

Working with Yasmin, Coral, and Aurielle, we selected a parrot's feather plant and took turns suggesting different conditions we could test it under. None of us had an affinity for aquatics, so we had to rely purely on science and the enhanced aspects of the academy's plants.

"This plant is considered invasive in a lot of areas. Maybe we should work on determining if we can find any way to penetrate the waxy coating. Non-magical botanists haven't had much luck with chemical control or herbicides," Aurielle suggested.

"Invasive," I mused, looking at the parrot's feather in a new light. "But the plant is not problematic here, at the academy?"

"Any invasive species that we work with here are well controlled by our magic. Dr. Lemna has all the invasive aquatics on lockdown. They can't reproduce without her allowing it. But we need to have them here for research purposes."

"And why can't those with aquatic affinities travel to places with invasive species problems and lock them down, like you're doing here?" I asked.

"Well, because we have to work within the confines of human scientific knowledge. And we don't want to push our control over plants too far, anyway. It's fine here, in a research setting. But in the real world, there are a million variables. We have to be more subtle and calculating," Coral said.

Yasmin smiled. "Can you tell Coral's parents work in international plant relations?"

"Sounds fascinating," I said, tucking away that piece of information for later. I had a million questions about this world, but my brain could barely process everything in the academy at this point, let alone the world beyond it.

"They seem to enjoy it. I think I'd like to pursue similar work. It's like peacekeeping but for botanists," Coral said with a shrug.

I followed their lead as we completed our work, but my mind couldn't help being distracted. It kept reviewing Yasmin's explanation the previous week about the verdant shield. Would it flicker again? And what did that mean for the longevity of the academy? I'd just been introduced to this place. The last thing I wanted was for its shield to be threatened.

"Coming?" Yasmin asked, breaking me from my reverie.

I realized that they were all standing, our aquatics research put away.

"Yeah," I said, glancing once at the sky, as if I'd see the invisible shield around us.

On Thursday, Alex sat by me in Psychology again.

"What are you doing this weekend?" he asked, easing himself into the seat.

I obviously couldn't tell him that I'd been invited to a garden party with magical botanists at a secret academy, so I improvised. "Mostly studying. And possibly hanging out with some friends tomorrow night. And I work on Saturday."

"Someone is busy." His voice was light, teasing.

He didn't know the half of it. "Just a bit."

"What time do you work at Vera's?"

"My shift is six a.m. to noon."

He whistled. "That's early for a Saturday. But maybe I'll get a craving for a lavender scone."

I smiled, the idea of him randomly popping by the café

surprisingly exciting. "How about you? Any fun plans this weekend?"

"Some friends from the dorms are having a barbeque. I was going to invite you, but since you're already booked up..."

I made an apologetic face. "I swear I never used to be this busy, but this semester is a whole other beast." I thought about Maci, and how she'd be falling over herself telling me to cancel my plans and take Alex up on his offer. A part of me wanted to. But Yasmin was looking forward to me joining her at the garden party, and I didn't want to disappoint her. My friendship with her—and everything about my experience at Evergreen Academy —was so new that I didn't want to rock the boat.

But here was Alex, looking adorable and inviting me to a barbeque. Something that felt so incredibly... normal.

"Maybe another time," he said, putting a pause to my inner dilemma. "See you later, B."

After giving him a little wave, I turned toward the parking lot, wondering if there was a way to make both my worlds balance in the boat that was my time and energy—and not tip myself into the ocean in the attempt.

Chapter Twenty-Four

On Friday, I showed up at Evergreen Academy first thing in the morning. Even though I didn't officially have Affinity Studies, I wanted to spend most of the day studying before the garden party that night.

As I walked across the campus, I noticed clusters of students in the forest, in the gardens, and out by the pond. Affinity Studies were clearly in full swing. I stopped into the teahouse to get a smoothie then made my way up to the library, which I found empty.

The morning sun was shining through the massive windows, the green of the plants adding to the sense of peace that I felt each time I walked in here. I couldn't think of a better place to tackle everything I needed to do.

I'd downloaded a language-learning app on Tuesday and had been practicing my Latin between classes at SCC and during downtime in the evenings, so I was starting to understand a few basic words and phrases. After a few moments of sorting through my journal, I decided to focus on Biostatistics, the area in which I had the most work to do.

The morning passed quickly, and I began to hear voices outside the library as students returned to their rooms before lunch. Soon, Yasmin popped into the library and whisked me downstairs, where we met Aurielle and Coral. The atmosphere in the teahouse was different today. Charged, somehow.

Once we got our food and sat down, it became clear why. Everyone was talking about the first garden party of the year that was happening that night.

"Should we all get ready in your room?" Aurielle asked Yasmin.

"Absolutely. And you too, B."

"Thanks," I said. "How late do these usually go? I have to work early tomorrow."

"That's totally fine. It starts at sunset, so you can be out of here by, like, eight or nine o'clock."

"If you're not having so much fun that you want to stay," Coral added.

"I always heard about these parties from my sisters. It's surreal to be going to one myself now," Yasmin said.

"You guys make this out like it's some huge deal. It's just a casual hangout in the forest," Aurielle said, and Yasmin shrugged.

I tried to suppress a thread of nerves. While I'd been getting along great with these three, this party would be my first real social interaction with the larger academy community. It didn't seem likely that everyone was as friendly as my fern-affinity crew. And with me not having affinity powers of my own, what would I have in common with the other students?

My attention was caught by a small gathering outside.

"So, what's up with those three?" I asked, seeing Callan standing with the two students he sat with in Basic Plant Biology. "I notice that everyone acts a little differently around them."

Coral lowered her voice. "Those three are all founders' descendants."

My pulse notched up, remembering what they'd told me about founders' descendants being more powerful than other botanists and being responsible for charging the verdant shield. Something had seemed different about Callan from the beginning, but I'd never been sure what.

"Callan descends from the tree founder, as you could probably guess. He's rumored to be the most powerful magical botanist in generations, stronger than any of the professors, even. Eli Quinn—" Yasmin nodded toward the tall boy with a sharp jaw, brown skin, and dark hair in a topknot "—comes from the herbal founder's family. He's also a member of one of the Northern California native tribes. Nevah Trinity"—her eyes shifted to the girl, and mine followed. She had warm brown skin and silky, wavy brown hair that reached her waist, even in a ponytail. "—is a descendant of the aquatic founder. She is a wiz with everything related to water, even those things that have nothing to do with plants. She swims like a fish."

"Wow," I said, watching as the three founders' descendants said a few words to one another then went their separate ways. Callan headed off toward the forest, and I assumed he was aiming for the tree houses.

"They're as close to royalty as you can get around here, not that botanists care about that sort of thing," she winked, and I smiled, though my head was spinning.

I thought back to when Callan had caught me as I'd fallen from the trees during my tree affinity test. Did all students with tree affinities have that ability or just the strong ones? And was this ability the reason he had been the one to charge my emerald gemstone? Instinctively, I felt for the gem on my finger and twisted it casually.

Just as I touched it, Callan glanced back over his shoulder to where we were all sitting in the courtyard. I realized I'd been staring, and I quickly turned my eyes back to my friends, trying not to wonder what he and the other tree affinities did when they went out to the woods. I had my hands full enough at Evergreen Academy without getting distracted by the mystery of the founders' descendants.

<h1 style="text-align:center">Chapter Twenty-Five</h1>

The ferns in Yasmin's room shimmied nonstop as the four of us got ready for the garden party. I watched in awe as Coral and Yasmin applied makeup from small vials.

"All of you have skin like glass," I said. "I'm so jealous."

"Oh, we're way ahead in plant-based skin care here. Like, decades beyond the most expensive products currently on the market. I'll get you some," Yasmin said.

Aurielle wiggled her eyebrows at Coral. "So, are you finally going to make a move on Waylon tonight?"

"I have no idea what you're talking about," Coral replied, dusting shimmering eye shadow on her lids. I caught the faint scent of roses wafting off whatever they were applying.

"You two never stop flirting with each other during Affinity Studies," Yasmin said.

"Wow. I didn't know everyone was so invested in our chemistry," Coral said, though she was trying to suppress a smile. "How about you, B? Has anyone caught your eye here? Or are you already dating someone outside of the academy?"

"Not dating anyone but... there is this guy at SCC."

Coral turned her freshly sparkly eyes toward me in the mirror. "Ohhh, a relationship with a regular human. How exciting. Time to spill."

"There's not much to tell," I admitted but shared about the few brief lunches we'd had together and his recent invitation to the barbecue that I'd had to decline.

"Do you want to wear something of mine?" Yasmin asked as the three of them finished accessorizing their outfits with nature-inspired jewelry. Coral was wearing a stunning pair of earrings that looked like wide golden ferns. I looked down at my jean skirt and white T-shirt, which I'd initially thought would be dressy enough for a party in the woods. It certainly was with my local friends, anyway.

"I guess I could borrow some jewelry."

Yasmin began to riffle through her closet. "And here's a jacket. It gets chilly out at night." She was right. The days were beginning to shorten now that October had rolled around. She handed me a trendy black jacket and waved to the jewelry box. "Help yourself."

While sifting, I landed on tiny white flower clips, which I dotted through the waves of my hair. Once I added a pair of delicate gold earrings, I instantly felt much dressier than I had before.

The four of us left Yasmin's room and descended the stairs. Other students were also making their way outside in small groups. I followed my friends' lead as they each grabbed a lantern from a table in the central vein.

"It's tradition," Yasmin explained. "No technology at garden parties, equinoxes, or solstice festivals."

Together, we continued out of the academy, past the back gardens and pond, and into a portion of the forest that I'd never visited before. By the starlight and lantern glow, I saw groups of students sitting on logs or in the gazebos that littered the area. Flowered vines stretched overhead across the clearing, like colorful and aromatic streamers. Music was already playing, though I couldn't tell where it was coming from.

"Pick your libation," Yasmin said, waving her hand toward the dozens of pitchers and punch bowls arranged on a flower-covered table. "Alcoholic, nonalcoholic, we've got it all. The drinks are made here and magically enhanced, of course. No one will be getting a hangover from these." She plucked a concoction off the table that appeared to be a mixture of pulpy orange juice, fresh cranberries and—I assumed—vodka.

I eyed the liquids, each labeled with a folded paper sign. There was everything from tequila mixtures such as Agave Attitude to Sake Secret to heather-infused beer. In the end, I settled on a sparkling lavender mocktail. Despite Yasmin's promises that the botanists had magically distilled out some of the more harmful properties of alcohol, I still didn't want to risk doing something stupid in front of a student body that I was just getting to know.

"Take a straw," Aurielle urged. "They're made of sugar and easily digestible cellulose. They disintegrate infinitesimally as you drink, so that by the time your glass is empty, they crumble into a little sugary ring that you can enjoy as dessert."

"There's Waylon," Coral said, taking a sip of her beer. "Couldn't hurt to go say hello when I'm looking this good. Anyone want to come?"

Aurielle nodded and followed her, but Yasmin and I found seats in an open gazebo. I startled when I heard a rustling above us and looked up to see two students walking across the branches overhead, lanterns swinging from their wrists.

"Tree affinities." Yasmin rolled her eyes. "They can never act normal at a party." As she said this, the ferns around the gazebo began to rustle, and I laughed.

"You're all magical botanists. None of this is exactly normal." I couldn't help but glance back toward the trees, wondering if Callan was up there, but the soft glow of the lanterns was gone.

"Touché. So, who would you like me to introduce you to? The academy's not that big, so, eventually, we'll all get to know each other. I'm most acquainted with the fern and moss affinities, of course, but I also have a lot of friends with harvester and herb affinities. My mom taught me that it's *always* good to be associated with the people who make the food."

"Your mom is a wise woman. My aunt's a baker, and she would say the same thing. Whoever you'd like to introduce me to is fine with me."

Throughout the evening, Yasmin led me around to various groups of people and worked me into the conversation. Whenever someone asked what my lead affinity was, Yasmin brushed them off with an "Oh, we're still working on that."

I wondered how long that line would work. Until the winter solstice when we changed classes? All year? Or had word already started to spread that I didn't have any affinity powers?

A few hours later, the volume in the woods had risen substantially. Students were singing and dancing to the music—which had a folksy undertone—and a group of students with floral affinities had started making flower crowns for everyone. I had to admit that, despite my initial nerves, I was having fun.

"Ah, the founders deign to make an appearance," Aurielle said just after nine o'clock, and I followed her gaze to see Callan with the two other students I was beginning to recognize. I ran through the names Yasmin had told me earlier. The boy was Eli Quinn, and the girl was Nevah Trinity. Nevah's curls were sleek and silky, as if her aquatic affinity kept them perfectly moisturized.

The three arrived together but went their separate ways, mostly gathering with others with their affinity powers. Many of the tree affinities were lounging around the campfire now, tending it, and Callan joined them.

It seemed like the clearing was quiet for a few moments when those three arrived, but then a boy who I'd met earlier—one of the aquatics—yelled, "Who's up for late-night pond races?" and the volume rose again as most of the aquatic affinity students ran after him.

"Pond races?" I asked.

Yasmin rolled her eyes. "It's hard to keep the aquatics out of the water, even when it's only fifty degrees and dark out."

"That reminds me, I have to get up for work at five thirty tomorrow. I should probably get going."

My three friends whined but also expressed their sympathy for my lack of ability to sleep in the next day, and we bid one another farewell. I didn't tell them that I would likely wake up naturally at five whether I was working or not.

"See you Monday!" I called over my shoulder then returned my mason jar glass to the receptacle on the table. At the last second, I remembered Aurielle's words from earlier and peeked at the bottom of my glass, spotting a peach ringlike gelatinous substance. I fished it out and popped it in my mouth, the not-too-sweet taste a perfect palate cleanser, like having a mint after dinner.

As I was leaving the clearing, someone strode up to my side. Thinking it was Yasmin, I turned toward her casually but then straightened when I recognized a deep voice.

"Hey, stranger."

"Hello," I said, not sure what else to say. What was Callan doing here? Yasmin's words from earlier rang in my ears. *The most powerful magical botanist in generations.* "Shouldn't you be walking the other way? You just got to the party."

"I was a little curious about why you're leaving so early."

"I have to work the morning shift tomorrow, so..."

"Got it." There was a hesitation in his voice, as if he wanted to say more.

"Yep, so no late Friday nights for me."

"How was your first official week here?"

I let out a breath, deciding to go the truthful route. "Well, the school's amazing. But I'm way behind on... everything. Especially anything related to math."

"Hmm," Callan said, and I stopped walking.

"'Hmm'? What does that mean?"

"Has Professor East said anything about it? Offered any... support for managing dual enrollment?"

"He did set me up with the stipend for attending here so that I can quit my job. I dropped down from three days a week to one, but I don't want to quit completely because—" I stopped then, not wanting to let Callan know that I wasn't sure I was going to last the entire year here.

We emerged from the woods, and I headed in the direction of my car. Callan stayed in lockstep with me. "Do you make it a habit of escorting everyone to their cars after dark?"

"Just the ones with no affinity powers to protect them."

My mouth fell open, and I quickly snapped it shut. So he knew about the results of my tests. "Protect me from what?"

"We're on a magically enchanted campus, but these are still the woods at night. The enchantments only work on humans."

I looked around us then, suddenly realizing how utterly dark it was and how thick the trees were. Cougars were known to roam these woods at night, but would they be inside the wall? "Well, thanks for the escort," I said as we reached my car.

He nodded, and as I drove away and checked my rearview mirror, I thought I saw him watching. What I couldn't understand was why.

Chapter Twenty-Six

During my Saturday work shift, I'd looked up hopefully each time the doorbell tinkled, wishing to see Alex. He'd alluded that he might stop by, but the closer it grew to noon, I realized that it had been more of a passing phrase than a commitment.

I spent Saturday afternoon and all of Sunday cranking out my SCC homework and flipping through the *Compendium Floracantus* when my aunt wasn't around. Any time I came across a Floracantus that sounded interesting, I wrote it down.

There was one for sustaining a flower's bloom for a long period of time, and I decided to try it out on one of the flowers on my aunt's balcony. Her petunias were still blooming, but it wouldn't be long before the colder weather caused them to die.

"*Longum flore,*" I whispered, even though my aunt wasn't home. I did my best guess on the pronunciation. Nothing happened, and I wasn't sure if I was even supposed to see anything visibly. The petunias didn't move or change color or do anything to indicate a magical botanical spell had been used on them. I made a mental note to try to observe if they bloomed

longer this year then put the *Compendium Floracantus* away for the night.

By the time Monday came around, I rolled from my SCC history class to math class with a yawn. I was starting to wish I had my Evergreen Academy classes in the morning instead of the afternoon just so I could have some of their magically enhanced coffees and teas.

Despite my tendency to wake up early, I required a dose of caffeine by midmorning. The caffeine from my cup of basic light roast barely seemed to be taking effect this morning, and the hard seat of my math chair felt like an assault on my senses.

"You look like you need one of these." A far too familiar voice came from my left, and I looked up to see Callan sliding into the desk next to mine, his hand outstretched with a paper to-go cup stenciled with leaves.

I stifled a gasp but attempted to pull myself together quickly. "Callan, hi. Um, what are you doing here? Do you have a message from Evergreen?" I whispered the last question, taking a furtive look at my SCC classmates. Most were slumped in their chairs or nursing their coffees, trying to wake up for the early morning math class.

"You assume I'm here because of you? Maybe I need remedial math." He nudged the cup onto my desk, and I wrapped my hands around it instinctively, inhaling the sweet scent of orange blossom tea.

I snorted. "Yeah, right."

Callan turned toward me then, one elbow resting casually on the desk as he eyed my textbook. "If I'm going to tutor you, it's easiest to know where you're starting from."

I flicked my gaze to his eyes, unable to continue feigning nonchalance. "What do you mean, you're going to tutor me?"

"Professor East thinks we need to help you get up to speed in some of your math and science skills."

I narrowed my eyes. On Friday night, Callan had asked if

Professor East had offered me any support, and now, here he was, being *sent* to tutor me. That couldn't be a coincidence.

"And you volunteered for the job." I said it flatly, but my brain was disbelieving. Callan was one of the busiest and most powerful students at Evergreen. He had founder duties that I didn't even know about. I couldn't imagine him having an abundance of time to tutor anyone, let alone me.

"Something like that."

My mind swam, trying to imagine what this was going to be like. With all the ways Evergreen Academy had upended my world in the past few weeks, my time at Siskiyous Community College felt like a sea of normalcy. I was an average student at SCC. Sure, I wasn't a star pupil in any class besides Art, but I wasn't a lifetime behind in magical scientific plant studies either.

And now, my two worlds were colliding.

"I'm assuming I don't get a say in this?"

Callan shrugged. "No one's going to force you into tutoring. But if you want to stay at Evergreen, you're going to need to keep up. Especially since you don't have any affinities yet."

I tried not to bristle. Did he really have to point out that we hadn't been able to identify any affinities for me? And what did he mean by "yet"? I swished my hair over my shoulder and turned my face toward the front of the classroom.

"I didn't even know you could still enroll this late in the semester."

"Professor East pulled some strings."

"Well, if agreeing to let you tutor me means you have to sit through classes that will probably be super boring for you, how could I say no?" I wasn't trying to be rude or snarky, but I really couldn't imagine why Callan would take the time to tutor me. Any number of students could do that. He must have had some ulterior motive. Besides, did I really want him to see how truly bad I was at anything to do with numbers or equations?

Callan hefted out a large book from his backpack, and from

the corner of my eye, I recognized the math text we were using for the class. He glanced up at the board then flicked to the page number that was listed there.

"I have the patience of the trees, remember? Now, drink up, local. Caffeine is going to be your friend this semester."

I frowned and flipped my textbook to the same page and tried to suppress a sigh. The patience of trees. Well, with my math skills, he was going to need it.

It wasn't until class had started and we were forced to be quiet that I realized he'd called me "local" like he had in the woods at the beginning of summer. All this time, I'd been wondering if he remembered, and if so, why he seemingly hadn't said anything to Professor East about it.

But based on his tiny smirk, I was pretty sure I had the answer to one of those questions. He remembered.

MACI WAS WAITING FOR ME WHEN I EMERGED FROM math forty-five minutes later. From the corner of my eye, I could see her studying us with interest as Callan said goodbye.

"Professor East gave me a copy of your schedule," Callan said. "I've got to get back to Evergreen for a few hours, but I'll be available this evening after our classes. Do you prefer to study there or here?"

I leaned back slightly, surprised that he was giving me an option and that we were getting started so soon. The answer was out of my mouth in seconds. "There."

Callan nodded. "See you then."

"Hope your patience is still holding up because you're going to need a lot of it to tutor me."

A ghost of a smile tugged at Callan's mouth. "Patience of the trees." He turned and walked away.

"Who was that gorgeous guy you were talking to?" Maci asked when I joined her.

"Just someone from my math class."

"It seemed like things were a little charged between you two."

"He's tutoring me, apparently."

"He works at the tutoring center?" I could see the gears in Maci's brain working in overdrive, wondering why she'd never seen him there.

"Not exactly. It's a private tutoring arrangement."

"Wow, I'm impressed that you're taking your grades so seriously." She gave me a high five. "Does he tutor for calc? He looks like he'd be more fun to work with than my current tutor."

"I think you're out of luck. I'm not sure that tutoring is usually his thing." I paused. "He actually attends Evergreen Academy with me."

Maci's eyes widened. "Why didn't you lead with that? He's the first person I've seen from that mysterious academy, besides you. You should introduce me."

I squeezed my fingers more tightly around the cup Callan had brought me, which I'd nearly finished. Callan's presence on campus was going to make it more difficult to fend off Maci's questions about Evergreen Academy.

"We're not friends or anything like that. He's just super smart, and they asked him to tutor me on some of the basics, since I'm, well, not doing so well in their classes."

Maci frowned. "You're not? What kind of classes are they?"

I stiffened, chastising myself for my slip. "It's mostly high-level science stuff. Way out of my wheelhouse. He's helping me with math."

"Well, don't stress yourself out about it. I'm sure you'll figure it out. Just give it time."

I forced a smile and tried to relax. "Thanks, Mace. Math and science just aren't my strong suits. I'm going to have to work hard to keep up."

Maci pursed her lips. I knew she was still confused about why I'd been selected for the "research project" in the first place, but she was too cognizant of my feelings to ask a second time. My flimsy explanation about Evergreen Academy being interested in my artistic skills was the best she was going to get.

We reached the tutoring center, and Maci darted her eyes to where Callan was disappearing around the corner of the math building. "Well, even if he's no good as a tutor, he's certainly fun to look at."

Chapter Twenty-Seven

Callan approached the table where I was eating dinner with Yasmin, Aurielle, and Coral that evening, seeming to appear out of nowhere. I felt my friends still, and the usually noisy table fell quiet.

"Ready?" Callan asked me.

"Sure. Just let me grab some more tea."

Callan nodded and moved away from the table, headed toward the central vein.

"What in the name of sweet rose petals was that about?" Coral asked in a loud whisper. All three girls leaned toward me, as if they were flowers and I had a floral affinity.

"Callan is going to be... tutoring me." It felt strange to say the words.

Simultaneously, all of my friends' eyebrows shot toward their hairlines.

"Seriously? I didn't know he tutored," Yasmin mused.

"I'm not sure that it's a usual thing for him."

Coral whistled. "Well, well, well. The mystery of the world's sexiest founder's descendent thickens."

I rolled my eyes but smiled. "I better get going. See you all

tomorrow." I refilled my mug with steaming periwinkle tea then found Callan waiting in the central vein.

"Library?" I asked, ready to head for the stairs.

But Callan nodded toward the door leading to the woods. "I have somewhere else in mind."

A few minutes later, we were in an empty tree house. Lanterns lit the space as the sun was rapidly setting. It was enchanting to be inside this environment that somehow seemed to have been built in conjunction *with* the trees.

"I thought the library might have too many prying eyes," Callan explained as I examined the space.

"Prying eyes?" What was Callan worried about? It was just tutoring, wasn't it?

"Some of the students here seem to have an... intense interest in me."

"Because of the whole founder's descendant thing?" The question slipped out before I could contemplate whether to bring it up.

"You heard about that." It was a statement rather than a question. He sat back and ran a hand through his dark hair. The tree tattoos on his forearms glimmered in the lantern light. Was he... shy about his magical lineage?

"Oh yeah. Apparently, you and the other two founders' descendants are much more powerful than all of us lowly botanical serfs."

Callan huffed out a laugh. "I wouldn't put it that way. But yeah, we have some advantages."

"And at solstice..." I began tentatively, thinking of the winter holiday that was fast approaching. "The three of you will recharge the school's verdant shield? What are we defending the school from, exactly?" I thought of his words as he'd walked me to the car after the garden party on Friday night.

He shrugged. "Lots of things. The elements are a big one. You haven't seen the academy in winter yet, but the plants will continue to thrive even when it's cold and snowy." He flipped his pencil through his fingers and continued.

"We have some protection from natural disasters as well. Wildfires and floods. And then there are the bits of our magic that keep non-magical people from seeing what's behind our walls. If they ever climb or peer over, they just see some nondescript cottage-like buildings."

Our eyes met, and I knew we were both thinking of the same moment—when I'd been snooping around the academy grounds with my friends.

I tried to hide the flush that I felt creeping up my neck. I was so close to asking him about that night—I wanted to know why he'd been there alone outside of the gates in the middle of the night—but I chickened out at the last second. He'd kept quiet about it to Professor East, as far as I knew, and I didn't want to give him a reason to change tactics now.

"Can you tell me how recharging the school's verdant shield works? Are you transferring some of your own magic? Pulling it in from elsewhere? Yasmin mentioned something to do with the soil."

Callan's eyes were still pinned to mine, as if he knew I'd changed my line of questioning slightly. "Are you trying to distract me from the fact that we have a stack of homework to work through?"

I sighed. So he was going to keep things close to the chest. "Polynomial equations are going to be the death of me."

Callan chuckled at my side, and I bit back a smile as I began to work.

Chapter Twenty-Eight

On Halloween, after weeks of a relentless pace of SCC classes, Evergreen Academy courses, and studying both on my own and with Callan, I was ready for a fun night out.

Alex had invited me to a Halloween party, and I'd accepted. I'd been excited all week, not completely sure if I was attending as his date or just as a friend. Either way, it promised to be a fun evening and change of pace. Plus, I'd always loved creating themed outfits, and Halloween was the ultimate dress-up occasion.

On my way out the door, my aunt tromped up the stairs, a small potted oak branch in her hands.

"What's that?" I asked, pausing to look at it.

"The town did the annual autumn tree cutting of Frank today. I grabbed us one of the cuttings, since you seem to be into plants lately."

I swallowed, glad her words were innocent enough. I'd been careful not to leave my Evergreen Academy books lying around where she could find them, but I supposed I *was* talking about plants much more than usual.

"Awesome. Shall we name him Frankie?" The town had been taking cuttings of Frank, the oak that had one of the letter boxes on the Wildflower Trail, for decades.

"How creative," my aunt teased. "It's perfect. Heading to the Halloween party?" She eyed my outfit. "Maybe you should take Frankie with you. It goes with the theme."

"Let's let Frankie adjust to his new environment before taking him to house parties, shall we?"

We had lined the steps to our apartment with carved pumpkins, and the candles inside were glimmering in the late evening light as I passed them.

I pulled carefully out of the parking lot, catching glimpses of children in costumes, trick-or-treating with their parents. I could practically feel the magic in the air, real or imagined.

I stopped by Maci's house to pick her up. Jace and Mitchell were planning to meet us there. As it turned out, those two had some overlapping friends with Alex, and we'd all been invited to the same party.

Maci looked stunning as she climbed into the car, long black boots stretching out in the passenger seat. She'd dressed as a pirate, with a short black-and-red dress and large captain's hat.

"Wow," she said, looking me over. "I wasn't sure how it was going to turn out when you said you were dressing as a plant lady, but you look totally adorable. The watering can is a nice touch."

I laughed. I was wearing a brown velvet jumper dress and had stuck plant leaves and vines all over my arms and hair. While I didn't have the power to have the plants twine around me, as many of the students at school did, I had gotten quite good at collecting plant specimens without damaging them, and I was proud of the display I'd crafted.

I wore potted plant earrings and had shimmering dark green powder dusted at the corners of my eyes, matching my emerald ring. My daisy-printed backpack was on my back, stuffed with a few essentials and my notebooks, which I hardly went anywhere without.

When we arrived at the house party, we could already hear music blaring from the street. I debated what the chances were that the cops wouldn't get called this evening and decided the odds weren't great.

Inside, I couldn't help but compare the dingy, sparse surroundings with the bright, warm atmosphere of the Evergreen Academy. Still, I had to give the guys who rented the house credit for taping a few Halloween decorations to the wall and getting an orange-and-black LED disco ball spinning.

"You made it!"

I heard Alex's voice and spun to see him wearing a baseball jersey from a Southern California team, black smudges of paint under his eyes.

"Nice outfit. Wonder where you got it," I teased.

"This was all I had in my closet that could be considered a costume," he said with a grin. "Are you... poison ivy?"

"A crazy plant lady, but poison ivy works too."

"Isn't she precious?" Maci said, and I couldn't help but feel slightly put off by her comment. But as I introduced my two friends, Alex slung an arm over my shoulder, and the feeling was quickly replaced by a flutter of nerves in my stomach. Maybe this was a date, after all.

"I'm going to go find Jace. He said he and Mitchell are here already," Maci said.

"Want me to come with you?"

"You two have fun." She wiggled her eyebrows and disappeared into the crowd.

"Let's put your backpack down in the coat closet," Alex suggested.

"Oh, it's fine. I can leave it on."

"It's no big deal. I want you to be comfortable. It's pretty crowded in here."

"Okay, sure," I said, not wanting to argue the point. Alex led me down a hallway to a coat closet, and we set my backpack up on a shelf.

"Let me introduce you to some friends," Alex said, and I followed him into the kitchen. "Fellas, this is Briar."

They took turns introducing themselves, usually adding their major. I wondered if it was an inside joke.

"Colin. Engineering."

"Aron. Chemistry."

"River. Political Science."

"How about you, Briar?" Colin asked. "What's your major?"

"Art," I said brightly.

"For now," Alex said with a grin as he cracked open a bottle of beer.

I turned toward him. "What do you mean?"

"No one actually majors in art, right?"

"I plan to," I said firmly, suddenly indignant. He'd known I was majoring in art. It had come up during our lunches together. So why was he changing his tune now, in front of his friends? He was ranging awfully closely to echoing the thoughts Maci had put more delicately over the last few months.

I could hear her voice in my head. *All I'm saying is don't put all your eggs in one basket. Art isn't that reliable of a career, is it? Maybe you should at least choose a high-demand minor.*

Alex put his hands up. "Sorry, Poison Ivy. No offense meant."

I nodded, and the conversation changed directions to talk of baseball, but an unsettled feeling remained in my gut.

The next hour was a swirl of unfamiliar faces, people laughing loudly, and turning down offers of beer. Finally, I'd wised up and filled a red Solo cup with soda so people would stop offering.

As the party progressed and the voices grew louder, I couldn't help but feel out of place. This was nothing like the garden party I'd attended with my friends at Evergreen Academy. After doing my best to socialize in the hot, crowded room, I decided I needed some air.

"I'm gonna look for Maci," I leaned over and said loudly in Alex's ear. It was hard to hear anything clearly over the pounding music. He nodded, and I began to search the house.

When I didn't find Maci inside, I went to the backyard, where a large portion of the party had gathered. Almost immediately, I spotted a familiar pirate's hat. That was when I realized that Maci was shouting. I moved toward her to see that she was arguing with Jace.

Oh boy. Trouble in paradise—again. As I took a step forward to join them and support my friend, a familiar voice spoke near my ear. "I see you decided to go on the nose with your costume."

I jumped and swiveled in shock to see Callan. I recovered, ready to assess his costume. But... he wasn't wearing one. He was in jeans and a T-shirt, looking like a model from a magazine, as always. "At least I have a costume! Didn't you get the memo that this was a Halloween party?"

He put his hands up. "I wasn't criticizing. You look... delightful."

I eyed him skeptically. So far that night, I'd been called adorable, precious, and delightful, and it all felt condescending. Couldn't one wear a cute, clever costume that wasn't sexy?

"Okay, why do you look pissed?"

I tried to relax my scowl. Callan had no way of knowing the odd feeling I'd been fighting that whole night. I'd always fit in in social situations in high school, but for some reason, I didn't feel like I fit in here at all.

I assumed that it might have just been because I'd been so put off by Alex's words about my major. But then, one of Alex's friends had been openly flirting with me and Alex hadn't seemed to mind.

In fact, he'd left me alone a few times, even though I'd come to the party to hang out with him. And throughout the night, I couldn't stop comparing my interactions here with those at the garden parties at Evergreen. The warm and fuzzy feelings I had at those gatherings weren't presenting themselves here.

Callan's expression had tightened, his eyebrows furrowed. He put his hands on my arms, and I tried to focus on what he was asking me. "Are you okay? Did something happen?"

I shook my head. "No, I'm fine. I just... I'm not sure that I really like being here."

"Then let's go."

I really looked at him then. "Wait, why are you here anyway?"

"Never been to a Halloween party. Decided to see what all the fuss is about. I can see the appeal because I get to see you with all this foliage in your hair." He touched one of my curls gently, and I shivered at the proximity.

"Ha ha," I said sarcastically, swatting his hand away to break whatever connection I was feeling toward him in that moment. This was Callan Rhodes, after all. Founder's descendant. Most powerful magical botanist in school. I was sure there was a reason he was here, and I was equally sure that reason had nothing to do with me.

"But aside from your costume, I'm not sure what else it has going for it. The drinks are laughable. I think it's more rubbing alcohol than plant distillation. I can't imagine the headaches all these people are going to have tomorrow morning."

"You're not wrong about that."

"Personally, I've seen enough. I need some food to wash down the sip of poison I just tried. Come with me?"

I glanced over at Maci. She was no longer yelling. Now, she was sitting on Jace's lap. I had no idea where Alex was. I still wasn't sure why Callan was asking me, but going with him suddenly felt infinitely better than the alternative.

Even if he was about to make me run some math drills or grill me on botanical trivia, maybe I would prefer it to spending the rest of the evening here. "Yeah, okay. Let me just say bye to my friend."

I approached Maci and Jace. "Hey, Maci. Is everything okay?"

She stood up and hugged me. "Everything is fine. Did you see us arguing? Turned out to be nothing... I think." She looked past me then and spotted Callan. "Oh my god, it's the hottie who tutors you. Did you know he was going to be here? Do you have two dates? You little boy magnet!"

I tried to shush her, wondering how much she'd had to drink. "No, I didn't know he was going to be here. I am ready to leave, though. Do you want to come with me? I can drive you home."

"No, we're all going to walk back to Jace's place after this."

I glanced at Jace and noticed that he seemed fairly sober, so I nodded. "Okay, but text me when you get there. If you end up needing a ride, call me."

She hugged me again and whispered in my ear, "Be careful, B. Managing two boys is fun, but eventually you're going to have to choose."

"What? I'm not—" I began to defend myself, but she laughed and pushed me gently away.

"Ready?" Callan asked when I returned to his side.

"I have to get my backpack and say goodbye to one more person. I just need to find him."

"Him?"

"A friend from SCC."

"I'll come with you."

We searched the yard and house for Alex, and I'd almost given up on finding him when I saw him emerge from the hallway.

"Hey, Alex, I'm leaving. Thanks for inviting me." I went to move past him, heading for the coat closet.

"Leaving so soon?"

"Yes," I said, making to move for the coat closet again, but Alex blocked the way.

"But the party is just getting started. We can—" At that moment, he noticed Callan behind me, and his eyes narrowed ever so slightly. "What are you—"

"See you later, Alex," I insisted, taking his moment of distraction to push past him and snag my backpack from the closet. I couldn't fault the guy for disappearing for a while and having fun at his own party. There was nothing official between us, anyway. We were just friends who hung out and did psychology homework together sometimes. I wasn't sure why I'd felt like I was coming as his date when clearly that wasn't the case.

Once I stepped outside into the crisp evening air, I took a deep breath, feeling ten pounds lighter already. I went to slip my backpack on my shoulders and frowned. It was halfway unzipped. I was sure it had been zipped all the way when I'd put it in the closet. Had it gotten jostled when I took it from the shelf?

"Who was that guy?" Callan asked, leading me to a black truck while flipping a set of keys in his hands. He opened the passenger seat for me, and I climbed inside.

"Just someone from school. SCC, I mean." I zipped the backpack closed and set it on the floor.

"Hmm." Callan's expression was tight, but I was used to the serious aura he carried with him.

"So, where are you planning to eat? There's nothing open this late around here except fast food."

"Oh, ye of little faith."

I glanced at him skeptically as he cruised away from the

house. "I grew up here, remember? I *know* nothing is open past eleven."

A smile touched his lips, but he flicked on the radio—which was set to a pop-punk station—and kept driving.

"Maybe there's a thing or two about this town you don't know, *local*."

Chapter Twenty-Nine

When we parked at the fanciest restaurant in town, a little boutique American place, I didn't move to get out.

"Yeah, this place is definitely closed." I eyed the empty parking lot and dark windows.

But Callan came around the side of the truck and opened the door for me. "I didn't say we were going somewhere that was open."

Before I could ask a follow-up question, he walked to the back door of the restaurant and pulled out a key.

"Wait, do you *work* here?"

"Not exactly. But Perennial Farms supplies some of their produce. I make sure they get top quality every week. It comes with some perks."

"Like a key to the restaurant?" I raised an eyebrow. That didn't seem likely.

"The owner is a family friend."

Right. Callan's family was bound to have made some connections with the locals over the years.

"But what are we going to do in a closed restaurant?" We

stepped inside, and Callan turned on the lights in the small commercial kitchen.

"I'm going to cook."

"You're going... to... cook?" I wasn't sure why I was so surprised. But the words spluttered out of me.

Callan smiled in a way that nearly stopped my heart. Then he slung an apron over his chest. "Don't look so shocked. I have herb affinities."

"You do? Trees are your lead affinity, right? What other affinities do you have?" I felt that we knew each other well enough for me to try broaching this subject again.

Callan busied himself pulling vegetables from bins as he replied, "All of them except for mosses."

I gasped. "All of them?"

"Except for mosses. The founders had all of the affinities, and that's why they considered themselves most suited to start the academy. While magical lines have decreased over time, we've kept our family lines... magically potent since then."

"Magically potent?" A thousand questions were stirring themselves up in my mind.

Callan sighed. "Has no one ever explained to you how magical blood works?"

"Not exactly." I thought of my conversation with Professor East that had been cut short by his needing to teach a class. With all of the other things I'd been learning lately, my magical inheritance was no longer top of mind.

"We think that, originally, every magical botanist had all of the affinity powers. Over time, as they married non-magical people, the genes were mixed with non-magical ones. Some families retained only a handful of the affinities. Many magical botanists these days only have one or two affinity powers. But my family and some others around the world have kept their powers up by only marrying other magical botanists."

"So you couldn't marry a non-magical person even if you

were in love with them?" I wasn't sure why the idea bothered me, but it did.

Callan whisked the vegetables that he had prepped in a ridiculously short period of time into a skillet then dumped some noodles into a pot of boiling water. "'Couldn't' is a strong word. But it would be discouraged."

I wanted to press, but something on Callan's face told me not to. "So, you have all of the affinity powers—except mosses," I added quickly when I could tell that he was about to say it. "No wonder you're such a wiz in every class."

Callan laughed. "That certainly makes it easier. That and the intensive tutoring I've had since I was a kid."

"And lucky me gets to be tutored by you." The words were out of my mouth before I could contemplate how he might interpret them.

"Depends on your definition of luck."

"Be honest. Why are you tutoring me? Wouldn't your skills be better used on someone who actually has powers?"

"Haven't you heard that the rarest blooms are the most interesting?" His voice was as smooth as silk as he whisked the food in the skillet.

"What is that supposed to mean?" Was it another one of those magical botanist idioms that I wasn't used to?

But Callan didn't respond. Instead, he plated us each a delicious-smelling mix of noodles, vegetables, and spices that would have taken me an hour to prepare.

"Bon appétit, local."

I bit into the mouthwatering meal, the atmosphere in the dimly lit kitchen a stark contrast to the pounding sounds of the Halloween house party.

"So, what was it like growing up here?" Callan asked.

We both reached for a shaker of pepper, and our hands bumped. I laughed and pulled my hand away quickly, trying not to notice the goose bumps that had pricked my arms when we'd touched.

"Oh, the usual. Friends you've known since kindergarten. Neighbors who watched you grow up. A whole town of people cheering for you to succeed. Nothing to do on the weekends except bowling, movies, or bonfires in the woods."

"So you're telling me it's the stereotypical small town?"

"Some things are, in fact, just like how they're portrayed in movies. But how about you? I take it you're not from a small town."

Callan waved a fork at me. "Nice try, but the conversation's sticking on you tonight. Who was that guy you had to say goodbye to at the Halloween party?"

"A friend from SCC." I briefly stuttered on the word "friend." I'd thought Alex and I were headed toward more than friendship, but after the way our first time away from school had gone, I wasn't so sure. But the change in conversation reminded me of something.

"Are you ready to tell me the real reason you were at that party? There's no way you just happened to pop by."

He seemed conflicted for a moment, but finally, he spoke. "I thought I sensed... Did you use your powers there?"

"What? No, of course not. I don't have any."

Something flickered across Callan's face. "I must have imagined it."

"Wait, you can sense powers? Can all magical botanists do that?" Admittedly, I wasn't far into my Evergreen Academy schoolbooks, but I'd never come across mention of anything like that.

His eyes rested on me for a moment, something like curiosity lingering there. "It's rare, but yes, I can."

"How rare are we talking? Seeing-a-comet-shower rare or witnessing-a-total-solar-eclipse rare?"

Callan tilted his face and looked bemused at my analogy but said, "The latter."

Holy cow. My friends hadn't been kidding when they'd said Callan was powerful.

We continued to eat, with Callan steering the conversation away from himself and the academy. He asked me about working at the bakery and what it was like living with my aunt. He deflected the remainder of my questions about himself so seamlessly, turning the conversation back to me so smoothly, that I hadn't noticed he'd been doing it until after we cleaned up from dinner and were driving back to Alex's house.

Alex, who had completely left my mind over dinner with Callan. How had this night flipped on its head so completely?

When Callan dropped me back at my car, the Halloween party was still raging inside. Before I could open my driver's-side door, Callan was there, doing it for me. He draped an arm across the top of my door as I got inside.

"Tell me I'm going to see that outfit again," he said in a pleading voice with a devilish smile. I touched a leaf in my hair, having completely forgotten that I was still in my plant lady outfit.

"Be careful what you wish for," I said in a singsong.

He didn't say anything, but his smile met the corners of his eyes, and I wanted to spend the rest of the night like this, even if he wouldn't answer my questions. But it was over as quickly as it had begun, and he closed the door softly and walked back to his truck.

And as he drove away, I had to sit in my car for a few full minutes, forcing my pulse to slow down. The night had taken a hard left turn—and not in a bad way. I sighed, trying to bring myself back down to earth. I was wading a little too deep into the allure of Callan Rhodes. I just hoped it wasn't a trap.

Chapter Thirty

The next week, Callan wasn't available to tutor me. He was away on a field study that was typically reserved for second-years.

I didn't like to admit it, but I felt a pang of disappointment when he didn't show up in my math class at SCC, and I missed our nights together in the tree house, studying by lantern light.

"Did you have fun at the party?" Alex asked, as we packed up our materials at the end of psychology class on Tuesday. I'd been worried it would be awkward to see him, given how things had left off between us at his party, but he seemed his normal, confident self.

I wasn't exactly sure how to answer. The party hadn't been my cup of tea, but the evening afterward, with Callan, had been one of the best nights of my life. "It was interesting," I said, deciding that was true enough.

"Sorry if it felt like I ditched you or anything. It got busier than I expected." He was watching my face closely, and I squirmed in my seat.

"No big deal."

"Lunch?" he asked, nodding toward the cafeteria.

I gathered my courage and shook my head. "Sorry, need to get going. Thanks again for the invite this weekend."

"Anytime. See you."

I watched him walk away for a moment and decided I wouldn't be accepting any invitations to hang out beyond our simple lunch and homework sessions.

As much as I'd thought I was interested in his contagious, upbeat personality for months, everything had shifted at the Halloween party. We wouldn't be a good fit—that had become clear. But he was still fun, friendly Alex, and I didn't want our friendship to change if it didn't have to.

I thought of Maci's drunken words at the party—"Managing two boys is fun, but eventually you're going to have to choose."

I shook my head at the absurdity of her assumptions. It looked like the choice, if there ever had been one, was going to be neither because Alex was just a friend, and Callan Rhodes was entirely out of my league.

When I got to Evergreen Academy, I took my usual seat at a lab table with Yasmin, Coral, and Aurielle.

"Let's try this again," I said, preparing to get a Floracantus to work for me for once. We were practicing a supposedly basic task of getting our affinity plants to speed up their rates of photosynthesis without sunlight present.

"*Accelerare comdere*," I whispered to a fern. Since I didn't have an affinity power, I tended to use the plants that Yasmin, Coral, and Aurielle were working with. My three friends were already jotting down notes. "*Accelerare comdere*," I said again, more firmly this time.

"How do you know if it's working?" I asked, not for the first time.

"You sense it," Yasmin said. It was the explanation they always gave. According to Professor East, I should still be able to do basic Floracantus like these, but I never felt the results that seemed to come naturally to my friends. A tiny voice in the back of my head continued to tell me that perhaps this was all a mistake and I wasn't a magical botanist after all.

I let out a breath of frustration and tried to focus on the scientific aspects of the project. My understanding of photosynthesis at the molecular level had increased beyond any I'd ever imagined having, and terms like "cytochrome complex" and "ferredoxin" now came to me with ease.

But the Floracantus were a different story, and I wondered if I would ever be able to conduct a simple spell. We cleaned up from class, and I left in a rush, not wanting to explain to my friends that I'd failed at using a Floracantus once again.

When I got home that evening, my aunt Vera was there with her boyfriend, Bryce. He greeted me warmly but quickly said goodbye once they both seemed to sense my sour mood.

"Sorry, Aunt Vera. I hope I didn't scare him off. It's just been a rough week."

"Is everything okay, love?"

"I should be further along than I am in my work at Evergreen Academy. I'm just a little frustrated with myself."

"I've seen how hard you're working. I was just thinking how I never see you studying at the counter in the café anymore, since you're always out at the academy. Has it become too much?"

I shook my head. "I can handle it."

Aunt Vera kissed my forehead. "Of course you can. Now, let's watch some trashy TV and forget all our problems."

We made heavily salted popcorn, and I smiled as we took our usual spots on the couch. At least, at the end of a hard week, I had this to come home to.

Chapter Thirty-One

On Friday, while everyone else was at their affinity studies classes, I took advantage of the empty library. First, I went to the magical botanist history section.

Ever since Yasmin had told me that Callan was a founder's descendant, I wanted to know more. I found a book on the history of Evergreen Academy and pulled it from the shelf.

I scanned the book, drinking in the history like it was a novel, not a textbook. I learned that the nine founders of Evergreen Academy were individuals with extremely strong lead affinities. One person with each lead affinity had come together to create the school and the verdant shield that surrounded it.

My eyes jumped to the name of the tree founder—Douglas Vitalis. That must have been Callan's ancestor. I skimmed the other names, jotting them down in my notebook before switching gears.

I wanted to do some sketching, so I sought out the section on botanical drawing. I'd already looked at some of the more modern books, but today my eyes were drawn to a section on the topmost shelf of books that were older, their bindings likely only

held intact with botanical magic. I used the rolling ladder to retrieve a few of them then returned to my favorite station at the table inside the tree's hollow.

I opened one book with drawings that appeared to be hundreds of years old. The pages were yellowed and the drawings a soft brown. Notes in a scrawling cursive in a language I couldn't read were crammed all around the floral drawings.

As I flipped to the second page, I felt a strange warmth in my hands. It was gone a moment later, and I continued to peruse the book, wondering what it would have been like to be the person creating these drawings.

In many cases, it was the first time certain plants had ever been drawn in detail. Without cameras, there was no other way to document what these species had looked like. Several of the plants were now slightly different from years of gene selection both natural and unnatural, and some were likely extinct.

I tucked the books in a drawer below the table to return to later and spent a little time in the sunnier part of the library with my drawing notebook, in which I sketched a massive bluebell flowering plant that was growing in the window. The dozens of bell-shaped petals seemed to be opening right toward me, as if begging to be drawn.

In that moment, I realized that even if I didn't have more than baseline magical botanist magic, the privilege of studying here would be more than enough.

Just as I was finishing my sketch, the lights in the room flickered, and my ring pulsed on my finger. I stood up, slipping my notebook into my backpack. Had the verdant shield wavered again?

I rushed down the stairs to see a few students returning from their affinity studies classes, chatting about seemingly normal topics. Otherwise, the place was fairly empty. Had the students who were outdoors noticed that the shield had flickered?

I looked around for a teacher to report the incident to, just in case. Professor Variegata was the first one I found, fiddling with the controls in Mendel's Atrium.

"Hi, Professor Variegata. Did you notice the shield flicker a few minutes ago?"

"Hi, Briar. Yes, I did. I'm resetting the controls in here because of it."

I knew I could leave now, but there was something deep within me that was both curious and concerned about these flickering spells. "Do you need any help?" I asked.

"That's very kind of you, but I'm almost done here."

After a moment's hesitation, I decided to go all in. "Do you know why the shield is flickering?"

Professor Variegata paused her work and turned toward me. "Most likely, it's a combination of soil deterioration and the weakening of magical botanists over time. The strength of the shield is directly proportional to the soil health and the power of the magical botanists who charge it."

"But I thought Callan Rhodes was one of the most powerful magical botanists in generations?"

Professor Variegata looked amused at my phrasing, but she nodded. "He is. We were hoping that his presence would slow the weakening, but sometimes, once things like this have started to accelerate, it may not be possible to slow or even reverse the decline."

"So then what can we do about it?"

Professor Variegata studied me, smiling kindly. "There's nothing you need to worry about, Briar. Professor East is taking care of it. Now go and enjoy your weekend."

I thanked her and left the atrium, but I couldn't quash the nagging feeling that her answer wasn't enough.

<h1 style="text-align:center">Chapter Thirty-Two</h1>

Three weeks later, I sat up in surprise when Callan appeared in math class at SCC, two cups of steaming tea in hand.

"Welcome back," I said when he slid into the seat beside me. He'd just dropped off a huge stack of papers at the instructor's desk, and I assumed it was all the homework he'd missed while on his research trip. It seemed so silly that he was keeping up on homework for an SCC class he didn't need to be enrolled in anyway, but I was secretly impressed that he'd done it.

"Was the instructor okay with you missing three weeks like that?" I asked.

"It's not ideal, but she can tell I've been acing all the tests up until this point, so I think she was more flexible in working with me."

"I'm sure your charm had nothing to do with it," I mused, and Callan smiled.

"It sounds like someone missed me."

"We had a test last week, and I barely scraped a B minus. I need my math savant around to carry me through this class."

"Don't worry. We'll double down to make up for it," he promised.

"Oh, joy," I said sarcastically, though my stomach did a little flip at the idea of spending more time with him. "So, what were you doing on the field studies trip?"

"I'm afraid that's only for the tree affinities to know." He smirked and glanced down at his textbook.

I rolled my eyes, ready to retort, but our math instructor started class, and I turned to the front of the room. I had to suppress a smile. Callan was back and teasing me again. All was right in the world.

Later that night, when we met in the tree house to resume our tutoring, I tried the line of questioning again.

"So, was what you were researching on the field studies trip really restricted to tree affinities, or were you just trying to throw me off before math class?"

"I was just messing with you." Callan flipped a pencil through his fingers, maneuvering it with ease. "We went to an area that experienced a large wildfire this fall. Our research group is working on some new theories in post-fire succession principles."

"Sounds... interesting?"

Callan chuckled. "It was. Sad, too, though. To see that such old forests have burned. They'll come back, but it'll take decades, and the ecosystem's composition will never be the same."

I wasn't sure at what point in my time at Evergreen I'd turned into a total nerd, but his science talk had me listening with awed appreciation. I switched to a question that had been bothering me for weeks.

"Did you know the verdant shield flickered again when you were gone?"

Callan looked down at my math book. "Professor East filled me in."

"Yasmin told me that it gets recharged on the summer and

winter solstices and the spring and fall equinoxes. If it's flickering now, do you think that the recharge on the winter solstice is going to be able to restore it to normal?"

"I wish I could say the answer is yes, but I'm not so sure."

"Professor Variegata said that sometimes once deterioration of a spell like this gets started, slowing or reversing it isn't possible."

Callan seemed to contemplate that. "She told you that, huh?"

"Is that a surprise?"

"I think you have a way of getting things out of people they didn't intend to share."

"This, from the *king* of undersharing."

Callan smiled lazily. "I'm just saying I'm impressed, that's all."

I glowed a little at his words, but I couldn't help feeling that they were countered by the fact that I had no affinity powers. Despite my doing my best to fit in here, could I ever truly be part of school when I didn't do affinity studies? When I couldn't even get a simple Floracantus to work for me?

The next words were out of my mouth before I could stop them. "Do you think I belong here? With no affinity powers, I mean?"

Callan kept his face relaxed, but I saw his posture tense ever so slightly.

"Professor East says you belong, so you belong. I know we've never had someone at Evergreen with no affinity powers before, but—"

"Wait? Never? But magical botanists with no affinity powers are a thing, right?"

Callan twisted away from me on his stool, casting his eyes down at his math textbook.

"Are you saying you've never met anyone else with no affinity powers? Isn't your family connected to tons of magical botanists on the East Coast?" My pulse quickened as I hoped for an answer that I had a feeling I wasn't going to get.

"Look on the bright side—you're an enigma, local."

My forehead scrunched as my stomach dropped. "Professor East said it was unusual, but he didn't tell me it was unheard of."

"Guess he wanted to spare your feelings."

Something like irritation began to form, and I looked Callan straight in the eyes. "Okay, what is going on? Is having no affinity powers rare, or is it... impossible?"

The feeling that I didn't belong, the one I'd tried to shove away over the past few months but that continued to nag at me every time I failed at using a Floracantus, forced itself back to the front of my brain. Had this all been a mistake? Was Professor East wrong about me?

"Whoa, slow down. I can see your brain going into overdrive. Just take a breath. It's obviously not impossible, if you're here. You responded to the initial test in Professor East's office, and the charged ring allows you to see the campus. That wouldn't work if you weren't a magical botanist."

He rolled his chair closer to mine, and he took my hands in his. Warmth flowed through me, and I sucked in a breath. I tried to send concentration to my brain instead of solely where our hands touched. He ran his thumb across my emerald ring.

"You *do* belong here. Your power is just somehow... different than everyone else's."

"One of your powers isn't mind reading, is it?"

Callan laughed and rolled his chair away from me again, leaning back to stretch his arms overhead. I felt a slight chill at the loss of contact and tucked my hands into the pocket of my sweatshirt.

"No, but it's not necessary with you. Your thoughts were written all over your face just then."

"Oh, really? And what am I thinking now?" I made a silly

face and tried not to think about the feeling that I wanted him to take my hands again.

"You're thinking that all these questions distracted me from your biostatistics studies. But you're wrong. I believe we left off on problem three."

I sighed dramatically, but my mind was still sorting through what he'd said when we got back to work. I had three takeaways from our conversation:

I didn't have any affinity powers.

That wasn't normal.

But I belonged at Evergreen Academy.

Could all three of those statements be true at once, or were Callan and Professor East telling me what they thought I needed to hear?

Chapter Thirty-Three

That week in Basic Plant Biology, we studied a rotting log in the forest. Professor Bowellia had us doing detailed drawings and documentation of plants that were making their home on the decomposing wood. Yasmin, Coral, and Aurielle were having a field day studying the ferns and mosses, and I was enjoying putting my drawing skills to use.

"How old do you think the tree was?" Yasmin asked, filling in a table in our notebooks.

"Fifty," Aurielle guessed.

"Ninety-one," I said, the number popping into my mind out of nowhere.

Coral's eyes widened as she checked the answer key. "It is ninety-one. Nice guess, B."

"So, Callan's back," Yasmin said. "Are you resuming your 'tutoring arrangement'?" She put the last two words in quotes, and I gently shoved her shoulder with mine. I glanced at the area where Callan was working with Eli and Nevah, making sure none of them were listening.

"Why the innuendo? He is tutoring me. *Only* tutoring me."

It was obvious to me that my skills had improved dramati-

cally since he'd started working with me, and Algebra and Biostatistics for Botanists were not as miserable as they'd once been. The truth was, I was starting to remember why I'd liked the patterns and logic involved in math as a kid, and my scientific skills were rapidly progressing under Callan's careful direction. My Latin was eking along at an infant level, but I was making progress.

"Sure, if tutoring entails being holed up in a cozy tree house together every night," Coral teased.

I rolled my eyes but couldn't help feeling a little glow at my friends' words. I glanced at Callan as he worked at the other end of the log, his hair a perfectly mussed chestnut brown as he carefully lifted a piece of moss, muscles flexing under his tattooed forearms. I blew out a sharp breath and refocused on my notebook.

It's just tutoring.

"I can't believe the winter solstice is next week," Yasmin said. "There are so many preparations to do. And we'll be switching classes after the solstice, so we need to wrap up all our projects. How are you doing with all this, B?"

"Not bad, actually," I admitted. And it was surprisingly true. Between Callan's tutoring and all the extra time I was putting in on my own on Fridays while the others were doing their affinity studies, I was at least able to keep up in classes. I still felt behind in Latin, but Professor Bowellia was happy with my progress. And we would take Latin all year, so I had more time to continue learning.

"I'm just glad finals are over at SCC so I can fully enjoy the solstice celebrations," Yasmin said. Grades had been posted the previous day. I'd managed to pull a high B average. But I'd signed up for three winter intersession classes—abbreviated courses in which you squeezed in a semester's worth of work in four weeks. I wanted to get as ahead on credits at SCC as I possibly could, since my regular semesters were so crunched with my Evergreen Academy studies.

"You're all going home for winter break, right?" I asked.

"Yep, I can't wait. As much as I love the food here at the academy, there's nothing like my mom's cooking, especially over the holidays," Coral said.

"My family is taking a trip to the fern conservatory for Christmas this year," Aurielle said.

Coral's eyebrows rose. "You're going to Alaska in the winter? That's brave."

Aurielle shrugged. "My parents are adventurous."

"I'm jealous," Yasmin said. "I've always wanted to go. Maybe I'll get the opportunity to intern there."

I'd been trying to track the conversation, but I needed clarification now. "Did you say 'fern conservatory'? What is that?"

"It's like the hub for all fern affinities. There's a conservatory for each of the nine affinities. They were set up by the founders and are hubs for each affinity's research and community. The one for the ferns is in Alaska," Yasmin explained. "Most botanists try to visit their lead affinity conservatory at some point in their lives. We're not allowed to visit the other conservatories unless by special invitation."

My brain snagged on that point. Without having a lead affinity—or any affinity at all—this was another part of the magical botanist world that I was never going to be able to experience.

"Please bring me back a souvenir from the fern conservatory, Aurielle. I've been dying to have something from there," Yasmin said.

"Me too!" I said, perking back up at the thought of the holiday season. Even with the SCC coursework I would need to crank out each day, between finals being over and thoughts of the winter solstice celebrations and Christmas, the end of the year was shaping up to be magical.

Nothing, not even a lack of affinity powers, could ruin it.

Chapter Thirty-Four

When I arrived at Evergreen Academy during the week leading up to the winter solstice, I could immediately sense that the mood in the air was different.

I entered the central vein to see students carrying large boughs of greenery. A few of the evergreen boughs were being floated through the air by the tree affinities.

Yasmin looped an arm through mine when she spotted me. "Want to make a wreath?"

"Absolutely." We gathered supplies and got to work at one of the tables in the teahouse.

Yasmin, Coral, and Aurielle all selected fern leaves so that they could magically enhance their wreaths, but I chose the local ingredients of spruce, fir, juniper berries, and holly. I threw in some ribbons to weave through the wreath and a dainty red bow for good measure.

"Drinks, anyone?" A first-year student who was currently on Kitchen Botany rotation stopped at our table, balancing a silver platter on one hand. Glass mugs of steaming cocoa and cider emitted an enticing smell.

"Both, please," I said, unable to decide. Yasmin laughed, and my friends each took turns selecting a drink.

"So, what all happens on the solstice?" I asked as we got to work braiding our wreaths.

"I only know what my sisters have told me," Yasmin said. "Lots of food, of course. A speech from Professor East. Then a few other activities that shall remain a surprise for our newest magical botanist."

"Fine," I said, fake grumbling. "And what about the charging of the verdant shield?"

"The founders' descendants will do that sometime between eleven and midnight. It's a strict time frame that the founders implemented."

"And how does it work?" I asked.

"They impart some of their magic into the original Floracantus that created the shield," Yasmin said casually, dabbing some moss onto her ferns.

"But *how*?" I hadn't been able to find anything about it in the library books I'd read. There was so much inherent knowledge in the magical botanist community that I was missing.

"Above our magical grade, B. None of us are founders' descendants," Coral said.

I pressed my lips together, not satisfied by the answer, but tried to suppress my curiosity.

"Well, let's hope whatever they do, it works, and there's no more flickering," Aurielle said.

We spent the next hour sipping our hot drinks and wrangling our wreaths into shape. I made mine in a petite size so that it would fit on the door of my aunt's apartment. "What are you all doing with your wreaths?" I asked.

"We'll hang them around here. Watch this." Yasmin signaled to one of the tree affinities who was roaming the room.

"Leif, can you hang these for us?"

Leif lifted his hands, muttered a Floracantus, and directed

their three wreaths—one by one—to hooks on the walls around the room, where they draped beautifully.

"Some students go all out and make a bunch. The school is going to be covered with these and garlands soon," Coral said.

I smiled. I should have known that, as magical as Evergreen Academy always was, this season would be even more enchanting.

As the week went on, Coral's words came true. The school's campus transformed into a cozy winter wonderland, incorporating hundreds of plants of the winter season.

When the night of the winter solstice finally arrived, we joined the procession of students bundled in coats, hats, and gloves, carrying the lanterns we used for the garden parties toward the forest. Most of us had decked our heads with crowns of greenery, holly berries, and tiny pinecones.

After a fifteen-minute walk through the forest, we finally emerged in a small clearing, and I sucked in a breath. A massive rectangular wood table was stretched out across the space, hanging lights decorating the sky above. Charcuterie boards and hot drinks decked the expanse of the table, which was decorated with fresh greenery nestled around hundreds of votive candles. The stars shone brightly overhead, as if they encouraged our gathering.

"It's like *Starry Night* come to life," I breathed.

"Did you know Van Gogh was supposedly tripping on absinthe when he painted that?" Coral said from my left. "They really should have had some magical botanists overseeing their production. We could have removed the psychoactive."

"Way to ruin a perfect moment, Coral," Aurielle said with a laugh.

We took seats on one of the long benches that spanned the tables, and I inhaled the rich smell of oranges, cinnamon, and cloves. Simmer pots were magically emitting the enchanting fragrance, even though there wasn't a heating coil in sight.

Professor East stood and cleared his throat. "Tonight, we celebrate the return of the light. The darkest days are over, and our plant friends will have more access to the sunlight that fuels everything we do here. Tonight, we enjoy a celebration of Midwinter's Eve together before you each depart to spend the holidays with your families. Take a moment to reflect on all we've seen, learned, and shared during this season." He lifted a glass, and we each raised ours in return. "To the returning of the light."

"To the returning of the light," everyone called out, and I joined in, warmth blooming in my chest as I said the words.

"Now, let's eat."

Chapter Thirty-Five

An hour later, after feasting and dancing as vines snaked around the arms of many of my fellow students and leaves floated in the air, the hour neared midnight, and the group began to make its way deeper into the woods.

"Is the party over?" I asked, disappointed.

Yasmin shook her head. "There's one final tradition." When she didn't say more, I followed along with the rest of the group. A few of the students toward the front of the pack were merrily singing a Christmas carol, and I caught a line about enchanted boughs of holly.

A few minutes later, we emerged by the creek, and I noticed dozens of pools of water, each with steam rising from them into the cold night sky. I whipped my head to Yasmin.

"I didn't know there were hot springs out here."

"There's a tradition that originated in Japan of celebrating the winter solstice with a soak in the hot springs with some citrus fruits."

Sure enough, I looked around and noticed that the professors were carrying baskets, and they began to drop a variety of

sliced citrus fruits into the water. The aroma hit me like an invigorating shower steamer.

"Um, we're not actually getting in there, are we?" I whispered.

"Of course we are."

"But I didn't bring a bathing suit."

"Don't worry. I packed you one." Yasmin slung a cloth bag off her shoulder. "I told you you'd be surprised."

We all scattered into the trees to change into our bathing suits, then I shivered fiercely as I ran to a pool with Yasmin, Coral, Aurielle, and a few of the other fern affinities. The water instantly warmed me up in a shock of heat, and I sank down, letting it spill over my shoulders. I relaxed my head to rest on the rock pool behind me, breathing in the fresh citrus scent. The experience was like being in an expensive spa rather than a hole in the ground in the middle of the forest.

"This is heaven," I said and sighed.

We soaked for a while then climbed out of the pools. Some of the tree affinity students dried us with their wind-maneuvering powers, and then I slipped my dress and coat on over my bathing suit.

As we began to walk back to the academy, Callan came up beside me and nodded toward the forest.

Yasmin gave me a questioning look, but I told her to go ahead.

"Happy Midwinter, local." Callan's voice held a note of amusement, and I thought back to the moment we'd first met. His words tonight mirrored those. *Happy Midsummer, local.* I still remembered it so clearly.

In all this time, we still hadn't officially acknowledged that day. Most of the time, Callan kept our tutoring sessions somewhat infuriatingly focused on school despite my attempts at having other conversations. Now, I wondered if that first encounter would ever come up.

"Happy Midwinter. This was…" I didn't have the words, so I left it there.

"I wanted to let you know that I'm leaving to visit my family for Christmas tomorrow morning, so I won't be here for a few weeks. You'll have to get through your winter intersession classes without me." There was a trace of amusement in his voice.

We walked toward the front of the grounds where my car was parked and stopped in the fields of flowers.

Something squeezed in my chest. The fact that he'd sought me out to say goodbye… It made me feel somehow excited and reassured all at once.

"Worried I'll be bored out of my mind with all of you gone?" I teased.

"Quite the opposite."

I was about to question what he meant when I remembered something. It was already past midnight. "Did you charge the shield? How did it go?"

He cast his eyes toward the building where I saw Eli Quinn, one of the other founders' descendants, entering the academy. The third descendant, Nevah Trinity, was nowhere in sight, presumably having joined friends or retired for the night.

"Everything appears to have worked. Did you feel the pulse?"

"No, but I was in the pools."

"Yeah, that will usually dim it."

"So your super founder duties are done for the night." I said it playfully, wanting to stand here with him for a few moments longer.

Callan snorted. But something near the ground grabbed his attention, and he stepped closer to me.

"I thought you didn't have an affinity for florals?" His voice was a sharp whisper, and I looked at him in confusion.

Then my eyes followed his, dropping to the tangle of deep-red flowers that were now leaning dramatically in my direction on all sides, forming a swirling circle around me. I drew a sharp breath and stepped back, but the flowers followed.

A smile pulled at the corner of Callan's mouth as he met my eyes. "Well, isn't that interesting?"

Chapter Thirty-Six

Ten minutes later, I was ushered into Professor East's office. Professor Tenella was in a chair at the side of his desk, a few leaves sticking out from her black curly chignon.

Callan slipped in at the last moment and took a seat next to me across from the colossal desk. He had told me to go inside then dashed off to find the teachers after the strange phenomena in the flower gardens.

"Mr. Rhodes has explained what he observed outside," Professor East said calmly. "He claims you demonstrated a floral affinity."

My head swiveled among the three of them. "That can't be right, though. Professor Tenella tested me…"

Professor Tenella nodded, and for the first time I noticed the large bucket of planted flowers near her feet. They were arched toward her. But she pushed the bucket in my direction, and they immediately switched their focus to me, as if we were two neighboring magnets.

"You're right, Briar. You didn't have an affinity for florals."

Professor Tenella smiled, her eyes meeting mine. "But now you do."

"Wh-what?" I stammered. "How is that possible?"

Professor East stood up and began to pace. "That's precisely what we'd like to figure out. Could we have missed something in the initial tests? Did your power take longer to manifest than most for some reason? Could your powers have been shielded somehow?" Professor East's eyebrows pulled together, and he shifted his gaze to his colleague.

"Perhaps her affinity power is tied to the seasons. Maybe it's not a coincidence that this happened on the winter solstice," Professor Tenella suggested.

Professor East steepled his fingers. "I suppose that's possible. Some affinities do manifest more strongly during certain seasons than others. But for it to appear so strongly, after not responding to the testing..." He sat quietly for a moment, and I cast a look at Callan. His eyes were fixed on the flowers at my feet, half of which were now arching toward him.

Professor Tenella spoke again. "Have you noticed any signs of affinity powers prior to tonight, Briar?"

I began to shake my head but then stopped, remembering. "There was a moment in class a few weeks ago when we were studying a rotting log. My team members took turns guessing the age, and it turned out that I selected the exact right number. I'd thought it was a lucky guess, but it was like the age had jumped into my mind out of nowhere."

I shot a glance toward Callan and saw a perplexed smile on his lips.

"Well, we have ourselves a bit of a puzzle," Professor East said, drawing my attention away from Callan. "But it's late, and we've all had a big day. Callan, I believe you're departing in a few hours."

Callan nodded, and my heart sank. For some reason, I felt

better about navigating whatever was happening if he was close by.

"Let's all take our planned time for the holidays, and when we get back, we'll run you through all the affinity tests again, Ms. Whelan. It's clear that something has changed, even if we don't yet know what."

I nodded, but internally, I was wondering how I would possibly manage waiting *weeks* without any answers.

Professor Tenella reached out and gave my hand a little squeeze, then she left the room with a "Happy Midwinter's Night!" The bells along the bottom of her dress tingled as she swept out the door.

Callan and I left Professor East's office together.

"Listen, I don't have to leave tomorrow." His voice was soft, softer than I'd ever heard it.

"Of course you do," I said, though I desperately wanted him to stay for reasons I couldn't fully explain. "Your family will want to see you for the holidays."

He sighed and ran a hand through his hair. "They'd survive, trust me."

"Well, I've agreed to work some extra shifts at my aunt's café to cover for the student employees who are going home. Time will fly." I didn't think it would, but I forced myself to pretend.

"Okay," he said slowly, studying my face. I put on a mask of calm and confidence. There was no need for Callan to know how curious and confused and maybe minorly terrified I was of whatever was going on with my powers. Powers. I had *powers*. A little shiver ran down my arms.

"Then I'll see you in a few weeks, Briar."

Before I could reply, he was gone.

Chapter Thirty-Seven

"Well, I must say that your mistletoe theme this year has reached a new level of whimsy, Briar Rose. Does someone have kissing on their mind?"

"Aunt Vera!" I faux gasped, snapping a tea towel at her.

We were putting the finishing touches on our Christmas cake decorating contest, a tradition my aunt had shared with my mom growing up. They would each make a cake, decorate it with as much festive pizazz as they could muster, and have their mom judge the winner.

A few years after my mom had passed, I'd taken her place in the competition with my aunt. She was always clearly the better of the two of us, but she called it a draw each time.

Aunt Vera put her hands up in surrender. "I'm just saying. You were really in the zone there. I wondered if your mind might be somewhere else."

My aunt was much too perceptive for her own good. There were multiple times throughout the evening when I wanted to tell her about Evergreen Academy, about what I was. The urge was much stronger now that I suddenly had powers. Had my power come from her side of the family? Could she shed any light on what was going on with me?

But Professor East had warned me about discretion, and I wasn't prepared to break that. Who would believe me, anyway? My aunt might just stick me straight into therapy and say I'd never properly processed my mom's death.

I guessed I should be glad she thought my distraction was due to something as normal as a love interest and not the sudden appearance of magical powers. While I'd been attending Evergreen Academy for months, the fact that I was a magical botanist had never felt real until my powers had activated. Now, I was scared to look sideways at a plant outside of the academy, wondering if it might do something that would give me away.

"Maybe I made the mistletoe cake for you and Bryce," I said, sliding it into a paper cake box and tying a ribbon around it. "He's coming over soon, right?"

"Yep. I guess that means he gets to choose between your darling mistletoe cake or this completely gauche gingerbread-man monstrosity." She eyed her creation as if regretting her design choices this year.

I peeled one of the fondant gingerbread men off the side and bit off his head, and my aunt made a shocked face before roaring with laughter.

"Hopefully, Bryce doesn't have any trouble getting here. The snow's really coming down now."

I looked out the window to see that she was right. Thick flakes were falling in front of the windows. We cleaned up the café and carefully walked through the slushy snow to climb the stairs to the apartment, cakes in hand.

Before long, Bryce gave a soft knock before pushing the door open. "Love the wreath, B. Vera said you made it at school."

"Thanks, Bryce. Do I have a future as a florist?" I teased. He gave me a quick hug before greeting my aunt with a quick kiss, and I made for the hallway, ready to make myself scarce.

"Make sure Bryce takes advantage of all that mistletoe I put on the cake," I called over my shoulder.

Even though I couldn't see her, I could practically hear my aunt rolling her eyes.

I got settled in my room with a warm blanket, the storm outside quickly increasing in intensity.

As I climbed into bed, I heard a loud scratching at my window. Thinking it was a wayward tree branch, I got up to ensure my window was shut tight against the incoming storm.

The scratching became more insistent, and I peered into the dark to see a volley of leaves swirling outside the pane as if of their own accord. I sucked in a breath, realizing what I was seeing.

Carefully, I opened the window, letting the small patch of leaves rush in before slamming it shut again.

Immediately, the leaves dropped to the ground. I riffled through them and noticed that one wasn't a leaf at all but a leaf-shaped piece of paper. On it, I recognized Callan's messy scrawl.

Merry Christmas. Hope you haven't caused any local calamities with your powers yet.
-C

My stomach twisted so tightly in delight that I had to sink onto my bed and suppress a squeal. Had Callan sent this note to me on the wind all the way from the East Coast? Or was he back?

The idea had a smile splashing across my face, but then I realized there was no way he had travelled back on Christmas. The academy didn't start up for the winter quarter until mid-January. I shouldn't expect to see him until well after the new year.

The leaves on the floor began to rustle again, swirling from my ankles up around my wrists. They tugged me toward my desk, and I picked up a pen. Were they prompting me to *write back?*

I searched for a small piece of paper then jotted:

None that I know of, at least. Merry Christmas!
-B

When I put the pen down, the leaves rushed around the paper and scooped it up then went zooming toward the window. I opened it, and with a loud rush of the storm, they were gone.

I flopped back onto my bed, unable to wipe the smile off my face. Callan could have texted me, like a normal person. But I was reminded again that nothing about him was normal.

He was a powerful magical botanist who'd grown up surrounded by other powerful magical botanists. And as far as I knew, he didn't have my phone number. Did he even *have* a phone? The idea that he might not was so shocking that it almost wore off the surprise of what had just happened.

Almost.

When I fell asleep that night to soft Christmas music, I dreamed of sugarplums and dancing leaves.

Chapter Thirty-Eight

When students began to return to Evergreen Academy after winter break, I met Professor Tenella in the flower garden. The blooms stretched their faces toward me as I walked past. Goose bumps pricked on my arms as it happened, and I wondered if I would ever get used to the sensation of being followed.

Over the break, I'd found myself grateful all this had occurred in winter, when my aunt's flowers were all dormant, so I wouldn't have to avoid the balcony on the off chance she noticed any errant flower behavior around me.

Professor Tenella reassigned the affinity test of planting a flower, and I went through the motions just as I had last fall. But this time, the tiny plant I buried in the soil shot up and bloomed within seconds.

"Let me see your notebook again, Briar."

I handed it to her, and she scratched out her original *Non par* and wrote *fortis compositus* in her looping handwriting.

"Strong match," she explained. "*Non par*, as you know, is no match. *Infirmi par* is weak match, and *Fortis compositus* is a strong match. Florals are likely going to be your lead affinity."

A little ripple of excitement went through me at her words. I truly had an affinity. I had a *lead* affinity. Professor East's insistence about me had been right all along. I really was a magical botanist.

I visited Professor Variegata next, who was gathering fruits with a group of students, her vine snaking around her wrist. When she directed me to touch the prickly pear cactus again, I expected the usual sharp poke, but instead, my hand felt like it met smooth glass. I pulled back in shock.

"Interesting," Professor Variegata mused. I collected a handful of legumes, and they softened and faded slightly in my hands, a sign that I'd inactivated the lectin. We went to the grassy fields next, and as I walked through them, the grasses paved a way for me, bending lightly so that I could easily pass. A shiver ran up my legs as I seemed to physically feel the presence of the grasses making way for me, like a gate creaking open with a sound you felt rather than heard.

"Well, you're sailing right through these this time. Last up is the storm resilience test." I remembered the not-quite-hurricane-level storm Professor Variegata had put me through in the fall, and I braced myself when we entered Mendel's Atrium. But this time, when she flipped the switch on the wall, the storm seemed to move around me. Wind and water brushed my cheeks and hair but then flowed right past, as if I were coated in sealant. When the storm ended, my hair was as untangled as when I'd first brushed it that morning.

Professor Variegata smiled and took my notebook. "*Fortis compositus* for all. And the same with Professor Tenella? Professor East wasn't joking when he said we were looking at an unusual case."

I thanked her, trying not to let the words "unusual case" echo around in my head as I hurried to find Dr. Lemna before lunch. The greenhouse by the lake had a few second-year students inside, conducting research. When Dr. Lemna saw me, she nodded. Apparently, she'd been warned about my second affinity test. "Let's get this over with."

We went to the pond, and I conducted the chemical tests. This time, when I finished, the water in the mason jar whipped into a whirlpool and changed colors.

Dr. Lemna assessed me carefully, as if seeing me for the first time. "I didn't believe it when Professor East said we should test you again." She looked at me more closely now, her sparkly blue eye shadow seeming to reflect in the late morning light. "Let's have you walk across the glass."

As soon as I stepped onto the glass that covered a portion of the pond inside the greenhouse, several plants seemed to rush over and position themselves under my feet, as if I were a magnet for their lush green limbs.

I looked at Dr. Lemna, and her eyebrows rose nearly to her hairline. "*Fortis compositus*. You are quite the enigma, Ms...?"

"Whelan," I responded. So now I was interesting enough for her to learn my last name.

"I'll be seeing you at Affinity Studies. We start at eight a.m. sharp. You have a whole quarter's worth of studies to catch up on."

And with that, I was dismissed.

"You've tested *fortis compositus* for all of your tests so far?" Yasmin asked, eyes wide as we met for lunch. Coral and Aurielle swiveled their bodies toward me, eager to hear the answer.

"Yeah." After the initial euphoria from my florals test, I was beginning to feel nervous about everyone's reactions. People kept using terms like "interesting" and "enigma." Those labels didn't exactly evoke reassurance. "And Dr. Lemna assumed I'll be in her affinity studies class for aquatics, but I also tested strongly for florals, harvesters, and grasses. How is the decision made on which is my lead affinity?"

"Usually, it's quite obvious. I think that's going to be a question for Professor East."

"Lovely," I said, drowning my sarcastic response with a bite of warm leek soup that was bursting with spicy flavor.

Aurielle reached into her bag then and pulled out three mason jars. She passed one to each of us, and I examined the glowing fern inside mine with a shiver of amazement.

"Fern lamps. They've been genetically engineered to glow. Fresh from the fern conservatory in Tongass National Forest, just for my best friends. And your cuttings are magically connected to the ferns at the conservatory they were taken from. As long as that fern is healthy, these will be too."

Yasmin's smile grew wide, and she hugged the jar to her chest. "You remembered! This is even better than I imagined. Thanks, Aurielle. It's going straight on my nightstand. I want to hear every detail of your trip. But first, I've been dying to tell you all about my trip to San Antonio. I saw Jordan, that guy I was telling you about." Yasmin filled us in on her winter break, and Coral and Aurielle shared their stories afterward.

As I ate my soup, I tried to let my mind relax and enjoy the stories my friends shared. But while I attempted to give them my full attention, the phrase *fortis compositus* continued to float around in my mind like lily pads on the pond, and a feeling that something wasn't quite right tugged from deep within me.

That afternoon, I tested for tree affinities with Professor Bowellia and then the mosses and ferns with Professor Sato. I passed with *fortis compositus* for all. It had been the strangest thing to be able to move through the trees as if I were walking on steady ground, the trees forming a path before me as I stepped. I was still afraid, but I had to admit that everything about the climbing and maneuvering in the trees now felt... comfortable. I was already thinking about ways to surprise Callan when he returned.

I gave a little squeal of glee when the adult sporophyte fern uncoiled for me, and as moss grew along my skin, the cells of my body seemed to embrace it in response. For the first time since I'd arrived, I finally knew what it felt like to be a magical botanist and have an unspoken bond with the plants around me.

Professor Sage invited me to help cook dinner to redo the herb affinity test. I crafted one of the dinner recipes and created another healing tincture then watched with a nervous flutter in my stomach as Professor Sage tasted the meal I'd created.

His eyes flew open in delight, and he rolled his wheelchair closer to the counter for another taste. "Marvelous," he breathed.

I chanced a tentative smile.

"A strong affinity for herbs, for sure. This is quite the turnaround."

"I'm not sure why," I admitted.

"Professor East will help you figure that out. He's not in today, so you'll have to do your defensive plants test tomorrow."

I breathed a sigh of relief, remembering my hallucinations from before and not eager to be poisoned again. Today had been overwhelming enough without adding that into the mix.

"I look forward to seeing what all you cook up with us this year, Briar." He packed away my soup and handed the travel pot to me. "Make sure your family gets a taste of this. They won't soon forget it."

Chapter Thirty-Nine

"Be careful on the roads this week, Briar Rose. There's supposed to be a big storm coming," Aunt Vera said as she came into the house after closing the bakery. She shrugged off her knee-length puffer jacket and unwound the scarf from around her neck. Even the short outside walk from the bakery to our upstairs apartment was cold enough to require bundling up.

People didn't tend to think of California as a cold state. But here, near the Sierra Nevada mountains and close to the border with Oregon, winters meant freezing temperatures and treacherous roads.

"I've got my snow tires on," I said, ladling two bowls of the soup I'd made at Evergreen Academy that day. I still hadn't tried it, and I was eager to see if either my aunt or I noticed anything out of the ordinary. I'd sliced up one of the fresh loaves from the bakery that was always in our bread box to go with it.

"And that's good, but it's the other drivers I'm worried about. You know how people can be on the highway when they don't know how to drive in the snow and ice."

"That's true. I'll be careful. I'm going up to the ski park with Maci this weekend. Hopefully, we get a powder day with the storms."

We took a seat at the table together, one of the rare occasions we were both here at the same time to share an evening meal. These moments had become even fewer and further between now that I'd been spending so many evenings studying at Evergreen Academy.

I watched as my aunt took a spoonful of the soup, and her eyes widened. "Did you make this?"

"Yep, it's a new recipe I tried at Evergreen."

"Wow, it's delicious. Is the recipe covered by that NDA? Because this would sell well at the bakery."

I laughed. "Maybe."

"Seriously, I had no idea they made food there. There's a kitchen and everything?"

"Yep," I said casually, and fortunately, she switched gears.

"Oh, I meant to tell you. I got a phone call from one of your professors. Professor East."

My head snapped up from the soup I'd just been about to taste, and I slowly lowered the spoon. Why was Professor East calling my aunt?

"He said you'd been doing well at Evergreen Academy and was hoping to meet me at some point."

I felt my eyebrows knit together but masked my concern by dipping a piece of bread into my soup and finally tasting it. An explosion of curry, cardamom, and more subtle spices melted in my mouth. Damn. This soup *was* good.

"He wants to meet you? Did he say why?"

"He left a message on my voicemail, so it was brief. I was planning to call back tomorrow."

I racked my brain for what to do. There was only one reason I could think of that Professor East would want to meet my aunt.

He wanted to know if she was also a magical botanist. Apparently, my newfound affinity powers were getting attention.

Chapter Forty

The next day, I met Professor East in the central vein, and we walked together to the Perilous Grove. My palms began to sweat as we approached the clearing, and I wasn't sure if it was in anticipation of the upcoming affinity test or because of the conversation I needed to broach.

I gathered my nerve and asked the question that had been on my mind all night. "My aunt told me you called. Is there some information you need from her?"

"Ah, yes. About that. Now that your affinity powers have emerged, especially after being dormant at first, a review of your family history might be in order."

"My aunt doesn't know anything about the academy. I didn't tell her on your advisement. I'm not sure how she'll react to all of this."

"I don't have to tell her anything in order to test her."

Test her?

"No," I said before I could think twice about it.

Professor East's pace slowed. "No?"

"Professor East, when you invited me here, you didn't mention any strings involving my family." I wasn't sure why my reaction had come so strongly, but the truth was, I was protective of my aunt. I envisioned Aunt Vera and how happy she was with Bryce, living a normal life. I didn't want it to be disrupted on my account more than it already had been. She'd rearranged her life to take me in. Now, it was my turn to return the favor.

Professor East bowed his head slightly. "That's true, and I don't mean to be invasive. Now, the stinging nettle."

"Sorry?" I asked, confused.

"See if you have a reaction to the nettle, like last time."

I finally noticed the plant we'd approached. I reached out and wiped my hand across the nettle, bracing myself for the burning pain that had accompanied it before. But instead of the hot sensation I was expecting, I didn't feel anything at all.

Someone dropped out of a tree behind us then, and Professor East straightened as I jumped in surprise.

"Mr. Rhodes. I didn't know you'd be joining us. Come to observe?"

"Just wanted to make sure you didn't poison her again."

My heart began to pound at the sight of him, at the sound of his deep, rich voice. He was exactly as I remembered—posture straight, clothes impossibly pristine even though he'd just been walking through the trees, and hair tousled. But a vein in his neck twitched, and I tried to keep my expression neutral. Was he... *worried* about me?

"I don't think that will be necessary. This test was conclusive, along with all the others she took yesterday. It appears that Ms. Whelan is *fortis compositus* for *all* of the affinities."

Callan took a half step backward but quickly straightened, face composed. He turned to me, and his eyebrows lifted ever so slightly. Well, there went my plans for surprising him with my tree-walking ability.

Professor East was silent for a moment, looking between the two of us. "Ms. Whelan, come see me in my office tomorrow after lunch. We'll need to work out a special affinity studies schedule for you. Mr. Rhodes, since you have experience with that, please join us."

Callan and I both nodded, and Professor East left us to follow him out of the Perilous Grove.

"I see you've been busy while I've been away," Callan murmured.

"This all just happened yesterday and today."

Without warning, Callan jogged toward a tree and scaled it in a few quick movements.

"Well, are you coming?" he called, and I looked up at him, startled.

"What do you mean? Coming where?"

"If you have tree affinities, local, we might as well start your training now."

Chapter Forty-One

Callan and I walked through the trees together as if we were strolling along a trail on the ground. We stepped from branch to branch, never once hearing a creak to indicate we might be a burden on the trees. While I was cautious starting out, Callan moved with the grace of a fearless child, like he'd been doing this since he could walk. It dawned on me that he probably had been.

We followed the tree trails all the way to the tree houses near the edge of campus and went inside our usual one.

"*Fortis compositus* for all. Really, Whelan? I knew you were interesting, but now you're going to have this whole place in a frenzy."

"A frenzy? Why?" I felt a little sweat form on the back of my neck, and I slumped into a chair.

"Because no one has affinity for all of the plants anymore. I'm the closest, with everything except mosses. But I don't have *fortis compositus* affinity for any except for the trees. The rest are just minor affinities. The same goes for Eli and Nevah and all the founders' descendants today."

I let out a deep breath, suddenly feeling dizzy. I wondered if I had overexerted myself in the trees. "Great. So you're saying I went from being an outlier with no affinities to an outlier with too many? What does a girl have to do to fit in around here?"

Callan laughed softly. "You weren't born to fit in, local. Get used to it."

Given the choice, I think I would have preferred being singled out for having no powers, not the reverse. At least then, most people didn't pay any attention to me. Most students didn't realize I didn't have an affinity power—they just knew I wasn't in their affinity studies class. But then I remembered the feeling of connecting with the plants for the first time during my affinity tests yesterday and the thrill of walking through the trees with Callan, and I wondered if I would really give that up to continue flying under the radar.

"How was your Christmas?" I asked, ready to change the subject.

Callan glanced out one of the round circles in the tree that served as a window. "It was fine. Yours?"

"My favorite part was when I received a message from some *leaves*." I eyed him with a smirk.

"Pretty cool what you can do with a strong tree affinity once you learn how to wield it."

I wanted to ask more about his trip home, but he seemed closed off about it, so I stuck with the change of subject. "Speaking of which, is there anything I should know? Do I need to be careful of anything... odd happening? Especially when other people are watching?"

He shook his head. "Not really. The main one that's visible is the flowers leaning toward you or the grasses leaning away. Or not being affected during a storm. But honestly, non-magical people never seem to notice subtle things like that. They're not conditioned to expect it, so why would they? Most of the changes that you notice will be internal. You probably don't feel it yet, since you need to hone your affinities, but any time you are near plants you have an affinity for, you'll be able to feel them."

"Feel them?" I asked, though I knew I'd already begun to experience it in a hazy sort of way.

"It's different for every type of plant. You might feel a subtle vibration coming off them, have an advanced ability to smell their fragrance, feel tension if they're in distress. You could become the best houseplant hobbyist in town. Eventually, you'll be able to sense if a plant needs water or fertilizer or more or less sun just by walking past it."

What he described brought an onslaught of anticipation mixed with nerves. It had always been a strange concept to me that plants were alive. But being able to feel them on such a level...

"Is there a reason you asked about things to look out for? Besides other people noticing?"

"I'm going snowboarding this weekend, and there will be trees all around. Just wanted to make sure I won't suddenly be compelled to take off my snowboard and start tree walking."

Callan let out a surprised laugh, and I bit my lower lip with a smile. "You're still in control of you, local. You'll have more sensations now, but you get to decide what you're going to do about them. Most of the time, outside of campus, you'll just have to ignore those feelings."

I let that sink in, and as we left the tree house, I had the feeling that my whole world was about to change. Again.

We left Professor East's office the next day with a plan for me to rotate my affinity studies. I would work with two different affinity groups each Friday, then another two the following week, and continue to cycle through. But because I was so far behind and had so many affinities, I was going to have to put in some extra time in the evenings. This meant that my tutoring time with Callan was going to have a new focus.

"I'll see if Eli and Nevah can work with you some too," Callan said. "We all have different combinations of affinities and different leads, so we can each provide insights the others might miss."

I swallowed. Eli and Nevah, the other two founders' descendants. I'd never actually met either of them officially, and in my mind, I held them up on a pedestal as nearly mythical beings. But Callan belonged on that pedestal, too, and the only reason that didn't completely distract me was how comfortable I'd become in his presence over the past few months.

The same couldn't be said for my friends, who still went totally silent whenever Callan stopped by our table at lunch.

"So, snowboarding. You said you're going this weekend?"

"Yes," I said suspiciously. Callan wasn't usually big on small talk that opened him up for personal questions. "Why?"

"I haven't had a chance to check out the ski park here myself yet. I mentioned it to some friends, and Nevah wants to join too."

My mind began to race. "Umm, I'm going with my friend Maci. It's been hard enough to fend off her questions about this place. If you and Nevah come, she's going to give you the third degree."

Callan simply shrugged, as if Maci didn't scare him. I pictured the four of us on the mountain. I'd never seen Callan outside of the academic settings of Evergreen Academy and SCC. Would anything about him be different?

I mulled over the idea, beginning to soften to it. If anything, this was my chance to get to know Nevah before she started tutoring me. But then another thought occurred to me. Did Callan and Nevah often hang out outside of class?

I mirrored Callan in shrugging. "Okay, you can join us. But you better have your cover stories prepared."

Callan gave me a dazzling grin and winked. "I'm the king of cover stories."

Chapter Forty-Two

I was prepping my snowboard gear on Sunday when I got a call from Maci. "This is really last minute, but you invited some friends, and I also invited someone to come with us, and I wanted to make sure it was okay with you."

"Sure. Who?" I asked because I knew that she and Jace had ended things shortly before Thanksgiving, and she hadn't mentioned anybody new. Plus, she and Jace were constantly on and off. I figured it was only a matter of time before they were *on* again.

There was a hesitation on the other end of the phone, and I sharpened my focus. "Maci?"

"It's... Alex. I invited Alex."

Alex? The guy who had briefly been a person of attraction for me but who I no longer saw since psychology class had ended? *That* Alex? My thoughts began to spiral. Since when were Maci and Alex friends? But all I could manage to say was, "Alex who?"

"*You know*, Alex. The one whose Halloween party we went to. We have a class together this semester and ended up sitting

206

together, since we already kind of knew each other. He's just so fun to be around."

I couldn't deny that. Alex *was* fun to be around, at least at school. A strange tension twisted in my stomach. There was no reason to say no. Alex and I had ended our minor flirtation on good terms. Any feelings I might have been developing for him had long ago fizzled out.

"Of course he can come." I tried to put more enthusiasm in my voice than I felt. With Callan and Nevah joining us, this was going to be an interesting crew.

"Great! We're going to have a whole group. I can't believe I'm going to meet some of your friends from the Evergreen Academy. One of them is your hot tutor, right?"

I rolled my eyes, even though she couldn't see me. "I better not hear those words come out of your mouth in front of him, Mace. I'm on my way to pick you up. See you in ten."

An hour later, Alex met Maci and me at the ski park, and we all exchanged hellos in the parking lot. Alex greeted me warmly, and I was glad that there didn't seem to be any strangeness between us. His familiar, friendly smile was back in place.

"Where are your friends?" Maci asked when Alex had finished buying his lift ticket.

"I'm not sure." But as soon as the words were out of my mouth, I felt a touch of air breeze across the back of my neck, and I turned to see Callan and Nevah, decked out in ski gear, walking toward us.

We did a round of introductions, with Callan introducing Nevah to me, me introducing Callan and Nevah to my friends, and Maci jumping in and introducing herself and Alex. Callan's face seemed to sharpen when he recognized Alex, but they nodded at each other casually.

"So, who's riding with who?" Maci asked when we all pooled at the bottom of the chairlift.

"You invited Alex, so why don't you two ride together?" I

suggested, knowing that was what my friend would want. And I wanted to take this opportunity to get to know Nevah better, since she'd be helping me with my affinity studies soon. I paused, examining the ease with which I'd sorted us. When had I started to feel more comfortable with Evergreen Academy students than with my non-magical friends?

I got on the chairlift with Callan and Nevah, Nevah sitting in the middle. "Did you grow up skiing?" I asked, glancing at her skis. Callan was on a snowboard like I was.

"Yep, I'm from Michigan and went skiing there on holidays," Nevah said.

"Nice. I've always wanted to try skiing, but I started snowboarding at age eight, and it stuck," I said.

"Same here. I'll get on a snowboard someday. But the idea of starting from scratch doesn't sound fun. I see the way snowboarders fall on their butts all the time when they're learning."

"It's true. And don't forget the occasional face-plant."

Nevah laughed softly, and I thought with a warm feeling that we were going to get along fine.

"Nevah's agreed to help you with your affinity training starting next Friday," Callan piped in.

"What are your affinities?" I asked.

"Aquatics is my lead," she said, and I remembered Yasmin telling me that. "And I have trailing affinities for florals, grasses, and defensive plants."

"She'll train you in aquatics and defensives," Callan said. "I'll take trees and florals, harvesters, grasses, and herbs. I know you've got friends in mosses and ferns and have been doing some work in that area already, so they can keep taking the lead on that. Eli's better at herbs than me, but he's busy with all the work he does in his community on the weekends. He said he's willing to assist if needed, though."

"Well, thank you both."

"It's pretty remarkable that you have all the affinities,"

Nevah said as we neared the top of the skill hill. "What does Professor East think about it?"

"I'm not really sure. We're still figuring it out."

We reached the top of the ski hill, and the three of us got off the lift, Maci and Alex a chair behind us. After we strapped in, Callan slid by me on his toe edge and said quietly, "See if you can feel the trees as you go down the mountain."

My head snapped up in response. "I thought you said I wouldn't have to worry about anything while we were out here?"

"You don't. But I'm not here just because I like to snowboard. Consider this your second lesson."

"But how do I fe—" I didn't get to finish asking my question because Callan was already gone, racing into the powder in the trees.

I hastened to follow him and do what he'd suggested, but by the end of the first run, I hadn't felt anything unusual. I'd enjoyed skimming across the sugary snow and slicing through the trees with my friends, but I hadn't felt anything out of the norm. I asked Callan and Nevah about it on the next chairlift ride.

"Am I doing something wrong?"

"It's probably hard for both of us to explain, since we've been doing this since we were kids," Nevah said, "but you've got to open yourself up to hearing from the plants you want to connect with."

"How do I do that?"

"Trees have an ancient lifespan compared to most other plants," Callan said. "Their presence is not so insistent as you'll find other types of plants to be. Instead, they are more of a steady drumbeat of a presence. When you're in the trees, try to tune everything else out, clear your mind, and allow yourself to be still. That's when you'll hear them."

I wasn't convinced that any of that was going to work, but I vowed to give it a shot. "Maybe we could go out to the chairlift that's tucked away on the other side of the resort. It's secluded and less busy. Would it help me tune out some of the noise?"

"Worth a shot," Callan said.

When we reached the top of the chairlift, I suggested it to Maci. "Want to do a run on Gray Butte?"

She turned to Alex and shook her head. "I don't think he can get over there yet." Maci had been patiently teaching Alex how to use the falling leaf method on his way down the hill while the three of us had been ducking into the powder between the trees. "Why don't you three go without us? We can meet up for lunch in a couple hours."

Alex looked like he was going to protest but ultimately turned and followed Maci as she began her descent.

Callan, Nevah, and I made our way to the chairlift that was tucked away from the rest of the resort, no signs of parking lots or lodges in sight. It was much less busy here, and the quiet could almost be physically felt. Only the soft whir of the chairlift and the low whistle of a breeze cut the stillness of the air.

"You got this," Callan said as we began our first run on the secluded hill. "Clear your mind."

As I sent my body down the hill, I pushed out all thoughts of affinity powers, of Maci and Alex, of the secrets I was keeping from Maci and Aunt Vera, of all the constant anxieties that simmered under the surface about my future, and focused instead on the cool air against my face, the sound of the snow as my board slid across it, the crisp smell of the mountain.

And then something shifted within me, and I felt my eyes grow wide as I experienced the sensation as clear as day. I could hear the trees... communicating with one another. I could sense the rustle of roots reaching out from tree to tree, the sound of water moving up from the ground. I felt like my heart was going to pound out of my chest. I slowed as I made my way down the mountain, taking it all in.

"You felt it," Callan said softly. I hadn't noticed that he'd come up beside me or even that I'd made it back to the chairlift. I nodded. "It's amazing, isn't it?"

"It's... It's like a whole new dimension has been unlocked."

Callan smiled, and I couldn't help smiling in return when he said, "Welcome to the world of magical botanists, local."

Chapter Forty-Three

The second session at Evergreen Academy began to pick up steam, and I got into the swing of my new classes—Chemistry of Plants, which took place in the greenhouse by the pond, my Kitchen Botany rotation with Professor Sage, Biological Applications of Physics, and Latin.

I worked with the various affinity groups on my rotating schedules on Fridays then alternated working with Callan and Nevah in the evenings. I was grateful that both were willing to dedicate so much time to me.

I quickly discovered that Nevah was a kind and dedicated teacher. Her methods were slightly different from Callan's, but I realized that Callan had been right. It was good for me to experience the disparate ways they approached their powers.

Callan's power seemed to flow naturally, as if using it were an extension of using a limb. Nevah, though, was more intentional. She chose which Floracantus to use strategically and taught me how to be methodical in researching the right Floracantus for the task at hand.

Under Nevah's direction, I learned that if I wanted a lily pad to spin in a circle, I needed to find a Floracantus specific to that species. If I wanted all of the lily pads in the pond to spin together, I needed to modify the end of the Floracantus to be plural.

I was quickly filling my copy of *Compendium Floracantus* with color-coded sticky notes and sketches around the margins. Leaves and pressed flowers had been inserted on vital pages as bookmarks. From the outside, it probably looked like I'd been in possession of the book for years, not a few months.

Nevah and Callan both knew most of the Floracantus they liked to use from memory, of course. I had fewer than thirty simple ones memorized by the end of our first month working together. I'd also taken to sketching drawings of what some of my favorite ones did in my notebook.

Today, Nevah and I stood in the Perilous Grove. "It's important to know that not everything to do with defensive plants is about defense at all. Sometimes, we're rendering the plants safer to use. Take the castor oil plant." She showed me a spiky orange plant. "Each of these spiny capsules has castor beans inside. Ricin, one of the world's most deadly poisons, is made from this. But castor oil also has an amazing ability to grow hair and eyelashes. With a simple Floracantus, you and I can dissolve the ricin and create potent eyelash serums that will quickly make you friends here."

I had noticed that Nevah's eyelashes were long, dark, and thick and had wondered if it was genetics or mascara. But it sounded like it was a magically enhanced super beauty serum. The potent plant-based skin care products Yasmin had given me already had my skin glowing. I couldn't wait to add this little gem to my routine.

"Is there a way to grow the castor beans without the ricin in the first place?"

Nevah looked at me strangely for a moment and shook her head. "There's no Floracantus for that. It'd be nice if there was. We could probably do it with genetic engineering, though.

Sometimes, modern science advances us more than magic, since we're limited to the Floracantus that exist."

"Does the school have priorities in what we research and create here? Do certain avenues take precedence over others?"

Nevah's face was thoughtful. "I think they let the plants and our powers decide. Plants have all different purposes, many of them medical or nutritional but others not. If they exist, even just to enhance beauty, we can't ignore that."

I nodded, taking the castor beans into my hands. I repeated the Floracantus Nevah told me and felt the ricin dissolve. We completed a few more steps and soon had a clear, viscous substance in a small glass vial.

"There's your first lash serum. Congrats." Nevah's words bolstered my confidence. As challenging as learning all these different affinities was, results like these made it all seem worth it.

The next evening, I went to meet Callan in our usual tree house. He was already there, jotting something in a notebook when I arrived.

"I think you're ready to try something more advanced," Callan said by way of greeting.

I eyed him skeptically. It was obvious that he and I had different definitions of the word "advanced." Was all the work we'd been doing to speed up the vascular system in trees child's play to him? I was usually sweating at the end of one of those meticulous sessions.

"What do you have in mind?"

"Let's see where your skills with herbals take you." He walked me through brewing up some herbal concoction that would supposedly stop an autoimmune response. But instead of paying close attention to the documented steps, like Nevah would have done, he encouraged me to feel the properties of the herbs as I touched them and prepare them based on that.

I struggled through it but eventually got a mixture heating in a pot on a camp stove. As we let the concoction simmer, I thought back to the day on the mountain when I had felt my first real connection to the trees. "Can I ask you something?"

"What's up?"

"Why did you have me practice opening up to the trees when we were at the ski park? Why not here at the academy? We've been out here in the tree houses dozens of times."

Callan spoke slowly. "Evergreen Academy is like an oasis for magical botanists. We have every plant, ingredient, and tool we could ever need. But it's not like that in the real world. Eventually, you're going to need to use your skills outside of here. I thought that trying things in your own environment, away from all the distractions of this place, might provide an opportunity for you to let loose, so to speak."

I contemplated it and realized he was right. I'd basically been ignoring plants outside of the academy this whole year, thinking of my skills as something that only applied when I was on the school's grounds.

Aside from the one time I'd tried—and failed—to make my aunt's petunias bloom longer, I'd never tried to connect with them. It didn't help that my affinity powers had become activated in winter, when evergreen trees were the main source of plant life available outside of Evergreen Academy's grounds.

"How are you so wise?" I asked, tossing a juniper sprig at him.

Callan leaned back against the interior tree wall, tattooed forearms flexing as he tilted his head back a little. "I wish my parents thought that about me."

I stilled. Callan rarely ever spoke of his parents or his personal life, and he always changed the subject when I tried. I'd never pushed because I was the same way when people asked me about my parents.

"You're joking, right? You're, like, the *best* student in school. They have to know how smart you are."

"Smart and wise are two different things." The timer

chimed, and Callan quickly moved over to take the lid off the pot. He stirred the contents. "Not bad, local. Not bad. Let's try another one." And just like that, the conversation about his parents was over, and my affinity studies took center stage once more.

LATER THAT EVENING, I APPROACHED THE POINSETTIA that my aunt had bought in the beginning of December. I'd been building a little confidence in my abilities, and Callan's words about practicing outside of the confines of the academy had struck a chord.

The velvety plant was perched on a corner of our counter, its red flowers bold and bright. I took a seat on the counter stool in front of the poinsettia then focused on tuning everything else out. Within a minute, I could feel the tissues of the plant, the tension of the roots embedded in the soil.

The plant had already been blooming for at least six weeks, which meant the leaves would start to fall soon. My focus cracked as I had the thought, and I took a deep breath. I focused on the plant again, opening myself up. Once I felt connected, I whispered, *"Longum flore,"* using the same Floracantus for blooming longevity I'd tried on the petunias last fall.

A tremor of excitement ran through me as I felt a satisfied hum push itself from the poinsettia's leaves and into the air.

"What are you doing?" Aunt Vera asked, and I jumped, quickly opening my eyes and leaning away from the plant. I hadn't even heard her enter the room.

"Just checking on the poinsettia. I think it needs water."

"I thought I watered it yesterday, but maybe I didn't give it enough."

Heart thundering, I shrugged casually, got a measuring cup,

and put a few drops of water in the pot. My magical botanist skills might be improving, but it was clear that my stealth operations could use a little work.

"By the way, I finally spoke with Professor East after playing phone tag for a while. That man is difficult to get ahold of. He said that he was just checking in to let me know you were doing well at school."

A feeling of gratitude toward Professor East grew like a well-nourished seed. I'd asked him to step back on approaching my aunt, and he'd followed through with that promise. I made a mental note to thank him the next time we spoke.

"So keep up the great work. He sounded kinda cute over the phone. Is he single?"

"Gross! That's my professor!"

"Sorry, just looking out for some of my friends. There aren't a lot of eligible bachelors around here."

I rolled my eyes but grinned as I shook my head, grateful that despite how much I felt I was changing, my aunt was exactly the same.

Chapter Forty-Four

"Apparently, I missed the memo about a Floral Fete where I'm supposed to present something," I said to Callan as we sat on a large tree branch, practicing a Floracantus that would extract willow bark without causing any damage to the tree. According to Callan, it was an important ingredient in the medical field.

Yasmin had filled me in on the upcoming festivity, which would fall on Valentine's Day.

"Yep, all lead floral affinities make something. I've seen perfumes, floral sculptures, even food."

I sighed, racking my brain for something I could pull together by the weekend. My affinity studies were spread so thin that I couldn't imagine finding time to do a whole project on such short notice, let alone one that was going to be on display for the entire school.

"Focus, local," Callan prompted.

"*Cortex removi*," I murmured. The bark gave a little shudder but stayed in place.

"Make sure you're focused while you're saying it. The tree knows your mind is on flowers, not it. *Cortex removi*," he said, and the bark peeled away in perfect curls that flew into his hand, the section of tree they had come from instantly growing back.

I sighed. I was never going to be a natural at this. My brain had always had trouble focusing on just one thing, which was one of the many reasons drawing appealed to me. I had to focus completely on that task. It helped drown out everything else for a short time.

"You're always drawing." Callan nodded toward my notebook, seeming to read my mind. "Do something with that?"

"For the Floral Fete? How is that going to be interesting to anyone?"

"Draw some of the flowers here. Show us how you see them. It won't be everyone's cup of tea, but nothing is." He bumped his shoulder against mine gently. "And I promise I will like it, so you'll have at least one fan."

I rolled my eyes but was inwardly grateful for the suggestion. I wasn't sure if it would rise to the level of expectation for the other floral affinities, but at least I could show I was making an effort. It was practically impossible to fit in with all of the affinity groups, but it didn't hurt to try.

"One fan? How could I say no?"

"He's a very impressive fan." His voice was as smooth as a river on a calm day.

"Then I'd better make something worthy of his interest," I mused. But my chest squeezed at the fact that my art might play a role at Evergreen Academy and that Callan might be interested in it. Reluctantly, I rose. "I have to run. I'm on Kitchen Botany rotation and in charge of setting out the evening tea and snacks."

"If you make honeysuckle and orange blossom tea tonight, I'll love you forever," Callan called out casually as I made to leave the tree house.

"Asking for favors now, Rhodes?" I teased over my shoulder, though I was secretly thrilled at his words.

"Just some good old-fashioned cronyism, local. Heavy on the honeysuckle, please."

I left the tree house with a roll of my eyes and a grin.

Chapter Forty-Five

I spent every spare moment during the final days of the week painting. Drawing had always been my forte, but I felt that a painting might be perceived as showing more effort at the Floral Fete.

After going back and forth about which flower to paint as I'd been sitting in the flower garden, a stunning pink foxglove at least four feet tall seemed to call out to me. The soft bells of its petals fluttered open, their fragrance drifting on the air to my nose.

The decision was made then and there. Yasmin had allowed me to store the painting in her room overnight, so I didn't have to haul it back and forth to campus. On Friday morning, I dropped off the finished painting—covered by a drape—to Professor Tenella. As I did so, I saw other lead floral affinities bringing in stunning floral wreaths, glass bottles of swirling fresh perfumes, floral-infused cosmetics and healing ointments, and even a few food products.

"I tried to raid the costume closet early," Yasmin said, entering the room with a stack of gowns over her arms. Coral

221

and I turned from where we were swiping magically enhanced cream eye shadow across our lids in Yasmin's mirror.

"Ohhh, let me see," I said, moving to help her make space in the closet to hang them. I'd learned that the Floral Fete did a period theme each year, and this year was Regency-esque. I eagerly sifted through the collection of stunning embroidered gowns in various colors.

"There's enough for us each to try on a few," Yasmin said.

As we took turns donning the gowns, I noticed that the soft plant-based fabric tightened and trimmed itself automatically to fit each of our different body shapes. Yasmin claimed the gowns had been charmed by Professor Variegata for the day. Automatic custom tailoring? Now that was something I could get used to.

In the end, I selected a pale purple gown with a modern twist. Instead of the traditional cap sleeves of a Regency gown, it had delicate straps that tied at the top of my shoulders with a bow. The ends of the gown trailed along the floor with wisteria flowers overlaying it.

We used the flowers Aurielle had brought to weave colorful blooms into our hair. I used my floral affinities to affix them firmly in place and plump up their cells so that they wouldn't droop throughout the night.

When we were all ready and turned to look at ourselves in the mirror, it was like we had stepped out of some kind of enchanted film set.

"It's nice having a floral affinity friend," Coral mused, and Aurielle gave me a high five on her way out of Yasmin's room.

The party was held in the flower gardens, which had been made over for the day. Flowers were *everywhere*, trailing overhead in an impossible fashion. The place smelled like the most perfect mixture of floral essential oils, not too overwhelming but just right. Students milled around in their dresses and suits, looking whimsical and dashing all at once.

And then I spotted Callan.

He was in a perfectly tailored black suit with a deep green tie that matched that of the leaves of the trees around us. He approached us and offered me his arm. I tried to calm the rapid way my heart was suddenly beating.

"You could have warned me you'd be showing up in a suit," I whispered.

"I'm the one who needed a warning. You look"—he let his eyes trail over my dress, my shoulders, and my hair and land on my eyes, where I'd taken special care with Yasmin's magical makeup and Nevah's lash serum recipe—"breathtaking."

"Well, it's amazing what some magic makeup and clothes that can automatically form fit to your body will do."

"You give magic too much credit," he said quietly, but he didn't explain what he meant. "So, where's this drawing I've been eager to see?"

"Actually, I ended up doing a painting." We followed my friends toward the gazebo where the various creations were displayed. My eyes widened when I saw that my painting was on an artist's gold easel trailing with flowers, right in the center of the display.

Whoever had placed my painting there had framed it with pink-and-white flowers that made the colors of my painting pop, perfectly accentuating the textured foxglove I'd painted against a dark background. With the arrangement, the bells of the foxglove seemed to jump off the page.

"Oh no," I breathed.

"Oh no?" Callan asked, confusion lacing his voice.

"I was hoping it would just be lying down on a table or perched casually against a wall, barely noticeable."

Callan nudged me inside the gazebo, and I saw that a few students were gathered around my painting, while others explored the various goods in the gazebo.

"Stunning," I heard someone whisper.

"The style is like something out of the Renaissance period," another commented.

Professor Tenella came to stand beside me then. "Absolutely lovely, Briar. Where have you been hiding that talent?"

"I usually stick to drawing, though I have to say I really enjoyed getting into painting again."

"Well, it's an absolute gem. Thank you for sharing it with us."

I let out a deep breath as Professor Tenella walked away. "She actually thinks it's good?" I breathed.

Yasmin and Coral caught up to us then.

"Oh my spores, that came out marvelous. I'd taken some peeks in my room but never saw the finished product. You're insanely talented, B," Yasmin said.

I flushed, unused to having such public attention on my art. Sure, it was my goal to go to art school as my mom had, but outside of my art classes at SCC, I'd never openly shown my work like this. And this was my first time doing a painting in this style. I'd been nervous to put it out here in the first place, and I wasn't sure how to react to the praise.

Luckily, I didn't have to be awkwardly silent for long, since my friends began to try on perfumes and ooh and aah over floral statues and cakes.

"How'd that feel?" Callan whispered into my ear, and I shivered.

"How'd what feel?"

"Putting yourself out there for the first time."

"Terrifying," I admitted, wondering how he'd known.

His mouth twitched. "I have a feeling this is only the start for you, local."

Throughout the afternoon, when we went our separate ways for afternoon tea and lunch, I caught glimpses of Callan with his tree affinity friends or chatting with Nevah. A little flare of discomfort arose at that, but I pushed it down, trying to be present in the moment.

The florals had outdone themselves, and this party wasn't one I would ever forget. We drifted to the dessert table, helping ourselves to some pastel-colored cupcakes.

A few minutes later, Callan approached and escorted me to the side of the building and under a covered trellis bursting with flowers, away from everyone else. We stood in the small space, the scent of rose and jasmine taking over nearly every other sensation. A few bees buzzed nearby but not in a bothersome way. The area was too saturated with pollen for them to notice us.

Callan tugged at his tie, straightening it. I suddenly had the strong urge to wrap my arms around him.

"How has your training been going with Nevah?"

I blinked. Nevah, of course. She was my tutor, like Callan was. That was all he was. And the two were far better suited for one another than he and I would ever be. They both had magical botanist families, lifetimes of experience. And their magic made sense. Nevah wasn't an enigma, like me. The thoughts festered out of nowhere, and I took a step back.

"Good, I think. Why? Has she said anything about it?"

A smile formed at the corners of his eyes. "Slow down there. I was just asking."

I let out a breath. "She's a good teacher. I see why you two are the perfect match." I clapped a hand over my mouth. Had I said that aloud?

Callan arched an eyebrow. "Why do you say that?"

"Well, you both look like models from a magazine. Then there's the fact that, along with Eli, you have the strongest affinities of anyone in the school. You're both from established magical families..." I racked my brain for more similarities to list, though there was a small feeling in the pit of my stomach questioning why I was saying all of this. Normally, I'd never voice this, but in this moment, it felt totally natural.

Callan made a confused face, then he looked at the half-eaten cupcake in my hand. His eyes widened, and he took the sweet treat from me. "So, someone spiked the cupcakes with *Scopolia* again. Professor East is going to lose it."

"What?" I asked, confused by every part of what he had said.

"*Scopolia carniolica*. Truth serum. People with defensive plant affinities can modify and use it. You'd be able to block it, since you have those affinities, but I'm guessing Nevah hasn't worked on how to block plant poisons that have been magically enhanced by other botanists yet." He swore quietly. "I'm going to have her move that up the list."

He took my hand and gently tugged me out from under the trellis. "I've got to find Professor East. Do you know if your friends ate any of the cupcakes?"

"Yasmin did, but Coral said she didn't want to end up with frosting in her teeth." Again, the response spilled out of me. Was I really under the influence of *truth serum*? I thought that was just the stuff of sci-fi spy-movie legends. Then again, I *was* at a school for magical botanists.

Callan navigated us through the crowd, where I started to overhear bits of arguments.

"You said you thought this dress looked good on me earlier today!"

"Well, I lied."

I gasped. How many people had eaten the cupcakes and were now saying things they'd never intended to share? I spotted Coral. Callan was making a beeline for her.

"Coral, I need you to look after Briar. And probably your other friends too."

"What's wrong?" Coral asked sharply, her eyes roaming over me for signs of damage.

"Someone spiked the cupcakes with *Scopolia*," he said quietly.

Coral gasped. "I heard that happened a few years ago."

Callan's face was grave. "I'm going to find Professor East. This can spiral out of control quickly."

Coral took my hand, and Callan disappeared into the crowd.

"But I want to go with Callan," I whined, unable to control my words.

"Come on. Let's find Yas and Aurielle and head back upstairs."

"Of course Coral's into you," Aurielle was saying to Waylon when we found her. Coral gave her a horrified look and took her hand.

"Sorry, it's the apple wine," Coral whispered to Waylon over her shoulder. "This is a disaster," she said to me. "We need to find Yas."

We spotted Yasmin a few minutes later. She was grabbing another cupcake from the garden table.

"I'll take that," Coral said, casually placing the cupcake back on the tray. "I should probably take all of these." She picked up the large tray and motioned for Yasmin to follow us. I felt like I was in a daze, not sure exactly where we were going or why Coral was acting so stressed.

"I want to dance," I said, and Coral shook her head.

"We need to go up to the room first."

"But the party's not over," Yasmin whined.

Coral sighed, looking frazzled. Then her eyes widened slightly. "I've got a surprise for you in my room."

We all murmured in excitement at that and followed Coral as she locked the cupcakes in a cupboard then climbed the stairs.

"What's the surprise?" Aurielle asked, looking around the room she shared with Coral.

"I'm going to brew y'all a special tea." Coral began to heat an electric kettle and sift through some canisters of loose herbs on her dresser.

"Ohhh, that sounds yummy," Yasmin said.

"And let's just hope Professor Sato is already working on brewing a batch for everyone else," Coral mumbled.

The three of us flopped on the two beds as Coral worked. My limbs were suddenly feeling tired, and I lay back on a large pillow shaped like a fern leaf. The ceiling began to spin as I did so.

"The room is spinning!" I shouted.

"You're fine," Coral insisted, shoving a mug of tea into my hands. "Sit up and drink this."

A few minutes later, my head began to clear, and I blinked at Coral in confusion.

"What the heck happened?" Aurielle asked.

"You were all drugged with enhanced *Scopolia carniolica*."

"The truth serum?" Yasmin sputtered.

"Thankfully, Callan noticed and asked me to get you all out of the party before too much damage could be done."

"Please tell me I didn't say anything stupid," Aurielle muttered.

"Oh, not much. You just told Waylon that I'm into him," Coral said in exasperation.

Aurielle winced. "I'm so sorry!"

Coral waved a hand. "It's fine. Maybe he won't remember in all the chaos."

"What did I say?" Yasmin asked, and I could see that she was racking her brain to remember.

"Not sure. I found you when you were about to eat another cupcake."

A fuzzy memory started to form then, and I moaned. Everyone turned to look at me. "I think I told Callan he looked like a model from a magazine."

Aurielle snorted with laughter, but Yasmin said, "I'm sure that's nothing he hasn't heard before."

"I think I want to crawl into a hole and never come out," I breathed.

"That's how a ton of people are going to be feeling," Coral said, then she walked to the window and peered outside. "I see teacups being passed around. Looks like Callan saved the day."

I groaned. "Don't speak his name."

"Can you imagine what truths came to light during the party? This place is going to be a mess tomorrow. My sister said this happened once when she was in school here. Some friendships ended forever." Yasmin's face was solemn.

"Well, at least the four of us are still intact," Aurielle said. "Sorry again, Coral." My stomach unclenched slightly at her words. Despite whatever embarrassing conversation I'd had with Callan, my friend group had survived the night.

There was a knock on the door then, and Coral opened it. I stood up when I saw Callan standing there with Professor East. The instructor saw the teacups in our hands and nodded. "Looks like you already got them the antidote. Well done, Ms. Day. Now, someone said they saw you with the cupcakes. I'd like to have a look at those."

"I took them and locked them in the spice cabinet after Callan told me they were laced."

Professor East nodded. "Very good. We'll make sure those are disposed of." He turned and left us then.

Callan made eye contact with me, and I went to the door. We stepped outside and propped it closed behind us. "I wanted to see how you were. Did the detox tea work?"

"Well, I don't feel compelled to spill my guts to you anymore, so I think so." I hoped to make light of the situation so my embarrassment didn't pull me under.

"Good. And just so you know... there's nothing between Nevah and me."

"Oh, okay. It doesn't matter if there is..." I felt my cheeks flush and internally cursed the *Scopolia* that had surfaced some deep concern I hadn't fully known I possessed.

"Yep, now I know the truth serum has worn off."

I smacked his arm gently, and he chuckled. But then his expression tightened.

"Not that my parents wouldn't be thrilled if there was. Trying to keep magical bloodlines powerful and all that aristocratic BS. She'd be the perfect match, in their eyes."

"And in your eyes?" I couldn't help asking. He was opening up more than usual, maybe to spare me some of the self-consciousness I was feeling.

"Nevah's great, but I've never seen her as anything more than a friend. And the same is true for her."

"Got it," I said, biting my lower lip. I hoped the relief didn't show on my face.

"I'm glad you're safe," Callan said softly. And then he was gone.

Chapter Forty-Six

When I got home that evening, exhausted from the aftereffects of the *Scopolia* poisoning, Bryce was pulling up to collect Aunt Vera for a Valentine's Day dinner. He climbed the stairs to the apartment, arms full of two large bouquets of flowers.

"For you," he said, giving my aunt a kiss, "and for you." He handed the second bouquet to me, and I grinned.

"Ahhh, shucks," I said teasingly. "You know you don't have to keep buttering me up, Bryce. I've accepted that you're not going anywhere. Don't be afraid to keep the flowers coming, though," I added quickly.

Aunt Vera gathered both of our bouquets and took them to the sink, then began to fill two vases with water. Bryce followed her, stopped at the poinsettia plant, and felt its velvety flowers.

"Yours is still blooming? Mine died, like, a month ago."

Aunt Vera glanced at the plant over her shoulder. "I've never had one live this long. It must be happy right there."

I swallowed. When I'd extended the longevity of the blooms, I hadn't thought about when the blooming would end. Was this

poinsettia going to bloom indefinitely? If so, I'd have to sneak it out of the house and find it a place at the academy.

"So, where are you two going for dinner?" I asked loudly, drawing their attention from the poinsettia.

"Delilah's," Bryce answered.

"Fancy." I nodded approvingly, but my mind jumped to the last time I was there. It was the restaurant Callan had taken me to on Halloween, where we'd snuck in the kitchen and he'd whipped out a Michelin-star-worthy meal.

"One of you should order the Mediterranean veggie pasta. It's delicious."

My aunt, who had just finished arranging our flowers in the vases, raised her eyebrows at me. "When did you eat there?"

I blinked, realizing my mistake. "Oh, I went there last fall with some friends."

"Look at you, growing up and stuff. Going to fancy restaurants without me." She kissed my forehead and then walked past, grabbing her red leather jacket and slipping it over her black dress. She looked stunning, her dark hair curled and lips touched with a deep-red stain.

"Have fun. Feel free to stay out late," I called after them as they left. It was our inside joke whenever they went on a real date.

"Just late enough that you'll still be up to eat the dessert we bring back for you," Aunt Vera said with a smile.

I watched them leave from the balcony, giving a little wave and then sighing quietly as I returned to the house. I was thrilled that after years of raising me, my aunt had finally found love.

Her twin sister became a mom at the young age of twenty, and I always thought Aunt Vera swung the other way because of it. While my dad helped support us financially, he and my mom never married, and he lived in a different state, never taking to parenting.

In many ways, my aunt helped my mom raise me since birth

before she took over in full six years ago. The deep lines of exhaustion and grief that had sunk into her beautiful face for years finally lightened, and since Bryce had been in the picture, she was glowing.

Maci came over shortly after they left to work on an essay for an English class we were both taking this semester. We hadn't spent much time together outside of class since the day we'd gone snowboarding with Alex, Callan, and Nevah.

I tried to tell myself the distance was because we were both busy and not because I was getting so much more involved with my life at Evergreen Academy. But perhaps it was both. We'd known that our relationship would change as we started college and that we would be going our separate ways to our four-year schools.

When I'd talked to Aunt Vera about it, she'd said that being able to maintain friendships as they evolved in form and frequency was a sign of maturity, and I hoped that was true.

Still, the distance had me opening up to Maci more than I had in a while.

"How has everything been with you lately? I know we haven't had much time to hang out outside of English class. Have I missed any major life changes?"

Maci sat up from where she'd been sprawled in front of her laptop on my bed. "Actually, there is." Her brown eyes shone brightly. "You know how Alex came with us snowboarding in January? Well, we've hung out a couple times since. I'm starting to wonder if this is going somewhere."

"So you and Jace are officially over?"

She nodded. "Yep."

"Do you and Alex have similar interests?" For some reason, his comment about me majoring in art came into my head again. Maci was future focused, wanting to secure a career that would bring stability and financial security. From Alex's comment, it sounded like he had similar ideals.

"I mean, yeah. He's really smart and committed to school, like I am. He's planning to transfer to a four-year. We're even both interested in majoring in business administration."

I frowned. "I thought Alex told me he planned to major in engineering."

"Well, you know how it is your first two years in college. Plans can change."

I nodded, accepting her explanation tentatively. "True. Well, that's good, then, Maci. I'm really happy for you."

She smiled and then said, "And what about you? Are you still hanging out with hot tutor? I was squealing inside when he came snowboarding with us. That wasn't his girlfriend with him, was it? She was gorgeous."

I sorted through Maci's questions. "Yes, we're still hanging out, but it's just tutoring. And no, she's not his girlfriend, but I agree. She is gorgeous."

"You're into him, though, right?"

I let out a breath and fell back beside her on the bed. I hadn't admitted it to myself, but here, talking with my best friend of forever, it felt safe to voice. "I think I kind of am."

Maci sat bolt upright on the bed. "So are you going to ask him out?"

"No!" It came out of my mouth without question. "He's not the kind of guy you just ask out. Besides, he's my tutor. No need to complicate that relationship." I thought about the awkwardness of our conversation about Nevah. The last thing I needed was for Callan to get uncomfortable around me and stop tutoring me. I couldn't imagine how badly I'd be struggling at both SCC and Evergreen Academy without his support.

"Well, just remember that we're only here for another year and few months. So either you enjoy it now, or you might never be able to."

"What about everything you just said about having similar

interests and aligned futures?" I raised an eyebrow playfully, and Maci laughed.

"Do as I say, not as I do. But seriously, you deserve it."

"Callan's fun to daydream about, but nothing's going to happen." I gave a little wistful sigh for Maci's sake. She couldn't understand the complex family dynamics he dealt with, the pressures of being a founder's descendant. I didn't fully understand it myself, and Callan had only allowed me to see snippets of that side of himself on occasion.

I was still learning basic Floracantus and hadn't even known I was a magical botanist until last fall. I wasn't even approaching the caliber of person Callan was going to end up with one day. We were, quite literally, from different worlds.

"If you insist," she said lightly, but a smile played on her lips.

Chapter Forty-Seven

The following week, Professor East requested to meet with me, and I walked to his office with a nervous flutter in my stomach. It had been a long time since we'd had a meeting, and Professor East seemed to be off campus more than on recently.

"Hello, Ms. Whelan. I'm sorry it's taken me so long to get to this subject. Things have been busy. But I thought we should talk about your affinity powers again. It would be good to increase our attempts to figure out their onset. Without talking to your aunt, as you requested, I wonder if you'd be willing to explore your family history with me."

I studied Professor East, wondering why he was so interested. I'd been grateful that he'd backed off with my aunt when I asked him to, but where was the interest coming from?

Whether we knew the history of my powers or not didn't change how I would approach my affinity studies, did it? And if my powers had come from my mom's side of the family and she was no longer around... what difference did it make? I sensed that there was something Professor East wasn't telling me.

"Professor East, I understand that my powers are unusual,

but is there something else going on here?" I straightened my posture, hoping Professor East wouldn't be put off by my forwardness.

Professor East studied me for a moment before speaking, all the plants in the room seeming to freeze as if they, too, awaited his response.

"What we've seen in your affinity tests is extremely rare. The magical botanist community has always taken great care to document magical family lines, especially the powerful ones. Your family must have fallen off that chart somewhere. It's important to our body of knowledge to put those missing pieces back together."

"Is that the only reason? To fill in knowledge gaps for the magical botanist community?" I pictured some magical genealogy group combing through my family's history. But I still sensed there was something that Professor East wasn't saying.

As if on cue, I could feel that the plants in the room were producing more oxygen than usual, as if to calm the environment.

"That's an important reason, yes. But it could be important for you too. When you go to visit a doctor, they always ask about your family medical history. The same reasoning applies here. Knowing your family's magical history could be of benefit to you down the road."

"What, are there magical plant diseases that can run in families?" I said it jokingly, but my stomach swooped a little at the thought.

Professor East shook his head and smiled softly. "No, and I won't force you into anything. But can you agree to think about it? We can work through your family history together. I'll just need a few records from you, and we can attempt to do a deep dive."

I nodded, standing up. "Of course." It wasn't that I was against sharing the records. I could get him basic details without issue. In fact, he could probably do some digging without me. In that regard, I was glad that he was including me in the search. But it was the lingering question of why this was important that was unsettling me.

"Good. And think quickly, please, Ms. Whelan. I'd like to start all of this before the spring solstice."

I wanted to ask why the spring solstice was the deadline, but I felt that I'd pushed my luck already. When Professor East returned his gaze to the papers on his desk, I took the hint to leave, wondering what he wasn't telling me.

Chapter Forty-Eight

I sat on the tailgate of Callan's truck, twisting pine needles into tightly braided coils to try to temper my curiosity about our tutoring session this evening. He'd sent a note to me in the library via the leaves, asking me to meet him in the parking area after dinner. When he approached, he was wearing a backpack.

"What's that for?"

"We're going to collect some letters."

"Letters?" I repeated, confused. "Does Evergreen Academy receive mail?"

"Not directly. They're from the trees on Wildflower Trail at SCC."

I hopped off the tailgate and dropped the pine needles, which fell and splayed out on the ground. Callan loaded his backpack into the truck and opened the door for me as my first question burst out.

"*That's* where the letters go?"

I thought of all the tree drawings I'd slipped into the letter boxes over the years. The most recent one had been the sketch of Frank, the oldest tree in town, that I'd done toward the begin-

ning of the school year, when my biggest concern had been alleviating Maci's fears about calculus.

Callan nodded as he eased out of the parking lot and through the gates that separated Evergreen Academy from the rest of the dense forest around us.

"But *why*? What does that have to do with magical botany?" Out of all the strange things I'd seen and heard since I'd come to Evergreen, this one felt the most discordant. Perhaps it was because I'd grown up with the tree-writing activity as part of my normal, non-botanist life, and I had never fathomed that it could be connected to this place.

"Our non-magical friends don't always remember to stop and connect with nature. The tree letter boxes are modeled off some experiments done in other countries. People felt more invested in their local environment when they connected personally with at least one plant. Trees make a great candidate for connection, since they're so enduring."

"So you're saying that Evergreen Academy installed the boxes?"

"It was the idea of a second-year student a few decades ago. He was researching the psychological and emotional effects of plants. It seemed to be a success in the community, so they left the boxes up."

"But what do you do with all the letters that are collected? You don't read them, do you?"

"We take them back to the tree houses. We don't read them all, but we do sift through. Sometimes, people leave poetry or interesting stories. Some even leave drawings for the trees." His eyes shot to me, and we held each other's gaze for a moment. Did he know? Had he seen my drawings? "It's more of a sociological study than anything now, but we tuck the letters away for posterity."

"How often do you empty the boxes?"

"Someone gathers them once a quarter. The boxes usually

don't fill up faster than that. I actually wasn't supposed to be doing this today. It was scheduled to be the student who spiked the cupcakes with *Scopolia*."

"Whatever happened with that?" Yasmin had passed along a little gossip about some of the friendships and relationships that were now strained due to the truth serum, but I hadn't heard if the instructors had determined a culprit. Magical botanists were surprisingly close-lipped.

"Professor East traced the magically enhanced *Scopolia* to a second-year student with a trailing affinity for defensive plants. His lead affinity is trees, so it's kind of embarrassing for us. But it is actually impressive that he was able to pull it off without a lead affinity for defensives."

"Did he get in trouble?" I assumed so, given that the student wasn't here to do letter-collecting duty today.

"Professor East was not messing around, since this happened a few years ago, and it appears the lesson wasn't strict enough. The student was expelled."

I inhaled sharply.

"Yeah. It's extremely rare at Evergreen. But the student essentially drugged all of us without our consent, so I think it's justified."

I nodded, suddenly feeling more solemn. Evergreen Academy had been mostly fun and games, but this was a reminder that plant magic had to be taken incredibly seriously at times.

We were nearly to town now, and I looked out the windows in wonder. What other integrations did Evergreen Academy have with the town that no one knew about?

Before I could ask more, Callan changed the subject.

"I heard you had a meeting with Professor East this morning."

I nodded, grateful that Callan had opened the door to this conversation. "He wants to do a deep dive on my family history with me, to try to determine where my powers came from."

"And you don't want to?"

"I'll do it. I'm curious about my history too. It's just that I don't understand *why* it's so important to know. How will knowing affect Professor East? Or affect my abilities? I can't shake the feeling that there's something he's not telling me."

Callan hesitated as he pulled into the parking lot of SCC and turned off the engine.

"What is it?" I pressed. If he knew something that would help me decide, I wanted to hear it.

"Professor East answers to the Magical Botanical Board of Regents. I'm assuming the pressure is coming more from them than him. If anything, I think he's probably shielded you from their scrutiny to the best of his ability."

My stomach clenched, trying to sort out what he'd just said. "The what of what?"

"The Magical Botanical Board of Regents. They oversee everything here at the school, as well as all magical botanical activity in the United States."

"And they're interested in *me*?"

"You have a strong affinity for every single plant group. We've been downplaying that here during your studies, but that is not something that Professor East would have been able to avoid reporting."

"But what does the Board of Regents want with me?"

"Probably nothing yet. Right now, they're seeking information. I imagine that once you're trained, they'll be lining up to recruit you for various high-level internships and careers." His voice was carefully even.

"*What?*" I choked out. I hadn't even thought about myself having a job as a magical botanist, let alone a high-level one, whatever that meant.

Callan seemed to sense my anxiety. "Right now, they're just

evaluating your potential. The next steps will really depend on you and the abilities you hone."

I chewed on my lip. In another situation, I would see this as an incredible opportunity. It was as if the biggest art gallery in the world was showing interest in my work. But I hadn't done anything to earn the recognition, and it didn't sit right with me. Plus, I was getting a strange vibe from Callan about the Board of Regents, though I couldn't put my finger on what it was.

"So you think the reason Professor East wants to research my family history has to do with the Board of Regents?"

"Possibly."

I let out a breath. I handled a lot of things coming my way in the past, but scrutiny from a powerful board like that? I wasn't ready for it.

"And what happens if the board doesn't get the answers they're looking for?"

Callan looked at me for a moment but didn't respond before proceeding to empty the first letter box, and somehow that was more ominous than any words could have been.

Chapter Forty-Nine

After a grueling Biological Applications of Physics class, where we worked on speeding and slowing the process of stomatal closure to study plant hydraulics, I met Nevah at the pond for an aquatics affinity session. My head was still spinning with recorded values and the strain I'd felt as the xylem tension approached an important threshold.

"You look peckish," Nevah said, tossing her hair over her shoulder in a cascade of dark ringlets.

"We were doing hydraulics testing today in Plant Phys," I said, using the common nickname for the course.

"Aw, enough said. Let's start with something easy, then. How about a Floracantus to scatter the floating plants so we can study the submerged ones?"

I braced myself to switch gears to Latin, trying to remember the Floracantus that would move the water plants along the surface of the pond. "*Per aquam labatur,*" I said finally, and the plants gracing the top of the water moved a few millimeters.

"Remember to connect with the plants. You have to feel them before you utter the Floracantus."

I tried again, reaching out to sense the tissues and then cells of the plants before uttering the words again. This time, they spread a little farther from one another, forming a small open circle on the water's surface.

"Better. Now collect some of the water. We're going to practice running a few tests."

We worked near the pond for nearly an hour before Nevah shifted gears. "Let's get some tea and go to the Perilous Grove."

Relieved at the prospect of a short break, I followed her into the academy building, and we brewed a strong concoction that should restore my energy and tighten my focus. By the time we walked out to the Perilous Grove, travel tea mugs in hand, I felt my brain begin to rev up and stood a little straighter, ready to give my studies a fresh start.

"Forewarning, Callan put the pressure on to up your training in this area," Nevah said once we entered the grove. "Apparently, the *Scopolia* incident really freaked him out. He is right, though. If you were far enough along in your training, you'd have been able to recognize the Floracantus that had magically altered the plant's properties and counteracted it immediately."

"We've been training as fast as we can," I said quickly, trying not to let feelings of being overwhelmed return.

"Agreed, but we may need to work harder. There is so much ground to cover with the number and level of affinities you have. And you're already years behind most magical botanists. Our time here is limited, and we have to make the most of it. I'm going to push you harder to memorize the core Floracantus." She flipped open her notebook and took a seat on a nearby tree stump, ready to observe my work. "Let's hope that tea has kicked in."

I nodded and slightly clenched my hands, letting my senses open to a nearby nightshade plant. "Let's do it."

Chapter Fifty

The first week of March brought Evergreen Academy's annual Capture the Roses game. I'd been anticipating the game ever since hearing about it and hoped I would get at least Yasmin, Coral, or Aurielle on my team.

When the day of the event arrived, we all gathered in and around the front gardens. Professor Tenella lifted her hands and magically clipped two enormous red roses from their bushes. She dropped them into two large jars, where they appeared to float in midair, petals outstretched in every direction.

"Welcome to our annual Capture the Roses competition. The area in play includes the entire academy grounds, outside only. No hiding your roses in the academy building itself. You will work with your team members to devise a plan to try to retrieve the other team's rose while protecting your own. All powers are allowed, but any that will result in an injury above basic bruises or scrapes are not permitted. Instructors will be monitoring and *will* remove botanists from the game if they are using affinities to injure others. We trust that you all will be more creative than that. As a reminder, the winners get easy entry to the vernal equinox celebration."

Excitement thrummed through the crowd of gathered students like bees flitting through the flower gardens.

"Now, for your teams." She began to call out names into Xylem and Phloem teams, and the group began to sort itself into two sides. Yasmin was called to Team Xylem and Coral to Team Phloem. I breathed a sigh of relief, knowing that I'd have at least one of them on my team. Aurielle was added to Yasmin's team.

"Callan Rhodes." I looked up at the sound of his name. "Team Phloem." I heard a few groans from Team Xylem. Eli Quinn had been sorted into Team Phloem a few moments earlier. But then Professor Tenella announced that Nevah was on Team Xylem, and there were loud cheers from that side that they had snagged one of the three founders' descendants.

With a last name starting with *W*, I was one of the last students called. Finally, Professor Tenella read my name, and I stood up straight.

"Briar Whelan... Team Phloem!" A few people high-fived me, and then I locked eyes with Coral and grinned as she moved to link her arm with mine.

"Thank spores you're on my team. I was worried you, Yas, and Aurielle were going to have all the fun without me."

"Circle up," Eli Quinn called, and suddenly we were all business. Team Xylem was dispersing into the woods, presumably to do its huddle out of earshot.

"We're going to break up into offensive and defensive teams. Defensive teams protect our rose at all costs. The offense goes for the other team's rose. If you have a preference, sort yourselves. Everyone else, stay here, and Rhodes and I will sort." I raised my eyebrows a little at Callan's name, realizing I shouldn't have been surprised. Of course, he and Eli were the unofficial team captains.

A handful of students split into offensive and defensive groups, but Coral and I remained in the middle with the others. Eli and Callan walked around the middle group, asking each person for their affinity powers and sorting them. When they reached Coral, she said, "Fern girly here."

"Defensive. Ferns are notoriously good at hiding things," Eli said, and Callan nodded. Coral wiggled her eyebrows at me and walked to the defensive team. "Where to put you?" Eli inclined his head toward me.

"Whelan's with me," Callan's decisive answer sent a pleasant jolt through me.

Eli nodded then said, "Defensive team, with me. Offense, with Rhodes."

Callan gave me a curt nod then shifted his attention to the group on our right. I glanced back at Coral, who gave me a wave of farewell as she disappeared into the forest.

"We're on offense, which means if we can't detect and capture their rose, we lose," Callan said, raising his voice so that everyone in the vicinity could hear.

"No pressure," a fellow first-year murmured from my side.

"As you can imagine, Eli Quinn isn't too keen on losing his last Capture the Roses game at Evergreen Academy, and I'm sure none of you are either. Let's hear your plans."

Callan allowed various individuals to share their ideas, nodding and asking direct follow-up questions. I got a glimpse of how sharp his strategic mind was, how he took a proposal and examined it from angles I hadn't even considered.

Finally, he turned to me. "And what's your strategy, Whelan?" I tried to suppress a smile at his use of my last name, assuming it was part of his *team captain* persona. Why did I enjoy every side that I saw of him?

"Well," I began slowly, "we can't win if we can't locate their rose. All the tree roots are interconnected across the grounds. Would the trees be able to communicate the location to us? Once we have that, we could put together a plan of attack."

A faint smile graced Callan's lips. "That's the best detection suggestion I've heard so far. Tree affinities, gather up."

I opened my senses as we gathered, reaching out to neighboring trees. Like me, most of the tree affinities used a few common Floracantus for communication, asking the trees to seek out the location of the rose and pass it back to us through their network of roots.

Callan used a complicated Floracantus that I couldn't understand, something to do with chemical secretions in the soil.

We waited a few moments, and then a shiver passed over me as, with a jolt of excitement, I sensed it. A tugging toward the eastern border of the campus. All of us with tree affinities turned our heads in that direction.

"It's over there?" one of the students with a lead aquatic affinity asked us.

"Seems like it. We can't pinpoint the exact location because they're shielding it with something, but that's enough to get us started. What do we know about the eastern edge of campus?" Callan prompted.

"A river runs through it," the same girl said again, rubbing her hands in anticipation.

"Exactly. Aquatics, you're gonna be the heavy hitters for this one."

Together, our group devised a plan, and we began to make our way through the forest. Those of us with tree affinities walked in the canopy of the trees, while the others moved on the ground below. Callan had recommended splitting like this in case any of us were caught. Those with lead grasses affinities used their powers to silence the ground so that the earth was eerily quiet as they walked below.

I followed Callan through the trees, walking along the path made of tree limbs as naturally as strolling through the park, though my heart was beating rapidly in anticipation of going on offense against Team Xylem.

As we approached the eastern side of campus, a strong wind kicked up. "The harvesters must be creating a storm," Callan whispered. Around us in the trees and down below, most of the students' hair was beginning to whip around wildly. Callan's, an aquatic affinity student's, and mine stayed perfectly calm. Our lead harvesters had stayed behind to perform defense with Eli Quinn.

"I can't take another step," one of our teammates on the ground whisper yelled.

Callan's jaw tightened, and he glanced at me then at the ground. We climbed down, and he spoke to the aquatic girl who, like us, wasn't struggling against the prevailing winds. "Moira, I think it's going to have to be the three of us who go." She nodded, seeming to understand the logic.

One of the second years with a lead grasses affinity said, "We'll act as decoys here and move in from a different vantage point if we get an opening. Good luck."

I followed Callan and Moira as we crept through the forest and knelt at the edge of a stream, staying out of sight as the wind ripped around us. Callan surveyed the area like a hawk assessing his prey, shrewd and calculating.

"The rose is there." He nodded toward a tree house about fifty feet up the river.

"How do you know?" I asked.

"Can you sense it?" he asked me, and I reached down deep within myself, blocking out all the commotion around me to focus on the image of the rose Professor Tenella had clipped and encapsulated at the beginning of the game. There was a strong tugging in my center toward the tree house, much stronger than when we'd been on the other side of the forest. I nodded.

"There's guaranteed to be booby traps all around it. Defensive plants, if they have any, but also possibly some florals and tree affinities. That's what I'd do. We'll have to get to it from the water." He looked at Moira, who nodded.

"How do you two feel about swimming?" Moira asked.

I'd done a little aquatic plant studying with Nevah and no swimming at all, but I'd always been a strong swimmer, and this was just a small creek. I nodded that I was in, and Callan did the same.

"It looks like we can hold our breath the whole way. I'll have those American lotuses provide cover."

"What if the other team has people in the water?"

Moira grinned. "Then we show them who's boss."

We slipped into the stream, and the sensation was unlike any I'd ever felt. Unlike the previous occasions when I'd gone swimming, when I got in the water, I didn't feel wet. Similarly to how the storm flowed right around me, the water seemed to glide past me as if my entire body were a wet suit. Moira took the lead, and Callan signaled for me to follow her. He brought up the rear.

We moved quietly through the river for a few minutes and were nearly to the tree house when Moira began to thrash in front of us. We stuck our heads out of the water, still hidden by the leafy lotus plants.

I noticed with horror that vines were wrapped around Moira's wrists. With a flick and a whisper, she threw one of them off. A vine snaked toward me from another direction, and I stifled a scream as I scrambled toward the bank.

"You two go," Moira said. "I'll hold them off!"

"Are you sure?" I asked, panting as adrenaline coursed through me. Moira nodded, and suddenly Callan was there, pulling me the rest of the way out of the water.

"We can't just leave Moira!" I gasped.

"She'll be fine. I've seen her skills. It's up to us now. Nevah could be around here somewhere, if she isn't on offense," he whispered, and a chill of nerves crashed over me again. Nevah was a formidable opponent, and as a second-year founders' descendant, she was eons ahead of my capabilities. If it came to a fight among the three of us, I wasn't sure who I favored to win.

"I need you on full focus now, local. Tap in."

Without thinking, I reached for his hand and instantly felt more grounded. I opened myself up, letting my senses be overwhelmed with the abundant plant life around us. I knew what we needed to do.

"We can climb the tree here then slide into the tree house. Nevah doesn't have a tree affinity. We'll have the advantage."

Callan nodded, and we scaled a nearby fir tree. "Wait here," Callan whispered, and before I could respond, he dove into the tree house heels first. A moment later, two large vines flew from out of nowhere and whipped inside the tree house.

"Callan!" I yelled, forgetting the warning to wait and scrambling into the tree house. My panic relaxed slightly when I took in the scene inside. Callan had secured the two members of Team Xylem who had obviously been stationed as the last line of defense. They were now tied to their seats, vines wrapped securely around their waists, hands, and mouths.

In the center of the tree house, on a small wooden table, sat the rose.

"We need someone with a floral affinity to break the enchantment and get it out of the capsule. Glad I know someone with one of those," Callan said, picking up the capsule and balancing it easily in one hand.

My eyes widened when I realized he was referring to me. "What? Can't you do it?"

"It'll be good practice."

"There's plenty of time to practice when we're not in the middle of a high-stakes game!" I looked around, expecting another member of Team Xylem to arrive in the tree house at any moment. My heart was still pounding from the chaos of the past few minutes.

"And that's why it's the perfect time to practice," Callan said. He passed the capsule to me. "There are a number of ways to approach this. Take your pick."

I let out a huff but then forced myself to concentrate. I relaxed my breathing and focused on the deep-ruby rose, willing myself to recall all I'd learned about the Rosaceae family. As if flipping through a mental drawing in my notebook, I pictured the spiral leaf arrangement, the hypanthium, the thorns that lined the stem—the one sharpness amongst all its beauty.

I zoomed into the aspects I'd seen through the microscope— the tissues then the cells—and envisioned the cytoplasm of each stretching. An idea came to me, and I formed the Floracantus I'd practiced with Callan.

"*Petala expandere*," I muttered.

The rose began to increase in size, filling the capsule. My palms started to sweat, and I nearly lost my focus when I thought it wasn't going to work, but with a few more centimeters of expansion, the petals and stem of the rose poked into the capsule, and it popped with a loud snapping sound. Whatever material the capsule was made of floated into the air like sparkling dust.

Before I knew what was happening, Callan's arms were around my waist, and he was floating us to the ground. For a moment we both stood there, grinning like frozen dolls, with me gripping the enlarged rose and Callan's hands still loosely grazing my hips.

Our eyes met, and my smile deepened at the playfulness I read in his expression. I so rarely saw him let loose like this, caught up in the moment of something simply... fun. And I was surprised I felt this way. The competition *had* been fun. Exhilarating, even.

"Nice work!" Moira shouted, appearing at my side. I was relieved to see that she'd managed to free herself from her captors in the river. She gave Callan a high five. We locked eyes for a second, and he smiled again, eyes crinkling at the corners. I lifted the rose into the air triumphantly.

Moira started chanting "Team Phloem" and led our celebratory crew back toward the academy, but all I could think was that I wished for a few more moments alone with Callan Rhodes.

Chapter Fifty-One

"That was epic," Coral said, scooping a heaping portion of fresh sorbet from her bowl. "I got to distract a bunch of harvesters who were trying to create a storm around us with the whispering of the ferns. It totally blew their concentration."

"Yasmin and I were preparing a bunch of herb bombs that we could toss at people as they approached the tree house, but Briar and Rhodes managed to avoid us by *creeping up the freakin' river.*" Aurielle glared half-heartedly at me.

"Hey, you had aquatics on your team too. One of them managed to temporarily sideline Moira."

"But not our B. She's a queen," Coral said, thrusting her cider glass into the air.

As soon as I lifted my glass to clink with hers, all the sconce lights that normally lit the teahouse in the evening went out. I felt a tug from my emerald ring. The lively chatter that had filled the room a moment before came to a halt.

Professor Sage rushed out of the kitchen, maneuvering his wheelchair faster than I'd ever seen. It was now too dark to make out exactly what he was doing, though. The only light in the room came from the moon and the stars that could be made out through the glass ceiling.

"The verdant shield went down again," I whispered, alarmed that the lights hadn't immediately come back on like they had in the previous flickers.

"Why haven't the lights come back on yet?" Aurielle asked, voicing my concerns.

"Have you seen Callan?" I asked. If the verdant shield was experiencing more than a flicker this time, Professor East might need him.

"I think the tree affinities went out to the tree houses after the game," Yasmin said, an anxious pull drawing her eyebrows together.

Just then, Professor East stepped into the teahouse, holding a large black flashlight. He spotted Nevah and beckoned her toward him.

"He's looking for the founders' descendants," I murmured, and Yasmin nodded.

"Great whispering vines," she breathed. "The verdant shield must still be down."

Professor Sage whistled and got the attention of everyone in the room. "Botanists, we're going to have to ask you all to stay inside for the rest of the evening. Here in the teahouse, your rooms, or the other common areas are fine. No one should leave the building. Professor Bowellia will alert any students who are currently in the tree houses to come in."

"How long are we going to be without lights?" Coral asked.

"As long as the shield is down, I'd imagine," Yasmin said.

"But how are they going to get the shield back up? I thought it could only be charged on the equinoxes and solstices," I asked, deep concern beginning to fill me. It had been minutes, and the lights were still off. This was nothing like the previous flickers. What did it mean for the integrity of the shield?

"I'm not sure," Yasmin admitted, worrying her bottom lip.

We waited in the teahouse, talking quietly, until Professor Sage flagged down the four of us about fifteen minutes later. Since we were all on Kitchen Botany rotation this session, he was calling us up for duty.

"There are chamomile citrus pies fresh out of the oven in the kitchen. Please pass them around. They'll help everyone to calm down." We filed to the kitchen, collected a tray of pies, and distributed them to the students in the area.

Just as the four of us sat down with pies of our own, the wall sconces flickered once then came back on. The students who remained in the teahouse cheered, and the volume in the room rose dramatically, as if the presence of light broke some unspoken rule of whispered voices in darkness.

A few minutes later, a frazzled-looking Professor East entered the room and climbed atop a small platform. All attention in the room turned toward him. After clearing his voice, he spoke. "I'm sure that was concerning to everyone. We will need to investigate this more closely, but it appears that the verdant shield temporarily fell. It has been restored. At this time, there is nothing to be worried about. We will proceed with classes on Monday morning as scheduled."

An abundance of chatter broke out once Professor East left the room.

"Well, that was enlightening." Aurielle snorted.

"Why did the outage last longer this time?" I asked, trying to keep the alarm out of my voice. "And how did they get the shield back up?"

"I'm not sure. And I don't think Professor East is going to share what he knows until things are more... stable," Yasmin said.

"So what do we do in the meantime?" I asked.

"Nothing. You heard the man. School as usual. This one's beyond our magical grade," Coral said, the relaxing properties of the pie apparently settling in.

"But what about the founders' descendants?" I pressed.

"Professor East is probably having a meeting with them right now."

I desperately wanted to see Callan. I knew this wasn't my issue, but I didn't feel as cavalier about it as Coral was acting. Everything about this felt... wrong. Another thought crossed my mind, and I straightened.

"What if someone had been walking by outside when the shield went down? Would they have seen the academy? What it really looks like, I mean?"

"That's why we have the brick wall surrounding the property," Yasmin replied. "They would have had to have been looking right through the gate when it happened. That's probably why we were all required to stay inside as well, in case our voices drifted out. Plus, it's dark out, and the academy is set really far back. I think we're safe in that regard."

I toyed with the emerald ring on my finger, wondering if it was useless without a verdant shield. Just another gem, although a beautiful one.

As I walked back to my car after finally leaving the teahouse for the night, I felt a swirl of leaves grace my calves. I stooped to pick up the note that was mixed with it.

Congrats on the win tonight. Sorry the celebrations were interrupted.

I hurriedly reached in my bag for a pen and scribbled a response on the back.

Are you okay? What happened to the shield?

I sent off the message and by the time I'd started my car, the leaves were back, this time pooling on my windshield.

Feel like ditching class on Monday?

An excited tremor ran through me at the words. Callan wasn't usually one to recommend skipping academic studies. But I was dying to know whatever he had to share.

Since when are you the bad influence? I'm in.

I sent the response into the wind and, a minute later, received a reply.

Meet you at the tree house. 8 a.m.

Chapter Fifty-Two

Callan was waiting for me in the tree house when I arrived on Monday morning, bent over a microscope.

"I thought we were ditching class, not doing extra studies," I said as I settled onto a stool next to him.

"Just doing a quick check of the soil," he said, looking up from the microscope and closing his notebook.

"What happened on Friday?" I blurted. I'd had homework and my Saturday shift at the café to distract me over the weekend, but my mind was never far from the question of what had occurred with the verdant shield after our game of Capture the Roses.

"Let's go off campus for a bit."

"You're really going to drag this out, aren't you?"

A tiny smile grazed his lips, but I noticed a slight twitch in his forehead, just above his left eyebrow. What did that mean? Was he stressed? Nervous?

"I think a history lesson is in order today."

I sighed but couldn't squelch the little thrill of anticipation I felt at the idea of spending more time with just him.

We went to Callan's truck, and he navigated off campus, out of the woods, and onto the road that led toward a popular send-off point for hiking the mountain.

A nervous clenching of my stomach formed as we approached the bends that would wind up the mountain. I didn't know exactly where it had happened, but my mom's car accident had taken place somewhere along this road on that horrible winter night. I gripped my seat belt and closed my eyes for a few moments until I thought we had passed it.

"You okay?" Callan asked when I opened my eyes again and inhaled a deep breath.

"Car sickness," I lied, not wanting to explain. Not wanting to dampen whatever he had planned with the memory of the worst day of my life. I threw out a joking line instead, ready to shift the atmosphere in the truck.

"Please tell me we're not hiking Mount Shasta today. I'm not in that good of shape."

Callan smiled, and my chest relaxed. The moment of dread had passed, just like every other time I'd forced myself up this highway. And this time, I let myself get lost in Callan's smile, in the woodsy smell of his truck, in the way there was a loose wave on the top of his chestnut-brown hair that flopped to the side with the mild breeze that rushed through the open window. I was okay. I was safe.

"Not today. But now that you gave me the idea..."

I groaned. "Just rewind the last minute and pretend I never said anything." We reached the parking lot, which wasn't full on a Monday morning.

Callan parked then led me to a trail that I knew led to a base camp of sorts. We'd taken field trips to do this hike in high school, and back then, I'd squeezed my eyes closed and held my breath on the bus as I'd done in Callan's truck, not letting the emotion overwhelm my entire experience of the day.

"Don't worry, we're just walking a ways. I wanted to tell you more about the history of the academy. You know that it was founded by several powerful botanist families, one for each of the nine lead affinities. One of the reasons this region was selected for the academy was the ecology of the area. The remoteness was an important factor, too, but the natural conditions were primary. This area is at the top of the water table for the state."

I nodded, having known that people traveled to our tiny town from all over the world just to try its pure mountain spring water.

"The quality of the water is an amazing source of life for the plants in this area, and the conditions of the soil here were perfect for embedding the verdant shield that protects the school. Over time, the conditions of the soil around the school have changed due to periods of drought, contamination from fires, and other factors. You can think of it like the verdant shield no longer having as firm of a grasp on the soil as it once did."

"But what about when the founders' descendants recharge the shield on the solstices and equinoxes?"

"That has always helped, but our families' powers have not maintained their potency. Many of our affinity powers have weakened since the founders originally created the shield. Between that and the weakening soil, it's been difficult to keep the verdant shield operating at full capacity."

"Why do you think it went down for so much longer last night? It doesn't seem like the steady trend downward we'd expect from something like this."

Callan's shoulders tightened. "We're looking into some leads."

"Is that what you were doing at the tree house? What kind of leads?"

"Based on what happened last night, we're looking to see if the levels of soil contamination have increased substantially. Professor East should have results soon."

"Soil contamination? Like, if there was a chemical spill near the property?"

"Something like that."

"So what happens now? Aside from running the tests, I mean. Is there a plan for getting the shield up to operational power?"

"At the spring equinox, a handful of other founders' descendants are going to come to the school and join us for recharging the shields. Professor East did not want to get the Magical Botanical Board of Regents involved unless as a last resort, but after Friday, we've reached the last-resort stage."

"The Board of Regents?" I asked, feeling a spike of anxiety based on what Callan had told me about their interest in me. "Why can't alumni or upcoming founders' descendants come to recharge it, like they do in years when no founders' descendants are attending?"

"Professor East had to report the development with the shield to the board, and they indicated that they'd prefer to come and handle this on their own." There was a tension in Callan's voice that I could tell he was trying very hard not to let on.

I tried to put aside my personal concerns for a moment to pinpoint Callan's reluctance. "Is it a bad thing if the board comes to help recharge the shield?"

"Evergreen Academy has always operated on the expertise of its instructors, with little oversight from the Board of Regents. And that has led to a lot of innovation over the years. But there are some on the Board of Regents who would like to take a... more direct role in the school's day-to-day."

"And you think that would be a negative thing?"

"Having people step in with their own agendas for the future of magical botanists beyond the pursuit of knowledge? Yeah, I think that would be a bad thing."

I let out a deep exhalation and looked around. The forest that blanketed the base of the fourteen-thousand-foot mountain was beautiful in the spring. I knew that, not much higher up, snow still settled across the ground and wouldn't be fully melted until well into the summer.

"Is there anything we can do to prevent it? It sounds like the shield can't be fully restored without them." My mind snagged on something then. "Wait, how did you all get the shield back up on Friday night if you're not strong enough? It wasn't a solstice or equinox. Recharging is only possible on those four days of the year, right?"

"Eli used an old Floracantus that didn't recharge the shield but rather infused the soil with enough nutrients to get the shield going again. It's a secret Floracantus that's been passed down through the magical botanists in his tribe who have been working with the soil in this area for hundreds of years. It was actually a brilliant idea, but it drew on too much of his power. He passed out afterward. He's currently at the health clinic of his tribe, recovering."

"What?" I looked at Callan in alarm. He'd sure been keeping this little tidbit tucked away nicely.

"He'll be all right. But obviously, we don't want that to happen to any of us next time. Eli has a lead affinity for herbs, and his body is more adept at healing because of it. We can't say that for the rest of us."

"Which is why you need more people."

He nodded, and I sighed, still thinking about Eli Quinn. I was glad that he was going to be okay, but I hated that he'd had to put himself in that position in the first place. I felt so helpless, and I remembered Coral casually saying that all of this was above our "magical grade." But was it fair that it all had to fall on the shoulders of Eli, Nevah, and Callan? Were they really so different from the rest of us?

"I wish there was something I could do."

Callan stopped walking and turned toward me. "That's

what I wanted to talk to you about. Well, Professor East wants to talk to you. He thinks you *could* help. You have a strong affinity for each type of plant."

"But I'm not a founder's descendant." I narrowed my eyes in confusion.

"That you know of."

I froze.

"You're joking. Hasn't the school been tracking the descendants of the founders carefully ever since the school opened? I think they'd know if I was one of them."

Callan shrugged. "Most of the lines have been carefully tracked for generations, like mine, but there are two or three founders' lines that have gotten fuzzy over the years."

I inhaled sharply, understanding the implication of his words.

"It's still a long shot, though. Back when the school was started, there were plenty of powerful botanists, not just those who founded Evergreen Academy. You could be descended from any of them. But Professor East still thinks it's worth pursuing, just in case."

Callan stepped off the path then and into a meadow, which was already blooming with wildflowers. The scenery here was so much different than at the academy. Instead of the overwhelming colors and smells that came from a property brimming with plants both native and non-native, magically enhanced and natural, the meadow and the forest that surrounded it were peaceful and calm, with nature in control of what survived and thrived.

When I took my eyes off the meadow and turned back to Callan, I saw that he had spread out a blanket and was removing containers of food from his backpack.

"What's this?" I asked.

"I think we've had enough talk of verdant shields and

lineages for one day. Even magical botanists take time to enjoy a picnic every now and then." He popped the lid off a glass bowl and began to dig into some fruit salad.

With a smile that I thought must have taken over my entire face, I joined him.

Chapter Fifty-Three

"Thank you for agreeing to work with us, Ms. Whelan. I know that you have had some questions about the reason for researching your lineage that I was unable to satisfactorily answer before. I didn't want to concern you, but now that the shield is showing signs of more severe damage, I felt that it was time to share." Professor East sat behind his broad desk the next day, Callan and I seated across from him.

"As Mr. Rhodes explained, the original magic that created the protections here at Evergreen Academy has been diminishing over the years as the environment has changed. Between wildfires, drought, and reduced soil quality, that magical connection to the soil is slowly seeping away."

"And it's getting worse lately, possibly because of a chemical spill?" I asked. Professor East shot a look at Callan, as if he wasn't supposed to share that bit of information.

He turned back to me. "That's correct. I was going to fill Callan in more completely after our meeting, but since it seems that you're already in the loop, I'll tell you both. The results from the soil testing are back. Compared to the samples we took at the winter solstice and fall equinox, the soil has extremely high

levels of salt and an uptick in cadmium. This is likely what's causing the soil's grip on the shielding Floracantus to slip."

"Do you know where the contamination is coming from?" I asked, thinking that if we had the source, we could possibly slow and eventually stop the deterioration.

"Unfortunately, we do not. That will be our next line of inquiry. In the meantime, the vernal equinox is quickly approaching. Even with the founders' descendants recharging the shield, it's not going to be enough for much longer. If your power could contribute in some way..."

"Of course I want to help," I said immediately. I realized that the time for hesitation about sharing my family history was over. Evergreen Academy needed help, and if I had any power to provide some, I would. "But can I ask, why can't we just test it out on the spring equinox? I could join Callan, Nevah, and Quinn in charging the shield, and we can see if it works."

"Two reasons, unfortunately. One, if you do have the ability to help charge the shield, I won't need to call out others to assist. So if we can determine that in advance, it's to the benefit of all. Second, the founders were somewhat... protective of what they created here. If someone attempts to charge the verdant shield who is not one of their descendants, there are... repercussions."

"Repercussions?"

"They worked in a component to the enchantment that the soil on campus would turn on someone who presumed to recharge the verdant shield that wasn't a founder's descendant. If you don't have the soil on your side, most of the plants here would be inaccessible as well. Without their cooperation, studying here at Evergreen Academy would be very difficult."

I sucked in a breath. *Those sneaky, petty botanists.* How old had they been when they'd created the school? Twelve?

Professor East took my shocked silence as a sign to continue. "You and I will review your family history together, starting tomorrow. Additionally, I'd like you and Mr. Rhodes to retrace your steps leading up to the winter solstice. There might be something we missed that activated your powers. That could be important in determining your heritage."

"We can try, but I don't remember everything I did." I attempted to rack my brain, barely able to remember the details of the previous week, let alone months ago.

"Do your best. Consult your notebook. Many of your activities should be dated. Do you keep any kind of calendar?"

When I nodded and mentioned my phone, he said, "Good. Comb through that. Mr. Rhodes will be your second pair of eyes. Try to retrace your steps physically as well as mentally. There is a bit of urgency now, before I contact the Board of Regents, so I'd like you to get started today."

He didn't have to add that if I didn't figure this out prior to the spring equinox, life as we knew it at Evergreen Academy might never be the same.

Chapter Fifty-Four

I spent the next few weeks splitting my increasingly limited time among my SCC classes, Evergreen Academy courses and Affinity Studies, meetings with Professor East to review my family tree, and retracing my schedule leading up to the winter solstice with Callan, which I was struggling to remember. We'd already combed through my school notebook, my SCC class schedule, and my phone calendar. We had a few leads to explore but nothing that seemed promising.

"What are we going to do if we don't figure this out in time?" I asked Callan. "Professor East is going to have to alert the Board of Regents, and some of them are going to have to come out here. And it's all going to be my fault."

"Your fault? There are many interesting things about you, local, but the fall of the verdant shield is not one of them. If you weren't here, it wouldn't even be a question. Professor East would have contacted the Board of Regents already, and they would already be planning their trip for the spring equinox."

I supposed Callan had a point, but I still couldn't help feeling there was more I should be doing. I dangled my legs back and forth over the tree branch we were currently sitting on. Callan had my notebook in his hands.

"The equinox is next week. How much notice does he have to give them?"

"I think he's going to hold out on you as long as possible, but... he'll probably give them at least two days' notice."

I clenched my hands. We were running out of time.

"Try to relax. You being a tangle of stress doesn't help the situation."

"But that's the problem. Most people on campus don't even know there *is* a situation. I can't talk to Yasmin, Coral, or Aurielle about this. I mean, they know the shield flickered after Capture the Roses, but it was so quick that I think most of them have already let it pass from their minds entirely." Professor East had asked me not to discuss what was going on with anyone other than him and the founders' descendants, since he didn't want there to be panic around campus.

"I'm sorry you can't tell your friends. But it's just a few more days. Then, hopefully, everything with the shield will be back to normal. For a while, at least."

For a while. The words were ominous. Was all of this just a short-term solution? Would it be the new normal for alumni founders' descendants to travel to Evergreen Academy to help charge the school at each equinox and solstice? And what if even that stopped being enough?

"What about the soil method that Eli did? Is that something that could be refined and repeated?"

Callan let out a breath. "After what happened to Eli, the tribe does not want to share the Floracantus he used. Officially, that Floracantus doesn't even *exist*, since it's not in the *Compendium Floracantus.* They don't want to be seen as responsible if the outcome was worse for another student who used it." Eli had made a full recovery and was attending class again, most of the school seeming to be none the wiser about what had happened.

"And I don't blame them," Callan continued. "Plus, soil can only hold so many nutrients. Eli wasn't fully restoring the quality of the soil, more like giving it a brief boost with fertilizer. So that's not a permanent solution, either, and not worth the risk."

"But there has to be a way." I was mulling it all over in my brain, trying to search for a solution, but I came up short. Besides, what could I come up with that Professor East, the other instructors, and all of the founders' descendants couldn't? I was a novice here, barely educated on matters of magical botany. Still, my desire to help was almost overwhelming.

Callan turned and took my face in his hands, and I stopped breathing. I met his eyes, reminded of how full and dark his lashes were. His palms were warm against my cheek, and I savored the feeling of rightness of his hands on me like this. His voice was gentle when he spoke. "This isn't on you, okay?"

I nodded, unable to speak. Callan had successfully calmed the anxiety of my thoughts, though he'd sent my heart rate spiking for a whole other reason.

We stayed like that for a moment longer, my breath stalling in my chest, everything in the room blurring so that all I could see were Callan's eyes, and all I could feel was the sensation of his warm skin on my face. Callan gently removed his hands, closed my notebook, and handed it back to me.

"I've got to go do some research with Eli. See you later, local."

Before I could blink, he was back on the ground, but my heart was beating as if he were still right next to me.

Chapter Fifty-Five

On the morning of the vernal equinox, I sunk my hands into the dirt of one of the planter barrels on Main Street in Weed. The students of Evergreen Academy were starting the day's festivities with a planting party in the local community under the guise of being SCC college students doing volunteer work.

I busied myself filling my barrel with sweet peas, tulips, and begonias, trying to distract my mind from thoughts of the verdant shield. Despite our best efforts and late nights, we'd made no progress on my family history or powers. Professor East hadn't been able to make any connection from me to any of the founders, and Callan and I had had no luck with determining what might have triggered my powers.

Two days earlier, Professor East had made the call to the Board of Regents, and three of their members were scheduled to join the equinox celebrations. They were continuing to test the property, but so far, they hadn't been able to determine the source of the excess salt and cadmium, which did not bode well for the strength of the shield.

Despite Callan's assurances, I couldn't help feeling that I had

let everyone down, and I was approaching the evening's festivities with a sense of melancholy and a slight creeping dread that I couldn't explain.

The flowers perfectly situated themselves in the soil, their roots already beginning to stretch out under the guidance of my hands. A little thrill of delight went through me at the feeling of connection between myself and the flowers, easing some of my worried feelings.

The flowers had been pre-enhanced at the academy and were both weed resistant and drought tolerant but not in any kind of obvious way. Down the road, a handful of students were passing out packets of wildflower seeds to those strolling along the sidewalks.

Spending a few hours planting at a regular human pace—since we weren't allowed to use any noticeable magical botanist powers in front of the townspeople—helped me to settle down and get lost in the rhythm of digging and planting. The earthy scent of the soil grounded me, a potent reminder that working with my hands was healing for the spirit.

At some point, my shoulders relaxed, and thoughts of the verdant-shield recharge settled into the back of my mind.

Before I knew it, our service project was wrapping up, and we were all to return to the academy grounds to clean up and change. I gazed down the street through the iconic Weed arch—the town's quirky name emblazoned across the entrance to Main Street on a painted backdrop of trees and the mountain—to the row of barrels and hanging planter baskets spanning either side of the street, each overflowing with different color combinations of bright, happy flowers. The street had been transformed in a matter of hours.

Yasmin caught me admiring them. "The real party begins at sunset," she said, linking her arm through mine as we walked to the academy vans. "We're entering the most productive time of the year for plants in the Northern Hemisphere, and they like to show off a little."

"Show off?" I quirked an eyebrow at her.

"With the temperatures rising, the plants will enter their rapid growing phase, and we'll see new stems and leaves everywhere. With the flowers, it becomes a bit of a competition to see which ones can bloom biggest and brightest early in the season. The floral affinities are helping them along, of course. Starting now and through the rest of the spring quarter, the campus is about to be the greenest, most vibrant place you've ever seen."

I'd felt that way about the campus all along, especially since the plants were able to bloom year-round due to the verdant shield. The reminder of what was at stake with the verdant shield tonight crept into my mind again, but I forced myself to stay in the conversation.

"And what about the humans? Do they show off for the vernal equinox too?"

"The florals are always showing off, so that will be nothing new. Remember the Floral Fete? But the herbals and harvesters will be bringing their best dishes out for a potluck competition and tea party, and the aquatics usually have some kind of surprise planned. Plus, all the second-years put the research they've been working on this year on display."

"How about the ferns?" I asked, thinking of her lead affinity.

"We will be in charge of making you feel like you've stepped into an enchanted land. And fortunately, ferns don't need much help to provide that kind of ambience. There's a reason fern fever swept England in the 1800s."

When we returned to the campus, we took showers then dressed for a spring party, Yasmin in a dress with a tiny fern pattern and me in a corduroy skirt and floral top that hung off my shoulders. We took turns magically braiding vines into each other's hair and dusting some glitter across our eyelids.

Finally, all dressed up and ready to welcome in spring, we approached the clearing next to the pond, and my eyes lit up. The shoreline was lined with glass-bottom boats, and some of the aquatics were already standing by, ready to give tours of the pond.

"Sign me up for that. And Dr. Lemna is nowhere in sight, so maybe I'll be able to relax around the water for once."

"Amen to that," Yasmin said. We approached a blooming trellis, where Professor Tenella was admitting students one at a time. Yasmin let out a loud sigh. "I wasn't on the winning team for Capture the Roses, so I'm going to have to answer a plant trivia question to be admitted. You go ahead. This could take a while."

I didn't want to leave her, but she joined Aurielle to wait their turns, and Coral spotted me and pulled me through the fast-track line for winners.

"I've heard that sometimes it takes people all night to get in. The difficulty of the question depends upon how much Professor Tenella likes you. If you've been a pest in her class this year, you might be in trouble."

I turned back to glance at Professor Tenella with a newfound respect.

"Come on, let's get drinks while we wait." I followed Coral to the drink stand, taking in our surroundings as we went.

The Apothecary Arts Club had set up a large booth overflowing with ingredients and glass jars of various shapes and sizes. They were offering to help us make perfumes, lotions, teas, and other items as gifts for our families or souvenirs from the vernal equinox. I made a mental note to stop by and create a perfume for Aunt Vera. With all the various extra studying I was doing, I hadn't had much time to experiment with plant-based creations just for the sake of it.

I ordered an elderflower spritz and clinked glasses with Coral. We glanced back toward the trellis and saw that Aurielle and Yasmin had both made it in.

"That was quick," Coral said as they approached. "Professor Tenella must approve."

"She threw me a question about ferns," Yasmin explained, "Total softball. And she asked Aurielle a photosynthesis question that a high schooler should be able to answer."

Once Coral and Yasmin had their drinks, we took turns making cosmetics and perfumes at the apothecary booth then got in line for the glass-bottom boat rides. I made sure to admire the spectacular potted ferns that were scattered around the area, shimmying nonstop.

Just as I was about to climb in with my friends, Nevah cut to the front of the line and looped her arm through mine. "Mind if I steal her?"

My friends widened their eyes at the sight of the second-year founder's descendant, suddenly shy in the presence of the most powerful aquatic here, but they all nodded simultaneously. "Thanks," Nevah said sweetly and took over the wooden paddle from one of the other aquatics.

"I was hoping to catch up with you today. We can squeeze in another lesson."

"You don't even take the equinox off?" I asked her playfully.

"It's not as much of a holiday when you're a second-year. I spent the last hour setting up my research for display."

"What are you planning to do next year?" I asked, surprised it had never come up before. I didn't know much about the internships that occurred during the third year.

Nevah easily rowed us away from shore, and we took off in the opposite direction of the boat my friends were in. "I want to combat invasive species. Invasive aquatic plants are some of the most detrimental to native habitats. I'm hoping to get an apprenticeship with the magical botanical field office back in Michigan. The Great Lakes could use some support. If I don't get picked up for an internship with the aquatic conservatory, that is."

"Wow, good for you. That sounds like important work."

"Look down," Nevah said, and I peered at the glass along the bottom of the boat. Tiny fish were zooming by, and plants were brushing along the bottom eagerly, as if saying hello. "It never gets old. *Mundare aquam*," she said, and the water beneath the boat became even more clear.

"A purification Floracantus?"

"It's the reason my hair is so silky. Keep some aquatic plants in your shower, and have them purify your water before you wash."

"Thanks for the tip." I looked down again, now able to see all the way to the bottom of the pond. The fish and plants moved around in all their colorful, viscous glory.

"So, why did you really invite me out here?" I asked. I'd sensed another motive from her the moment we climbed into the boats, and I noticed a slight shake in her hands as she'd first dipped the oar into the water.

"That obvious, huh?" Nevah sighed and studied the water. "I'm nervous about tonight. I don't know how much Callan has told you about the Board of Regents, but they've been wanting to get a tighter grip on this place for years. I feel like having them assist with the recharging of the verdant shield is going to open the door for more oversight."

"Yeah, Callan mentioned that some of them might have personal agendas."

"That's putting it mildly. They have different priorities for graduating magical botanists than the school, which has historically allowed us to explore any avenues we are interested in."

"Like what?"

"They want magical botanists to have more influence in the world. They'd like to see more of us in government positions or situated on the boards of influential private companies and nonprofits. That's not always a bad thing, but that can't be the only path. Magical botanists are not a monoculture. Some may be suited for leadership, but others want to do field work in remote villages, or open restaurants, or pursue art. It's always been the academy's mission to support space for all of that."

I swallowed, the sense of foreboding that I'd felt that morning returning. I was one of those students who planned to pursue art. If the Board of Regents took over and things changed next year, where would that leave me?

"Is there anything we can do to stop it?" I wondered why Nevah was telling me all this.

"I'm graduating this year, and my internship, if I get it, won't have me returning here very often. Eli Quinn will be gone as well. But you'll be here next year. You and Callan. I know you're not a founder's descendant, but with you having all of the affinities, I think you've got an important role to play here, should you choose to."

"So you want me to... keep an eye on things?"

"I'm not even sure what I'm asking. I mostly wanted to give you a heads-up. Callan already carries a lot, and it would be great if he didn't feel he was on his own next year."

My eyes met her dark-brown ones, which seemed to gleam like the clear liquid of the water. "He won't be alone. I'll make sure of it."

Nevah nodded and began to turn our rowboat back toward the shore.

WE SPENT THE REST OF THE LATE AFTERNOON VISITING the various activity stations and the research booths that the second-year students had put on display. We tried the potluck appetizers from the harvesters and the tea innovations from the herbals, casting votes for our favorites. At sunset, we all took seats at a series of large circular wood tables for dinner.

Professor East rose, and we turned in his direction. The pond was at his back, and the sunset and the mountain reflected majestically onto the water. I had a strong desire to pull out my notebook and sketch the scene—or even paint it. The sight lent itself perfectly to watercolor, a medium we'd been exploring in my Art II class at SCC this semester.

Professor East clinked his glass, and the group quieted. "We have some very special guests celebrating the vernal equinox with us tonight. I'd like to welcome three members of the Magical Botanical Board of Regents. Oliver Saxson." Professor East nodded toward a tall Black man wearing a deep blue suit that appeared slightly whimsical in its stitching, who stood and nodded then took his seat.

"And Solomon and Wendy Rhodes." The two stood up, and my eyes gravitated to the woman, who had sun-kissed olive skin and dark locks pulled into an effortless, loose, wavy bun.

Wait. Had Professor East said their last name was Rhodes? My eyes shot to Callan, who was sitting across the clearing with some of the other tree affinities. His eyes met mine briefly, and his jaw tensed ever so slightly.

"I see where Callan gets his looks from. His dad is kinda hot, and his mom is a smoke show," Coral whispered, confirming my suspicions.

The hot bloom of surprise formed in my stomach and planted a seed of disbelief in my brain. Solomon and Wendy, two members of the Magical Botanical Board of Regents, were Callan's parents.

Chapter Fifty-Six

"You never told me your parents were on the Magical Botanical Board of Regents!" I whisper-hissed when Callan approached me after the dinner.

"It never came up." He put a hand on my back, gently guiding me away from any prying ears.

"Never came up? Surely one of the times we were discussing the board would have been a good time to mention it."

Callan winced. "I wasn't sure how to... explain it."

I let out a deep breath. I wasn't truly mad at Callan. He was even more tangled up in all of this than I'd realized. I thought about everything Nevah had said on the rowboat, about not wanting Callan to be alone next year. Had she truly thought that his own parents were going to cause a problem for him?

"Let's just hope everything goes smoothly with the recharging. Your parents have agreed to help?"

"My father is just tagging along. He's not a founder's descendant. But between my mom and Saxson, Professor East thinks it should be enough."

Saxson. He said the name of the other regent so casually, I

realized that he must have grown up in a circle of people even more powerful than I'd assumed from a founder's descendant.

I nodded, my brain processing the increase in power the founders' descendants would have. With two more people, their odds of charging the shield successfully were greatly increased. I was about to ask Callan more about his parents when Eli Quinn appeared at our side. "It's time."

Callan nodded and squared his shoulders. "I'll find you after," he said to me.

"Shouldn't I come, just in case?"

"Just in case what? You know the consequences if you aren't a founder's descendant. We can't risk it. It's out of the question." His jaw clenched again.

I nodded and watched Callan and the rest of the group walk away until they disappeared into the trees, then I quickened my pace to follow.

I found a hiding place behind a massive lilac bush and watched as the five founders' descendants—Eli, Nevah, Callan, Oliver Saxon, and Wendy Rhodes—surrounded the stone circle on the ground. Professor East and Callan's father stood off to the side. A breeze blew a few sprigs of lilac into my hair, and I inhaled deeply, the delicious scent calming me slightly.

The founders' descendants stepped into the ring and knelt, touching their hands to the soil as one. I felt a vibration around my ring finger, and I nodded with relief. It was working.

But the sensation lasted for only a second, and the warmth that usually accompanied it petered out.

"The charge isn't holding," I heard Eli Quinn say. "We don't have enough power."

Their heads collectively turned to Professor East, who stepped forward. He looked at the sky and then at his watch, expression grave. "There's less than an hour left of the equinox. We won't be able to get another founder's descendent here on time."

My hands clenched into balls as I saw the realization wash over each of them. They weren't going to be able to charge the verdant shield tonight. The salt and cadmium that was poisoning the soil had increased to such a level that even this group wasn't going to be able to establish a full recharge.

That meant the school was going to be without magical protection until the summer solstice.

I inhaled another strong whiff of the lilacs and rolled my shoulders back. Without pondering it for another second, I stepped out from my hiding place.

"I'm here too."

All heads in the circle whipped to mine, though no one removed their hand from the soil.

"Briar," Callan said quietly, pronouncing both syllables of my name so distinctly that it sent a shiver down my spine.

"I have to try." The words came out in a whisper, but with the silence that had fallen over the area, I knew they'd all heard me. I looked to Professor East, our eyes meeting, and he nodded, though his expression was tight.

"Wait—" Callan said sharply, but before he could reiterate all the protests I already knew, I thrust my hand into the circle and touched the soil inside the ring of stones.

Chapter Fifty-Seven

At first, I didn't feel anything out of the ordinary. But then a vibration seemed to roll slowly from my hand and up through my arms, and I was cast backward with such force that I found myself sprawled on my back. I gasped as the wind was knocked out of me.

Distantly, I heard Callan curse from his place in the circle. Professor East ran to my side, but I sat up, protesting against the throbbing in my head, anxious to know what was happening with the shield.

I cradled my wrist, knowing something was wrong with it but not being able to process anything but the group of people in front of me, their hands still touching the soil.

Callan locked eyes with me, and something flickered across his expression that I couldn't read. I realized what he was going to do a second too late, and my entire body tensed. I opened my mouth to ask him to stop, but I wasn't quick enough. *Don't do it.*

Wordlessly, he thrust his second hand into the soil. Everyone in the circle gasped as something I couldn't feel passed through them, and I felt the surge of energy on my ring finger again.

I leaned forward, heart racing. I didn't know all the intricacies of how charging the verdant shield worked, but I did know that the founders' descendants always charged it with one hand, careful to let the soil take only a fragment of their magic.

Callan had just blown through that rule. A tremor passed through his body, and I struggled to my feet, fear spreading through my veins.

And then Callan fell to the ground, unconscious.

"WHY DID HE GIVE SO MUCH? DIDN'T HE LEARN FROM Eli?" I was barely avoiding shouting as I spoke to Nevah outside of the healing room where Callan was being treated by Professor Sage.

"He didn't feel he had any other choice. I was considering doing it myself, but I didn't gather the courage before Callan did. The window of the equinox was closing." Nevah turned toward me and looked me up and down.

"The real question is why did *you* do what you did? You're not going to be able to work with any of the plants on academy grounds now! My stupid, elitist ancestors have essentially cursed you."

I cringed and leaned my head back against the wall. I'd been so focused on what happened to Callan that I hardly had time to process the fact that I'd gambled my heritage... and lost.

"I just felt like I had to. As you said, the window was closing. If the school doesn't have a shield..." I flexed my wrist, nothing but a slight soreness there now. Eli had healed my aching wrist with a salve of herbs he slathered across my forearm and hand. I'd barely noticed him doing it in all my fear of what was going on with Callan.

Nevah sighed, but she slipped her arm around my waist.

"Let's get you a warm shower. Can you stay the night here? I don't think you should be driving."

When I nodded, Nevah guided me into the elevator, apparently deciding the stairs were too much for me at the moment. On the second-floor landing, I saw Yasmin, Coral, and Aurielle gathered outside Yasmin's door.

"There you are!" Yasmin whispered, a relieved note in her tone. "We've been so worried. Our gems did something weird, and then we couldn't find you anywhere." She seemed to notice the way Nevah was steadying me. "Are you okay? What happened?"

"Briar needs a shower and another dose of healing salve before she explains anything. I'll bring her back to your room after, if she's up to it."

"Another dose? B, are you okay?" Yasmin's eyes were wide, and concern flooded each of their faces.

"I'm fine. I'll fill you all in soon, okay?" My friends stared as we walked past them. Nevah's room was larger than Yasmin's, and she had her own private bathroom. The founders had been elitist indeed.

I used her shower, which was filled with aquatic plants and herbs, and hoped that my hair would come out as silky as hers always was. Then I shook my head at the ridiculousness of that thought after everything that had just happened. Maybe it was my brain's way of trying to calm me down—focus on things like vanity to distract myself from my worry.

Once I was dressed, Nevah brought the remaining healing salve Eli had given her.

"I think Eli took care of your wrist in his initial pass, but you were thrown back pretty hard. This will help with any potential bumps and bruises in other places."

I slathered the salve all over my tailbone, arms, and hips, which had broken most of my fall. The soreness that had started to settle in during my shower began to ease.

"Thanks, Nevah. I guess I'd better go explain what happened to my friends."

She nodded. "Just ask them to keep it to themselves, okay? I don't know what Professor East is going to want to share with the broader school."

I nodded in agreement. "But Nevah... why didn't it work? With five of you, I mean?" As I asked it, though, I already knew the answer. The soil was deteriorating more quickly than anyone had anticipated. But if there were a nearby chemical spill, shouldn't those impacts be slowing by now? Was the spill somehow increasing in intensity? But I didn't voice those things. I wasn't sure if Professor East had discussed the salt and cadmium levels with Nevah.

Her expression darkened. "It should have worked. At the fall equinox and winter solstice, the three of us charged the shield on our own. The charging from the solstice didn't seem to hold, though, since the shield flickered and Eli had to do that old Floracantus to enrich the soil, ending up nearly as hurt as Callan was tonight. But with five of us... it should have worked. It doesn't make sense."

Her words followed me as I went to my friends and filled them in on what happened, only omitting the privileged information about the soil contamination.

Yasmin made up the spare bed in her room for me, and I climbed into it gratefully after answering their questions to the best of my ability and asking them not to share with anyone else.

Mind and body exhausted, I fell asleep as soon as my head hit the lavender-infused pillow.

Chapter Fifty-Eight

It took Callan a few weeks to recover, and as far as the broader school knew, he'd gone on a trip with his parents after the equinox. Rumors about why our gems had flickered twice that night died out quicker than expected as the students were distracted with our new spring classes.

But there was one thing we couldn't cover up, and that was that something had happened with me. I was still attending classes, but I couldn't work any botanical magic on the school's grounds.

In the new quarter, I was taking Latin, Flowering Plant ID, Ecology in Action, and Affinity Studies. I could continue to learn Latin, even if I couldn't use any of the Floracantus that were derived from the language. And Flowering Plant ID was feasible to work through without powers as well. Professor Tenella assigned a lot of group work, so I teamed with Yasmin, Coral, and Aurielle. They would do any magical investigations required, and I would do all the drawing for our group.

Ecology was a different story. That class took place out in the forest, fields, greenhouses, or on the pond, and I couldn't conduct any experiments beyond the non-magical measurements.

Fortunately, the instructors were supportive of my continued learning, and Professor Bowellia helped to ensure that I continued to participate, though at a level equivalent to what I would have learned in a non-magical SCC class.

Affinity Studies were the final thorn, and at times I wanted to throw in the towel on being a magical botanist altogether.

I'd started the year unable to do Affinity Studies because my powers had been locked away—for reasons still unknown. Then my powers had been unlocked in a flood, and I'd had affinities for everything. Now, I still had those affinities, but I couldn't use them. At least, I couldn't use them on Evergreen Academy grounds.

Professor East was determined that I be able to continue my studies, so he was encouraging me to practice discreetly off campus grounds. Still, this would severely limit what kinds of plants and equipment I had access to. But it was better than nothing, and I was just glad that he wasn't mad at me for my unsanctioned attempt at charging the verdant shield.

I caught a few sideways glances from other students and murmurs of "Did you hear she tried to help charge the shield?" or "Have you ever heard of someone getting cut off by the founders?" right after the equinox, but thankfully, the comments died down as the new session went on. Magical botanists had the rapid growth phase of their plants and a new set of classes that drew their attention away from me before long.

It was exactly two weeks after the equinox when Nevah informed me that Callan was ready for visitors. Professor East had let it leak that Callan had returned to the academy the previous day, for the sake of any curious students.

I practically skipped to Callan's room, though there was a slow coil of nerves there too. I entered his suite when I was sure the landing was empty.

"Hello, Briar," Professor Sage greeted me. "Callan is doing much better now, but please keep your visit short." He rolled out of the room and closed the door behind him. Once I left the entrance area and fully took in Callan's living quarters, I inhaled sharply.

Yasmin's room had blown me away the first time I'd seen it, and Nevah's was a work of art, but this was something beyond my wildest imagination. Callan's bed was circular and filled the inside of half a tree, which stretched to the high ceiling of the room.

I forced my eyes away from the tree bed to examine the rest of the space. Callan was nowhere in sight, so I assumed he was in the bathroom, and I took the opportunity to take in the notes and drawings on his desk, the tree sketches and diagrams pinned to the walls, the remnants of experiments that littered the various tabletops. A book on herbal healing concoctions was propped open, sticky note tabs peeking out of its pages. In the corner was a small table bearing a two-foot-tall bonsai tree, pruning shears on a tray next to it.

A door clinked closed behind me, and Callan appeared, along with a fresh woodsy smell, as if he'd just stepped out of the shower. He was wearing sweatpants and no shirt, and I quickly looked away from his toned stomach. Unlike his arms, his abs were free of tattoos.

"Sorry. Professor Sage let me in."

Callan didn't say anything at first. He just walked to his closet and slipped a shirt over his head.

I took all of him in, studying to make sure he truly was okay. It had been hell the past few weeks, wondering if he would recover in full, as Eli had, or if there would be permanent damage from what he had done. Aside from looking a little tired and his hair being disheveled, he appeared like I remembered.

"What were you thinking, trying to charge the shield like

that?" The words were out of his mouth so quickly—and so sharply—that I flinched.

"I had to try, Callan. So that one of you wouldn't end up doing what *you* did." I put an emphasis on the word "you," making sure he knew I wasn't the only one who had done something reckless.

Callan let out a breath, and I sensed the anger draining out of him, transforming into a determined resignation. "We both did what we thought we had to do. But what about your studies? With the affinity powers you have, it's essential that you train them. And you only have a little over a year left in this school before you'll be expected to—" He cut himself off then, and I narrowed my eyes.

"Expected to what?"

"I told you that Professor East couldn't keep your powers from the Board of Regents. There are people out there who want to dictate our futures more closely than they have in the past."

"Nevah mentioned something about that. She said that they want to encourage more magical botanists to go into positions of power."

"It's worse than that. If some of them have their way, they'll force graduates on a career pathway depending on their affinity powers."

I tensed at the words. "Force? How?"

"These people are connected. They can ensure graduates get the jobs they want them to... and that they don't get other jobs that they don't find suitable."

"This sounds like some secret-society nonsense."

Callan hesitated and looked out the imposing glass window. "Magical botanists basically *are* one big secret society, Briar. And their influence is strong, whether society knows it or not. With some of the environmental destruction we've seen over the past few decades, they want to make their presence even... stronger."

"What would they do with those of us with multiple strong affinities?"

"We'd be tapped for top missions and careers of their choosing."

"And are your parents in the group pushing for this change?"

Callan sank onto the large cushioned window seat, seeming to deflate. "Unfortunately, yes."

"What about you? Do they want to force you into a field you don't want to go into?"

His jaw clenched, and I knew the answer. "I've always wanted to go into medicine. I've known that since I was a kid." He paused, turning his face away from me as he looked out the window again. "When I was young, I watched a friend fall prey to a cancer that could have been cured if we'd been a little further along in our alternative-therapies studies. We can do so much good with our medicines. The potential is there to heal incurable diseases. But that's not what my parents want from me."

Goose bumps popped out all over my arms as Callan spoke of his childhood friend, and I wanted to wrap myself around him. But I stayed a few feet away as he gazed out the window into the forest beyond. It was hard to imagine not supporting your child who wanted to go into a field as noble as medicine. Most people would be thrilled if that was their child's dream.

"What do they want from you?" I tried to ask it tenderly, but my blood was starting to boil in anger toward his parents. Couldn't they see what an amazing son they had? Didn't they trust him to make decisions about his own future?

"They've tossed around a few ideas. Politics or something similar to what my brother is doing."

"What does your brother do?"

Callan froze and then said smoothly, "I don't have the clearance to talk about it."

Someone cleared their throat, and I turned to see Professor Sage in the doorway. "Callan, we need to do your last therapy session. Briar, I'll have to ask you to come back later."

"Sure," I said, though I desperately wanted to continue the conversation with Callan. I felt like he was finally opening up, and I wanted to hear anything he was willing to share. Callan stood and walked me to the door.

"I'll do whatever I can to help you keep your affinity studies going despite the curse or whatever you want to call it. And we'll continue to research what's going on with the soil. Just don't let your guard down, okay?" His voice was gentle but serious, and the smell of his freshly showered skin enveloped me like a calming hug.

I wasn't sure what he meant by his warning, but I nodded, trying to shake the feeling, once again, that there was more going on than I knew about.

Chapter Fifty-Nine

Callan returned to classes the following week, and no one—aside from my friends, Nevah, Eli, and a few of Callan's closest tree affinity friends—knew what had really happened. I was impressed with the ability of our small group to keep a secret but decided maybe it was inherent in our DNA. Plants were natural secret keepers. Maybe that meant magical botanists were more inclined to be too.

As April rolled into May and we approached the end of the school year, I tried not to be disheartened at how much my progress had slowed.

Callan and I sat in the library one night—he not being medically cleared to go back to the tree houses yet—and I expressed my frustration. Candles flickered in their sconces on the walls, and a pleasant, jasmine-smelling breeze drifted through the space. We had the place to ourselves, most students choosing to study outside on such a brilliant spring evening.

"I know I did this to myself, but things are so much harder without access to my affinity studies on campus. I don't get to train with Nevah anymore, and the sessions I've been doing on my own on the Wildflower Trail at SCC have been pitiful at best. At least my painting skills have improved a ton this quarter, since I don't have much else to focus on."

Callan's eyebrows pinched together, and he reached across the table to flip through my notebook. "You have gotten really good. Even better than you were with the painting you submitted at the Floral Fete, and that was pretty incredible."

"Um, thanks," I said, shifting uncomfortably under the praise but smiling nonetheless. I was used to Callan pushing me to do better, not reflecting on how far I'd come. "But I'm not sure how much good that will do me in the magical botany world."

He skimmed the early pages of my botanist's notebook and paused on one of my sketches. "Where did you get the idea for this plant sketch?"

I leaned over to see which sketch he was pointing at and scanned my memory through the early days of the school year, before my powers had been activated. I'd picked that sketch to mimic because of how unusual its markings were. It almost looked like tiny fairies were drawn on the inner side of the petals. "I saw it in a book here in the library."

"It looks like a genie violet." Callan's face scrunched up in concentration. "Those went extinct shortly after the Renaissance period. They were so rare that non-magical botanists still don't have a record that they ever existed. What book did you see it in?"

I wasn't sure where he was going with this, but I let my mind sift through the memories of that time, trying to place what my days had been like then. I sat up a little, remembering something. "I'm pretty sure I copied that one from a botanical art book. There's a collection of really old ones. I remember them because I was trying to be delicate with the pages."

"Show me."

I nodded, and we wound our way along the circular walls of the library atrium. I led us to the tucked-away table inside the tree where I'd spent most of my first quarter when I didn't have any affinity studies. Some of the books I'd been studying were still stored in a drawer underneath it. I pulled them out and slid them across the table to Callan.

"Here they are. These books inspired the painting I did for the Floral Fete, actually."

Callan bit his lip, face screwed up in concentration.

"What is it?"

"I'm not sure. It's just a feeling."

I waited, hoping he'd say more. I was utterly confused about why we were even standing here, looking at these ancient botanical books that I hadn't touched in months, but I trusted Callan's instincts.

"Let me go get Professor East. Wait here."

A few minutes later, Callan returned with Professor East and Professor Tenella. He indicated the heavy, weathered books on the table. "Briar was studying botanical art books and journals this fall. These are the ones she was referencing just before the winter solstice."

"And you think this has something to do with her powers?" Professor East asked. I could tell he was having trouble making whatever leap Callan had made, just as I was.

But then Professor Tenella slid one of the books toward herself and opened it. She looked at me curiously, her head tilting slightly to the side. Finally, she spoke. "We haven't heard of this for centuries. But maybe..." Her words were directed at Professor East, who waited patiently for her to continue. She glanced toward the library door and whispered. A ribbon of nearby viny flowered plants slid across it, and it softly closed.

"There are stories of magical botanists who had the ability to store their affinity powers in the pages of their botanical drawings. The rumor was that powerful botanical artists of the Renaissance period weaved a bit of their affinity magic into the pages when they created their books. The abilities to extract the magic from the books ran through a few family lines for some generations then disappeared. The theory was that the magic stored in the books had dried out. But maybe..." She turned toward me then. "Maybe the family lines just went missing for a while."

I struggled to comprehend everything she had said. "You think that, by reading these books, I drew magic out of them?"

"Less drawing the magic out, I think, than activating the magic that was locked in you. An epigenetic change, perhaps, though they wouldn't have known that back then. But these lines have been little more than myth for centuries. The details have been lost to time."

"Fascinating," Professor East murmured, running his hand along the pages as if searching for power he hadn't known was there. "If that kind of affinity only ran in family lines, that means she'd be a descendant of one of the great botanical artists, correct?" He eyed some of the portraits that clung to the library's walls.

Professor Tenella nodded. "That's my understanding. Some of the most powerful magical botanists of the Renaissance period dabbled in art. Many of them became obsessed with botanical drawing."

"And Ms. Whelan would be a descendant of whoever's book activated her powers?"

I sucked in a breath as Professor Tenella nodded almost imperceptibly.

Professor East gently turned to the first inside page of each book—pages I'd always skipped right over—and I held my breath.

"These two books"—he turned them toward me and lifted his eyes to meet mine—"were authored by Leonardo da Vinci."

Chapter Sixty

"Leonardo da Vinci?" Yasmin gasped as I filled her in on what had happened in the library earlier that night. "As in *the* Leonardo da Vinci? The one who painted the Mona Lisa?"

I nodded, and her hands moved to her mouth.

"Many of the students here have interesting magical ancestry, but this is a whole other level," she said. "Your artistic skills must be a family trait, then."

"This can't be real, can it? I didn't even realize how precious those books were when I was flipping through them last fall. Hand drawn and annotated by *the* Leonardo da Vinci? They should have had a sign on them! I should have had to wear special gloves!"

I felt borderline hysterical now, talking to Yasmin. In the library with Callan, Professor East, and Professor Tenella, I had heard but not absorbed. Now, though, it was starting to sink in.

"Oh, don't worry about that. All the books here have been sealed by natural protectants. You couldn't even light them on fire if you tried."

"Well, that's a relief," I said, though I didn't feel much

better. How important was having this history, anyway? I wasn't a founder's descendant who could help with the problem of the school's verdant shield, and despite my affinity powers, I was falling further behind the other students because I could no longer do botanical magic at the academy. Aside from my heritage being a fun trivia fact, I couldn't see how it improved the school's situation or mine at all. Still, I couldn't deny that the connection fascinated me, and I was already formulating a plan to research my ancestor—if that was who he truly was.

"By the way, can you keep this to yourself for now? I'm not sure if this information means anything yet, and I'd rather not be more of an outlier here than I already am."

"But *darling*, don't you want everyone to know that not only do you have all the affinity powers, you can't use them on campus grounds due to trying to help save the school on the vernal equinox, and oh, by the way, you're also a descendant of one of history's most famous painters and your magic was activated through some form of magical storage that most people don't even know exists?" Yasmin's voice had taken on a dramatic flair.

We exploded into laughter, and I relaxed at the experience of discussing this so playfully with her. Everything she had just described felt like less of a confusing burden when it came out in a humorous waterfall of words.

"It *is* kind of ridiculous," I said once I'd caught my breath from laughing.

"Of course, your secret is safe with me, B," she added in a more serious tone, and I gave her a hug before leaving her room.

When I left the academy, I headed straight for the bakery. While I couldn't talk to my Aunt Vera about this new information in detail, I could at least try to gather some insights.

My aunt was kneading her famous olive bread when I stepped into the kitchen. The café was busy preparing extra baked goodies for the variety of graduation parties that were already starting to happen at the local schools. After exchanging a few pleasantries, I dove in, trying to keep my voice casual.

"Aunt Vera, do you know much about our family history? I know we're Italian on your side, but do you know any more details?"

"Nonna always told us we were mostly French and Italian but probably a mix of some other things too. Belrose is French—I know that much—and that came from her husband. The Italian was on Nonna's side of the family. Beyond that, I don't know much."

"Thanks. That's what I thought." None of this was really news to me. My family had been passing down Italian recipes and phrases for decades, and my grandma had always joked about marrying the least romantic Frenchman on earth. But apparently, his baguettes were to die for.

"Now that you bring it up, I think your mom was doing some kind of ancestry project for one of her college classes before she left the university. I can't remember what she found out, though."

My ears perked up at that. My mom had been researching our ancestry? If it was when she was in college, that would have been eighteen to twenty years ago. Was it a coincidence? Lots of people researched their family history. My stomach dropped in a familiar way. For the millionth time in the last seven years, I wished my mom were here to ask her.

"Any reason you're wondering?" Aunt Vera's voice was gentle, and her eyes flicked up to mine as she continued to work the dough.

"We were talking about ancestry at school a bit. Famous people we might be related to, that sort of thing," I said, trying to keep my explanation close to the truth.

Aunt Vera snorted. "My bisnonna Marie used to say that we were descended from some old prominent Italian families, but who knows? Every family has their stories, and they tend to get exaggerated over time."

"Mm-hmm," I murmured, thinking that Great-Grandma Marie may have been doing the opposite of exaggerating.

"Are we still on for your birthday tradition next week?"

I sat up in surprise, for the first time in my life having forgotten that my birthday was drawing so close. As a kid, I'd been the type who started planning my birthday party months in advance.

The tradition—of us taking a midnight plunge, the exact time of my birth, into Castle Lake—had been started by my mom when I was five, and Aunt Vera and I had kept it up, even in those first few years when doing it without my mom had been like doing it without a limb. After the plunge, we each gobbled down a piece of confetti cake as we towel dried under the light of the moon.

"Of course," I said, tinkering with the emerald birthstone ring. Amazingly, my aunt had never asked about its origins.

"How are you feeling about finals at SCC? And is there anything you need to do to wrap up the year at Evergreen Academy?"

"I think finals will be okay. They're next week." My answer was truthful. Thanks to Callan's brilliant tutoring throughout the year, I was excelling in most of my SCC classes. "Oh! That reminds me." I pulled a flyer out of my bag and held it up to show her. "My art class is having a gala to showcase the work we did this year. It's next Thursday at six. Do you want to come?"

My aunt's face split into a smile. "You're finally showing some of your work! Absolutely. I'll be there."

I realized I hadn't answered her question about wrapping things up at Evergreen Academy. In truth, I didn't know what the end of the year there held in store. I knew that the top-achieving second-years were being selected for internships with the conservatories and field offices. But since we didn't have finals, I assumed the spring classes were going to end like the fall and winter anno uno classes had—with students creating summaries of their learnings and detailed descriptions of questions they wanted to pursue on the subject in the future, all carefully catalogued in our botanist journals.

The idea that my first year at Evergreen Academy was drawing to a close brought on a surprising sense of melancholy.

I'd always looked forward to summer vacations in previous school years—and I was still excited about the upcoming trips to the lake and long summer nights—but this year felt different. Despite the challenges I'd had, I was going to miss the magic of the academy and all the people in it.

One person in particular.

I said goodbye to my aunt and went up to our apartment, where I grabbed my notebook and headed for the balcony, a drawing session the only thing I could think of to calm my warring mind.

Chapter Sixty-One

"Race you back to the shore!" my aunt shouted, immediately breaking into a freestyle stroke.

"No fair!" I shouted back, beginning to pull myself through the water. My aunt had won more than one regional swimming award in high school, and she definitely still had her skills. But despite my desire to catch her, I couldn't help slowing down, just a little.

This was the first time I'd really swum since discovering my powers. The only other time had been sneaking through the river during Capture the Roses, and there hadn't been time to take it all in then.

I marveled at the awareness of the aquatic plants in the lake below me and wondered if there was a Floracantus that would allow them to bend in a certain direction, swaying the water—and me in it.

My body felt like it buzzed with energy, as if being cut off from my affinity powers at Evergreen Academy had affected me more than I realized. Other opportunities to spend time in nature in my tight schedule were few and far between. Now, my powers were ready to go.

"Winner gets the biggest slice of cake!" Aunt Vera called over her shoulder, and I picked up my pace again, reluctantly leaving the connection with the aquatic plants behind. By the time I reached the shore, my aunt was already drying herself off with a towel.

"Haven't you heard of letting the birthday girl win?" I grumbled, though I was grinning. My aunt was glowing in her element like this. She passed me a piece of cake—the smaller of the two.

"Where would be the fun in that?" She took a huge bite of the confetti-flecked concoction. We finished eating and drove back into town through the darkness of night, blasting a birthday playlist that was years out of date.

When we got home, we finally wound down, preparing to shower and grab a few hours of sleep.

Even without a midnight birthday dip to keep me up, I'd been staying up too late. Between studying for various exams, I got sidetracked reading about Leonardo da Vinci and his family history.

As far as historians knew, Leonardo had never had children, but he'd had a large number of half brothers and sisters. If I truly were related to him, it had to be through one of them. Which one? And would I ever know?

According to Professor Tenella, Leonardo was one of a handful of Renaissance artists and scientists who had woven botanical magic into drawing books. From what I could piece together, however, Leonardo had set it up so that only those with his DNA could access his magic.

I couldn't be the first person in history to have experienced this. In all likelihood, the magic had passed through the family like that for generations and then had disappeared, like so many family secrets did over time.

Was there a reason it had emerged now? Why was I the one from my family to attend Evergreen Academy and find Leonardo's books? Was my mom's genetic research still hanging around somewhere?

The more I thought about the situation, the more questions came to mind. And with the summer break from Evergreen Academy imminent, it was unlikely that I would get answers soon.

The only concrete action I'd taken outside of my own research was to put a book about Leonardo da Vinci on order from our local bookstore, Ink and Parchment. Mara, the owner, informed me it was back-ordered due to being out of print, but she promised she'd find me a copy. At least that was one thing to look forward to this summer—more time to attempt to learn about my family's history.

Just as I was getting into bed, an incessant tapping of leaves at the window caught my attention. With a smile, I rushed to open it.

Happy birthday, local. - C

My smile widened and I bit my lip, amused at the fact that, even though he was the only one who sent me messages like this, he still felt the need to sign them with his initial. I sent off a quick reply.

Thanks, night owl.

I checked my clock. It was nearly two in the morning. What was Callan doing up, anyway? I tried not to let that thought—or any of the others crowding my mind—keep me awake. Instead, I imagined the pull of the plants from below my body as I'd swum through Castle Lake and drifted into gentle dreams.

Chapter Sixty-Two

Finals week at SCC went by quickly. I managed to keep my focus locked in all week, and by the time I left the final for my last class, I felt confident that I'd passed them all and possibly even done well enough to get As in most classes.

"How'd it go?" Callan asked as we stepped out of the math classroom for the last time.

I grinned. "I think I nailed it. Our study guide basically covered everything that was on there."

Callan raised a hand, and we high-fived. "Nice work, local. You'll be acing calculus next."

I eyed him skeptically. "Don't push your luck."

As we left campus, there was a slight ache in the pit of my stomach. It was possible this was the last class I'd take with Callan at SCC, and while I knew I'd still see him at Evergreen Academy next year, there was something about our time on my normal human college campus that felt sacred. He was there only for me—though I still couldn't understand why—and his presence had bridged the gap between my two worlds. That bridging had grounded me much more than I realized, and the idea that it was coming to an end brought a strange feeling of nostalgia and loss.

In that rare moment of serious reflection, I wanted to thank Callan for everything he'd done for me this year. But before I could do so, he spoke.

"I gotta run. Let me know once you've checked your score online. Let's see if you managed to match me."

I rolled my eyes and bit my lip, suppressing a grin. "Maybe I beat you. Bet you don't even think that's possible, do you?"

"Everything's possible with you, local." Callan winked and left the SCC campus, possibly for the last time.

When I got to the Evergreen Academy campus later that day, a student approached me—a fellow first-year I recognized named Porter. "Briar Whelan?" he asked tentatively.

"Yes?"

"Professor East would like to see you. He's in his office."

"Thanks, Porter," I said. He raised his eyebrows, reddened slightly, nodded, and walked away.

Yasmin let out a little giggle. "I think he was surprised you knew his name."

"What? Why? This school isn't that big."

"Yeah, but you hang out with Callan all the time. That puts you in an elite tier at this school. Plus, you have all the affinity powers."

I wrinkled my nose. "I'm not a founder's descendant. And everybody knows I can't even use my magic on campus. And I'm *definitely* not elite."

Yasmin shook her head. "Keep telling yourself that."

We went our separate ways at the top of the staircase, and just before I prepared to knock on Professor East's office door, Callan joined me.

"Do you know what this is about?" I asked.

"I have an idea," Callan said tersely. A moment later, the grand door was tugged open by a tendril of a trailing vine inside the room. We entered the expansive office, and Professor East put aside a laptop he was working on.

"Is there news about the chemical spill?" I asked once the door was closed.

"Yes, though 'chemical spill' may not be the right term."

"What do you mean?" I asked. A look passed between Professor East and Callan before he responded.

"We managed to trace the source of the salt and cadmium to a specific location just outside the academy's grounds. There is evidence that someone has been... magically poisoning the soil there."

I gaped at him even as what he said filled in the gaps of what had been going on. If someone had been poisoning the grounds intentionally, that would explain why the strength had been increasing. And if it had been done with magic, that could explain why it took so long for Professor East to trace.

"But who would do that?" I asked, genuinely appalled. Evergreen Academy was a place of beauty, of inquiry, of comradery. Why would someone want to poison it?

"We can't know the motivation until we determine the culprit. I've increased security around the grounds outside the wall, but if the poisoner is observant, they may pick up on this and stay away."

"At least that should stop the poisoning, right?" I asked.

"I think we can be confident that we'll be able to prevent any further poisonings now that we know what to look out for. Hopefully, the soil will have a chance to recover with the influx of toxins abated."

"But if we don't find them, we won't know why they were doing this," Callan said, and Professor East nodded. Callan's muscles flexed under the tattoos of his forearms as he gripped his thighs.

"We may be able to trace them based on the evidence we found"—he glanced toward Callan, and I was reminded with a jolt that Callan could sense power being used—"but I'm not confident of it. Whoever did this, they were quite skilled. I doubt they'll make it easy for us to find them. Plus, the academy is about to break for the summer. For now, we may have to be satisfied that we determined what was happening and focus on strengthening the soil quality so that the summer solstice recharge will go off without"—he glanced at me this time—"a hitch."

A hitch. That was putting it mildly.

"The reason I wanted to fill you both in is because I appreciate how much work you put into determining where Ms. Whelan's powers came from and in going above and beyond to recharge the shield at the vernal equinox." He turned to Callan. "Should our work in this investigation require your services, I will reach out."

Callan nodded then stood and left the room.

Professor East shifted his gaze back to me, steepling his fingers. "As for you, Ms. Whelan, I wanted to talk about your summer plans."

I nodded for him to continue.

"I know that this last session was frustrating for you, with not being able to perform your magic on campus. Your instructors all tell me that you made the most of it and still managed to make some forward progress. Thankfully, next year is a bit different. Second-years spend a lot of time on field studies, many of which are off campus grounds."

I sat up straighter, excited at what seemed like the first bit of good news in weeks. In my worst moments, I'd doubted if I'd even be allowed to come back to the academy next year, after decimating my prospects of using magic on campus.

"Additionally, I think you should consider taking a heavy load of summer courses at SCC. Balancing your courses there with field studies here next year is going to be a challenge. I'll get them to work with you, of course, but it would be ideal if you could take a lighter load there next year. I know you took a few winter intersession courses this year and some summer courses right after high school. Plus, your transcripts show a few AP credits. With a large summer load, you'll be close to completing the full number of credits needed to graduate from SCC."

"I can do that," I said quickly, wanting to appease his every request. Throughout this year, I felt that Professor East had bent over backward to help me, even if I hadn't always seen it at the time. And the fact that he was already planning for my success next year made me that much more eager to follow his suggestions.

"Summer enrollment has already started, so I'll see what classes I have remaining and take as many as I can." I remembered Callan's push for me to continue math and take Calculus. Dare I take it over the summer, without his help? Part of me was scared to attempt it while the other part was eager to do it, just to show him I could.

"Good." Professor East rapped his knuckles against the desk in a quick, unconscious motion. "Things might be a little different around here next year, Ms. Whelan, but I want you to know that you've exceeded my expectations in every way this year. You put your head down and put in the work. You're going to have to double down on those efforts next year, but you have already shown that you've got it in you."

I tried not to blush, surprised by the praise he was lavishing on me. "Thank you, Professor East. I won't let you down."

"I know you won't. Have a nice summer."

The trailing plant tugged open the door again, and I took that as my cue to leave. I cast one last look over my shoulders and saw my professor staring out the window at the bright summer sky, fingers steepled and brow furrowed.

Chapter Sixty-Three

Nevah pulled me into a hug. "I'm going to miss you, Briar. Sorry I couldn't be more help this spring. But I know you'll do great next year." It was her last day on campus.

"Thanks, Nevah. I owe you a ton. So, where are you headed? Back to Michigan?"

Nevah's eyes brightened, and she gave me a sheepish smile. "Actually, I was selected for an internship at the aquatic conservatory in Florida, so my plans for the Great Lakes are going to have to wait."

"Nevah! That's amazing! Congratulations." It wasn't at all shocking that she'd been selected—she was one of the best in her year and a founder's descendant to boot—but the official announcement was thrilling.

She beamed. "Thanks. I'm excited. Hey, maybe you'll get invited there eventually. You do have an aquatic affinity, after all."

I startled at the idea. Aurielle had told us about visiting the fern conservatory in Alaska, but aside from that, the conservatories had pretty much fallen off my radar. I'd had too many other

things to focus on this year, and next year wasn't shaping up to be much different. Nevah didn't know about my newfound heritage—Professor East had kept an even tighter lid on that piece of information.

"Maybe. It'd definitely be fun to visit you," I said.

Nevah gave me one more hug, and then she was gone. Coral and Aurielle said their goodbyes next. We all had one final breakfast together in the teahouse.

"You all are welcome to visit me in Louisiana this summer, if you want to brave the heat and humidity," Coral offered.

Aurielle wrinkled her nose. "I'll be perfectly content in Connecticut, thank you very much."

"San Antonio isn't going to be much better, heat wise," Yasmin sighed. "But Jordan will be there, so that's all that matters."

"A whole summer with your love. Poor you," Coral teased.

"We're not official yet. It doesn't really make sense for us to date while I'm still in school. But he's hoping I end up working at a botanical field office in Texas when I'm done at Evergreen."

"Y'all are thinking way too far ahead." Coral pursed her lips. "We're young. Let's focus on one season at a time. I'm not even thinking about next school year, let alone what happens after that."

"Sure, you aren't, Miss International Plant Relations," Aurielle said, raising her eyebrows at Coral.

"That's a loose career goal, not wedding plans." Coral elbowed Yasmin, who rolled her eyes.

"Wedding plans? Now who's the one thinking too far ahead? What are your plans for the summer, B?" Yasmin turned to me, obviously trying to change the subject.

"I'll be working at the café, taking a large summer course load at SCC. You know, normal human things."

"And you'll be practicing your Floracantus, since you'll be off the academy grounds, right?" She said this part more quietly.

"Right," I agreed, excited at the thought. I'd already brought home all my textbooks, including my copy of the *Compendium Floracantus*, and carefully stashed them in my closet.

We helped Coral and Aurielle to the vans that were taking students to the small local airport, where some of their parents had chartered flights home. Our friends waved at us one last time as they climbed in the van.

After the vans drove away, I sighed. "It's just you and me, Yasmin. I'm glad you're sticking around for the SCC art gala."

"I wouldn't miss it. Though why anyone would want to see my work is beyond me."

"Do you mind if I break off here?" I eyed the tree houses, and Yasmin smiled.

"It's not truly summer until you wrap things up with your tutor, right?" she teased.

I shook my head and rolled my eyes, but there was truth to what she had said. I knew there was one more person I needed to say goodbye to before leaving Evergreen Academy for the summer.

Callan was boxing up supplies in the tree house when I found him. I'd had to climb the tree the old-fashioned way— using the rungs—since my tree affinity magic didn't work on campus. When I was with Callan, I mourned the loss of it more than any other time. I missed walking through the trees with him, practicing Floracantus in that unique, intuitive way of his.

"Were you planning to leave without saying goodbye?" I asked, quirking an eyebrow at the boxes he was filling.

"Hello to you too." He raised a hand and murmured words I didn't catch, sending the boxes drifting out the hole in the tree. They nestled softly on the ground below.

"Are you packing up the entire tree house?"

"Just my favorite bits," Callan said, but the spark of humor that I was used to expecting in his voice was gone. I studied him more closely then, stomach dropping at how tired he looked.

His hair was slightly disheveled, and there were faint circles under his eyes.

"When are you leaving?" I tried to keep my voice even, implying that the question was neutral, even though it wasn't. It had already been hard to say goodbye to Coral and Aurielle, and I was glad I had a few more days with Yasmin, but soon she'd be leaving too.

Once Yasmin and Callan left, all my friends from Evergreen Academy would be gone, and I'd be surrounded by people who only knew one side of me. I wouldn't be able to talk about magical botany, Floracantus, being descended from Leonardo da Vinci, or any of the other amazing discoveries I'd made this year. The idea made my stomach twist.

"This weekend. My parents have already planned networking activities for me over the summer."

"I'm sorry. Did you say *networking*?" I barked out a laugh, but Callan's face remained impassive.

"Their specialty. If I had it my way, I'd stay here all summer, continuing my research on the tree medicinals. But it is what it is." He rubbed at his jaw.

"So I guess I won't see you until August, then?"

"I thought I'd be back on the summer solstice to recharge the shields, but after what happened to me at the vernal equinox, I'm not sure if plans are going to change."

My heart leapt at the thought of seeing him again at the end of June—of being a part of this world again, even if briefly—instead of having to wait all the way until August. But then I remembered how injured he'd been after putting too much of himself into the recharge, and I told myself not to be selfish. Professor East would do what was right for the school and for his students. That included Callan just as it included me.

"Well, you have my number if you need to get ahold of me. Unless I should only expect messages to come through the leaves?" I was baiting him, since I'd given him my number but still didn't have his. We communicated only at school or during those few times he'd sent me leaf messages.

Callan smiled mischievously then, and I felt a tug of happiness that I'd momentarily drawn him out of whatever unpleasant place he'd been in his mind.

"Let's make a deal. If you initiate a message in the leaves, and it makes it to me, I'll text you once I receive it."

"But that's super-advanced magical botany! You know I don't know how to do that." My return messages had reached him only due to the complexity of his own magic. I'd had nothing to do with it.

He was leaning back against the interior of the tree, forearms folded over his chest, tattoos on display. His head casually rested on the wall. It was a stance I'd seen him take so many times, and yet it felt charged in that moment, like we were standing face-to-face.

Just then, a breeze whipped up, and a few soft green leaves rushed up and tenderly grazed the sides of my neck before falling to the floor. Callan grinned, and the sight melted my heart.

"Then I guess you'll need to practice, local."

Chapter Sixty-Four

When the night of the SCC art gala came around, I put on a black dress and some teardrop earrings and fixed my hair into an elegant updo, so unlike my standard casual waves. I even decided to wear kitten heels—usually totally off-limits—and hoped my feet wouldn't hate me by the end of the evening.

I met Yasmin at the library on campus where our class was hosting the gala. We set up our submissions along with our classmates, and our instructor came by to wish us luck on our public showing. We were each allowed to submit three works, so I had entered two of my drawings plus the painting I had done for the Floral Fete at Evergreen Academy.

"I shouldn't have put mine next to yours," Yasmin whined. "Yours are so much better."

"Stop that. You were working with *charcoal*. I haven't even touched that medium. I'm so impressed with how they came out."

Yasmin beamed and straightened her shoulders slightly. I wasn't sure if I should ask her if she had invited anyone to the gala. After all, she wasn't from the area, and I didn't know if her family was able to travel for something like this.

"My aunt is coming by," I said. "I've told her all about you, so I know she'll be excited to see your work."

"Oh, that's awesome. It will be great to meet her."

The gala doors opened then, and members of the college and local community began to filter through the rows of easels. We answered questions about our work and milled around with our guests to view our classmates' submissions. Aunt Vera was blown away by the foxglove painting I'd done for the floral fete, which I'd decided to title simply *In Bloom*.

We were an hour into the gala when I heard a voice I would recognize anywhere. I looked down the row and saw Callan greeting my art instructor with a small group of people. He had a small bouquet of wild white roses in his hand.

A moment later, he began to make his way toward Yasmin and me. He was wearing a suit that was perfectly tailored, and I was ready to beam at him when I saw that his smile was wary. My guard went up immediately.

That was when I noticed who was trailing him. The tall couple stepped out from behind their son, and Callan's mother spoke.

"Callan had told us you were a talented artist, but we had no idea he wasn't exaggerating. This is quite impressive." Her eyes shot to my painting of *In Bloom*.

My shoulders straightened at the sight of Wendy and Solomon Rhodes, both impeccably dressed, sipping sparkling cider that probably tasted like ground apple peels to them.

They were in town again? Had they come to escort Callan home, or was there another reason they were visiting? Had they come out to investigate the poisoning of the soil? But why were they here at SCC's art gala, of all places? My senses went on high alert, feeling like I was missing something.

Callan stepped closer, handed me half the roses, and leaned in to whisper in my ear. "I'm so sorry. I tried to stop them."

He turned to Yasmin and gave her the remaining flowers, which she took with a surprised smile. "Lovely work, ladies," he said, all hint of anxiety erased from his voice.

I swallowed and put on a bright smile. These were Callan's parents and prestigious members of the Magical Botanical Board of Regents. Whatever reason they had for being here tonight, I planned to make a good impression.

"That's very kind of you to say." I met each of his parents' eyes in turn. "It's nice to see you both again."

I got Aunt Vera's attention and waved her over. "This is my aunt, Vera. Vera, this is my friend Callan, and these are his parents."

My aunt stepped forward. "Nice to meet you all. Does Callan have a piece in the gala?"

"No, our son doesn't take classes here," Wendy said coolly, and I cast Callan a raised eyebrow, realizing he hadn't told them about the math classes he'd taken with me. "Callan studies with Briar at Evergreen Academy."

"Right," my aunt said, an easy smile slipping onto her lovely face. "She's been pretty tight-lipped about that place, but I know it's been a great opportunity for her this year."

"You have no idea," Wendy said, and her smile was bright as her sharp eyes locked on mine. "One might say her potential is *unmatched*." There was an emphasis on the last word that caused me to suppress a shiver. "We look forward to seeing you again soon, Briar."

And with that, the Rhodes family breezed out of the gala, Callan straightening his shoulders as he followed his parents. He turned and caught my eyes briefly before rounding the corner, and then he was gone.

"They seem a little... stuffy," Aunt Vera murmured once they were well out of earshot.

I choked back a laugh. The unexpected encounter had brought my two worlds together in an unsettling way, and it left me with a sense of unease.

"Maci and I will meet you at the restaurant after you finish up here," my aunt said, motioning between Yasmin and me. About halfway through the gala, when Maci stopped by, my aunt had decided the four of us needed an end-of-year celebration at Delilah's.

As we cleaned up the gala, a stir of emotions swirled through my core. One part of my brain couldn't stop sorting through the questions that clung to my curiosity like a climbing vine to a trellis. Questions about how I would go about studying on campus next year with no access to my powers, about who had been poisoning the school's grounds and why, and now, about why on earth Callan's parents had come to my art gala.

But when I took my painting of *In Bloom* from the easel and examined the intricate details I'd incorporated into the painting, a sense of hope kicked in across the curiosity.

I now knew about my ancestry, and I had a summer to dig into it further. Thanks to Callan, Professor East, and my three good friends, I felt more at home at the academy than I'd ever expected to. And lastly, no matter what schemes his parents were up to, next school year, I would see Callan Rhodes again.

I pulled one of the delicate white roses from the bouquet, murmured a Floracantus for longevity, and stuck it behind my ear, stepping out into the warm evening air. Tonight was for celebration, and this magical botanist was going to embrace it.

Unmarked Correspondance

Delivered via Wildflower Trail letter box
Written in code
Undated

Destroy after reading.

Due to recent events, we have redoubled our efforts to find the **[redacted]**. We have located the **[redacted]** but have not been permitted access. Will need your support in making arrangements. We need a botanist with access to **[redacted]**.

With verdant regards,

Cobralily

The end

The end... for now
The story of Evergreen Academy will continue in book two.

Want more magic?

Want to know what your plant affinity power would be?

Want to read what was going through Callan's mind when he first met Briar on Midsummer?

Want to join the Society of Magical Botanists reader group on Facebook?

Go to Heather Schneider's Bonus Content page on her website (heatherschneiderauthor.com) for access to all of the above!

Do you want to follow other writing projects Heather is working on?

Sign up for Heather's newsletter to stay up on the latest new releases and reader opportunities.

If you enjoyed the story, please leave a review. Reviews help indie authors find new readers, and help readers find new books to love.

Thank you for reading and being part of Heather Schneider's reader community!

Also by Heather Schneider

Books by Heather Schneider:

- Meet Me in St. Louis (young adult romcom-mystery)
- Chasing Cheer (Magical Emerald Hollow book 1)
- Finding Cheer (Magical Emerald Hollow book 2)

Acknowledgments

First and foremost, thank you to every single reader who has picked up one of my books and read it, told me you loved it, left a review, shared with friends, or supported my author journey in any way. I couldn't write books without people to read them, so thank you from the bottom of my heart.

Mom, you're always at the top of this list! Thank you for always reading, for loving my stories, and for encouraging me every step of the way.

To the rest of the fam, your love, support, and the amazing memories we make together make all of this possible.

Zach, for all our adventures, and many more on the horizon. What a year it has been.

Bethanie, for being such an amazing author friend. I'm so grateful for your friendship and for our coffee writing dates.

Danielle and Julia, for being my literary hype women! Seriously, thank you for always reading and sharing with everyone you know.

To Pamela, for your wonderful beta reading notes. Thank you for helping to make this story better.

To my ARC team and those of you who interact on my social media reader communities, your engagement inspires me to keep creating.

To my cover designer, Krafigs Design, thank you for creating such an enchanting cover. Seriously, the cover makes me feel like I'm stepping into the world of magical botanists.

To the editors and proofreaders at Red Adept Publishing, thank you for all your care with my work.

About the Author

Heather Schneider is an author of young adult and adult contemporary and cozy fantasy novels, always with a love story.

Heather lives with her husband and their Chiweenie, Toby. When she's not writing, you can find her reading, listening to podcasts, traveling, or spending time with family.

As an indie author, Heather would love to hear your feedback on *Evergreen Academy*!

Please connect with her on Instagram or Facebook @heatherschneiderauthor and leave a review wherever you review books.

You can visit her website and subscribe to her newsletter at heatherschneiderauthor.com.